Tardy Bells
And
Witches' Spells

WOMBY'S SCHOOL FOR
WAYWARD WITCHES

SARINA DORIE

BOOKS IN THE WOMBY'S SCHOOL FOR WAYWARD WITCHES SERIES LISTED IN ORDER

CONTENTS

ACKNOWLEDGMENTS

I am fortunate to have so many supportive friends and family encouraging my endeavors. From an early age I had a mother who was my number one fan. I appreciated the early years of encouragement and the later years of brutal honesty. I am thankful I have a husband who enables my creative addiction. I wouldn't be able to write if Charlie didn't go in his man cave and entertain himself with World of Warcraft during the long hours it takes to produce a novel.

Thank you Night Writers, Alpha Readers, Visionary Ink, Wordos, and Eugene Writers Anonymous for helping me make this series the best it can be. Justin Tindel and Daryll Lynne Evans, you gave me hope and a writing community at a time when both were lacking in my life. James S. Aaron, your suggestion that I'm writing a cozy witch mystery was brilliant.

Eric Witchey, your classes always inspire me to write better craft. If only I had been born with a witchy last name like you were. But one can't have everything.

PROLOGUE
Oops, I Did It Again

"Magic is not real," I said as I waited for my therapist to come in.

Magic wasn't real—because if it was—that would mean I was a witch. And if I was a witch, it would mean I had killed two people using my magic. It was better to be normal. It was safer.

But after everything I had experienced in my sixteen years, it was hard to believe magic didn't exist.

The antique clock on the wall ticked away, the rhythm slow and lethargic. Even through the haze of medications, my therapist's tardiness made me uneasy.

I hugged a potted orchid in my hands, trying not to damage the white flowers. It grounded me to hold onto something. Another orchid my mom had given Dr. Bach rested on his desk, stretching toward the cheery sunshine beyond the misty veil of curtains.

My mind dipped into the well of dark memories I wanted to forget. I pushed away unbidden thoughts of my older sister and what had happened to her and my first love, Derrick. I would not think about it. Dr. Bach said what had happened wasn't my fault.

I remembered Derrick's blue eyes, full of sunshine and optimism. The way he used to smile at me banished the cold cynicism of the world and reminded me anything was possible. I imagined his lips on mine, his arms pulling me into the sanctuary of his embrace. The old yearning returned, bittersweet and suffocating in its intensity. Tears filled my eyes.

The room grew eerily silent. The clock no longer ticked. The lamps in the corners flickered and hummed. Haltingly, the mechanisms of the clock started up again, but this time the beat ticked irregularly.

Tick-tick-tick-thunk.

Silence.

Tick-tick-tick-thunk.

The second hand spun counterclockwise in spurts. The scents of potted plants and dusty chairs faded under the sharp tingle of ozone and metal. Electricity tingled under my skin.

"Oh no." I flinched and looked around, ready for something to explode.

This was not happening again. It had to be one of my hallucinations. I didn't want to be crazy, but the alternative was worse.

Beyond the window, the black silhouettes of birds cast ominous shadows over the interior of the room. Their wings slapped against the glass as if trying to break their way in. I squeezed my eyes closed, my apprehension growing. Those were just birds. They were not evil Fae, I told myself. No one was about to abduct me like they had with my sister.

"Magic is not real."

I said it, but I was wrong.

CHAPTER ONE
If You Believe in Fairies, Clap Your Hands

"You're a liar, *ginger*," Karen Walker said as we walked home from school with her older brother and his friend.

"No, I'm not!" I said. No one managed to make my blood boil the way the neighbor kids did. Had it been anyone else, I could have ignored them. "And don't call me that, *squib*." I hoped I wasn't going to get in trouble for saying that word. My older sister said it wasn't a real swearword, but it felt like one.

"If you're a witch, prove it." A little smirk tugged Peter Walker's mouth into a sneer. "Do something magical for us." He nudged his buddy, Jordan Burke, like it was a joke. They were fifth graders, two years older than Karen and me.

"Maybe I will." I held my head up high, imagining myself impervious to the sting of insults in my witch hat, black cape and Gryffindor scarf. Even so, a prickle of hurt wormed its way under my armor of striped socks.

If I was going to prove myself, I would have to hurry before my parents came home from work and stopped me.

Our two-story brick house was a lush oasis surrounded by green gardens and shady trees in a desert of boring cookie cutter homes with dead grass. Once we'd made it through the gate of the white picket fence, the four of us kids dragged the large trampoline over to the side of the house, under the lower part of the roof where it was only one story. I tried to direct them so they didn't stomp through Mom's artful arrangement of flowers planted along the perimeter of the patio, but they didn't listen. Karen chewed on the end of her brown braid, listening as Jordan whispered to her. He usually didn't deign to speak to third graders, but today he had walked home with Karen's older brother, Peter.

They wouldn't be sorry they'd come. I was going to show them magic.

Awkwardly, I held the broom while I climbed up the ladder my dad had left leaning against the roof to fix the satellite dish. My heart hammered in my chest as I shuffled along the angled edge of the roof. I placed the broom between my legs. This would be like all those times I'd successfully practiced flying onto the trampoline before. Only, those times had been from the top of the three-foot brick wall that separated the patio and fire pit from my mom's garden.

I gazed down at my audience below. My witch cape billowed around my shoulders and my red hair danced into my eyes. This was the moment I would prove I was a witch. I would fly. Tomorrow they'd be nice to me and Karen would invite me to sit with her and the cool kids during lunch.

"Hurry up, Clarissa," Karen said.

A niggling doubt worked its way into my mind. What if I wasn't a witch? No, that was impossible. But if I wasn't, the trampoline would surely break my fall.

"Chicken," Peter taunted.

It occurred to me I might be wrong. I might be a fairy, not a witch. If that was the case, the broom wouldn't work. I needed to ensure I would fly. I poured the bottle of pixie dust from the amulet around my neck. I just had to have light, happy thoughts like in *Peter Pan*. Or was that *Mary Poppins*?

I closed my eyes and edged closer to the gutter. I had to concentrate. Magic only worked in stories when a witch focused— and when she needed it most. A door slammed somewhere behind me. I tried to ignore the sound. It probably was my sister getting home from her after school club. She would go straight up to her room to do homework like she usually did.

Another door opened and thudded closed.

"What are you doing over here, Karen?" my older sister, Missy asked. "Where's Clarissa?"

My accomplices chuckled.

"She's going to fly." Karen tee-heed.

"What are you talking about?" Missy came into view.

Her blonde hair was pulled up into a ponytail and she wore a blue and green dress that reminded me of water. She joined them out on the lawn, trampling through Mom's petunias.

Great. My sister was about to ruin everything.

Missy followed their gazes. Her curiosity transformed into anger as she shouted at me. "Oh, no you don't! You get down, this instant."

"Okay," I said. I inched forward, my toes over the gutter. My heart pounded in my ears.

"No! You go over to that ladder and get down. Right now." Missy punched Karen in the arm. "You should be ashamed of yourself, encouraging her like that."

"Ow!" Karen squealed.

Missy shoved Peter and rounded on Jordan. "You're all a bunch of jerks."

"It's okay, Missy," I called down. "I can fly. I'm going to prove it. Just watch."

It didn't count if no one watched. She had to be looking at me.

"I told you to climb down. You get off the roof before you break your neck. Now!" Missy pointed to the ladder.

I tried to explain why I needed to do this, but she talked over me. "Whatever these losers told you, ignore them. You don't have to prove anything."

"Missy, listen," I said. "You don't have to worry. I know I can do magic, and I'm going to show you all. I just need you to be quiet so I can concentrate."

"If you do this, I'll tell Mom and Dad." She started up the ladder.

"Good," I said. They would see it was true and stop telling me I lived in a fantasy world.

"No!" Missy said. "Do NOT do it. Stay where you are. I'll get you down."

"I don't need your help. *You*, stay where you are. Don't come any closer." Why did she have to embarrass me in front of the neighbors?

This wasn't going well. If she tried to stop me, I was going to have to leap off the roof before I was ready. My clammy hands gripped the wood of the broom.

She reached the top of the ladder. "If you don't stop, I'll make sure you get grounded. If you don't stop I'll—"

I inched away from her, slowly, not wanting to trip over the uneven shingles of the roof. "I don't care."

Only, I did. I didn't want to get in trouble. But this was going to be worth it. No one would punish me once they understood I had *powers.*

"Stop being like this." Missy inched toward me, arms out to balance herself on the incline. "If you do this, I'll be mean to you. I won't give you the toys in my Happy Meal. I'll take back that dress I gave you yesterday."

I chewed on my lip. Missy was never mean to me. We were friends.

My audience snickered below. I heard the words "gullible" and "moron."

Missy threw down her trump card. "If you jump, I won't be your friend anymore."

My feet rooted to the shingles. She couldn't!

She went on. "If you're going to be my best friend, you can't do something stupid like this. If you jump off the roof and die—"

"I'm not going to die."

"Fine, if you *fly* off the roof and survive, I won't ever speak to you again. I'll hate you, and you won't be my friend anymore. Is that what you want?"

I looked to the trio below and then to Missy. I shook my head.

She offered me a smile, holding her hand out to me. I trudged back to her and took her hand. She grabbed the broom from me and threw it at Peter. He jumped back. She guided me to the ladder and held it as I climbed down. Each rung brought me closer to my impending doom. Once I stood at the bottom, the three other kids whispered to each other.

Karen looked me over, her expression unimpressed. "I knew you weren't going to do it."

I hung my head with shame. Tomorrow it would be all over the school. People would have one more reason to make fun of me. Couldn't Missy understand how she had just ruined my life? I would never have friends now.

Missy climbed down after me. She picked up the broom from

where it lay in the tangles of thyme and rosemary, and swatted at Karen and then Jordan. They dodged back. Jordan kept laughing, even as she hit him. He stopped laughing when she smashed the wood of the broom against his nose.

He cried out and grabbed his face, blood spurting from between his fingers. I stared in wide-eyed shock.

"Get lost, all of you. If I ever hear about you egging her on like this again, I'll make you regret it. Understand me?" Missy's hair fell out of her ponytail and streamed around her shoulders in wild waves. She looked like she could have been a witch at that moment. She smacked Peter with the broom. "You're a bunch of jerks and bullies. Someone could have gotten hurt today. I won't let you pick on my sister." Her voice turned hoarse as she shouted and chased them.

They ran around the side of the house and out the gate of our white picket fence. Missy stared after them, waiting until they'd ran across the street. The wooden gate swung on its hinges.

"Wow, that was great," I said. My sister could be simultaneously terrifying and wonderful.

Missy stalked back toward me, dragging the broom in the dirt of the flower beds. Her cheeks were flushed. I smiled at her, grateful she'd told off those kids. Maybe they wouldn't tease me tomorrow.

As I reached out to hug Missy, she slapped me across the face, hard enough to bring tears to my eyes.

I stumbled back. "What was that for?"

Missy burst into tears. "Don't ever do anything stupid like that again. Promise me. I don't want to lose you." She grabbed me and clutched me to her.

I hugged her back and patted her shoulder.

"Do you know what Mom would have done to me if you had broken an arm when I was supposed to be watching you? Do you know what she would have done to you? She's one step away from taking away your *Narnia* books as it is."

"No! Not my books!" I said. "You won't tell Mom and Dad, will you?"

She didn't answer.

"Please?" I asked.

If she did, they would command me never to do it again. And then I wouldn't be able to because it would be bad if I didn't listen to them. I had to find a new way to prove I was a witch.

Missy sniffled and pulled away, wiping her face against her sleeve. "I won't tell . . . if you can tell me why you aren't going to do that again."

I tried to figure out what she wanted to hear. "You don't want me to get hurt. You think I can't really fly."

"I don't think. I know, dorkbreath."

"But I can! I did it before. I flew from the wall to the trampoline."

She grimaced. "No, you *jumped* onto the trampoline. Anyone can do that. Repeat after me, 'I cannot fly.'"

In my most petulant monotone I said, "Fine. I can't fly. Will you promise not to tell?"

She gave me a playful shove. "You're impossible." Her smile told me everything would be all right.

I thought that was the end of it. I went back inside to do my homework. Mom came home an hour later and Dad shortly after that. I didn't hear Missy tattle, so I thought I'd gotten off easy. It was after dinner as I was playing with my toys that I suspected something was wrong.

I was aware of the silence downstairs. The television wasn't on. I lay across my Tinker Bell bedspread, listening. Missy was on the phone in her room. That meant she wasn't squealing on me. I continued to play.

A procession of my Barbie dolls dressed in the gowns of a fairy court loomed over the My Little Pony pegasi and unicorns, dwarfing them. Footsteps creaked up the stairs. I lined up three storm troopers beside Darth Vader next to the model *U.S.S. Enterprise* I'd made with Dad. The two opposing forces faced off.

Dad leaned against the entry, the bulk of his frame taking up the majority of the doorway. His eyes raked over my tableaux. "Honey, come downstairs for a minute. Your mom and I want to talk to you." He rubbed at his golden beard and mustache, not meeting my eyes.

Cold dread settled like ice in my gut as I clutched Midnight Rainbow, my favorite unicorn. I followed Dad down. He moved slowly, lumbering toward the living room like a pack animal burdened by the weight of too many bags.

Missy had told. I was going to get in trouble. They were going to take my books away. I would have to lie. I didn't want to, but I would say Missy was fibbing. I didn't know what else to do.

They sat on the couch side by side. They never sat on the couch with backs straight and rigid, looking like someone had died. Unless someone had died. Mom smiled, or looked like she was trying to. Maybe my books were safe.

"There's something we need to tell you." Dad leaned his elbows onto his knees and rubbed at his face.

"We've been talking. . . ." Mom said.

My nerves jittered with anticipation. Missy had told them. I was certain of it, now more than ever.

"I didn't do it." I hugged Midnight Rainbow. "Missy made it up."

My parents looked at each other, confusion painting their faces.

"What?" Dad asked.

Mom's eyes narrowed with shrewdness. "*What* didn't you do?"

Immediately I could see my error. They hadn't been about to ground me from reading fantasy novels for the rest of my life. Missy hadn't told them. Only, I had blown it, and they were about to dig the truth out of me. That meant they were going to tell me some other terrible news.

I tried to cover my mistake. "Nothing. I mean, we were just playing earlier, and she got mad at me and. . . ." I tried to think of something, but all the imaginative tales stored up in my brain failed me.

Dad plunged on, unfazed, his eyes glued on the avocado-green carpet. "We've talked to you about some things in the past. Grownup things. We need to talk to you about something important."

Neither spoke. Mom swallowed.

"Something important," I repeated.

Wait a minute. . . . This was it! Finally, they were going to tell me I was special. I was a fairy or a witch or something magical.

I glanced over my shoulder. "Shouldn't Missy be here for this?"

"Missy already knows about grownup things," Mom said. She took my hands in hers, staring into my eyes. "Do you remember when we told you some things are for the imagination? Not everything magic is real."

"I remember," I said quickly. The anticipation was killing me. Surely they were about to tell me what was real—that I was a witch.

Dad pulled at a loose thread on the seam of the brown couch. "Do you remember last Easter when you found those white, powdery footprints leading from the living room out onto the lawn?"

"Yes. We looked it up in that book, and we identified it as the

Leporidae Eastarus—the Easter Bunny." Looking it up in one of Dad's books had been his idea. "Those footprints led to the best eggs ever!" I didn't know what the Easter Bunny had to do with anything important, though.

"That was me," Dad said.

"No, it wasn't. Those weren't your footprints."

Mom shoved a paper bag at him. He removed the talcum powder and bunny slippers.

I shook my head, refusing to believe him.

Mom nudged him. "Tell her about Christmas."

"That was also my idea," Dad said. "I ate the carrots you left out for the reindeer. And the cookies and milk."

"But you couldn't have. You're lactose intolerant."

Dad's eyes crinkled up with pity. "I poured the milk back into the carton."

"I don't believe you."

"Santa Claus, the Easter Bunny and the tooth fairy are stories," Mom said. "They're make-believe."

The fragile world I had always loved shattered before my eyes. I wiped a tear from the corner of my eye and held my chin high. I was a big girl. I could handle the Easter Bunny and tooth fairy not being real. I'd already suspected as much from the gossip of third graders in my class. I was fine with that creepy guy at the mall who always waved at me and invited me to sit on his lap not being the "real" Saint Nick.

Everything would be fine if magic still existed in the world.

I drew in a shaky breath, afraid to ask. "But Hogwarts—that's real, right?" It wasn't like I was asking if Harry Potter was real. Even if he was fictional, it didn't mean the place he went to school couldn't be real. The place I would be going to school.

My parents' nervous glance at each other said it all. Mom fidgeted with the frizzy tail of her long red braid. My heart plummeted to my stomach and settled like a pair of concrete shoes in a river.

"I'm sorry, Clarissa." Dad sat me between the two of them. He kissed the top of my head. His beard tickled my face.

My mother muttered under her breath. "See, I told you those books were a bad idea."

Those words were more powerful than Missy's slap to my face earlier.

I covered my eyes and bawled. "What about Jesus? Is he a lie too?"

Mom said nothing.

"No, honey. God is real," Dad said.

Yeah, right. See if I believed anything they said ever again.

I squirmed out from between them and threw my toy unicorn on the floor, about to run out of the room.

"Not so fast." Mom grabbed the back of my shirt and tugged me onto the couch beside her. "It can be hard to tell the difference between what is real and what we want to be true. Sometimes there are strange things that happen in the world that we don't understand. Don't try to take care of these things by yourself. If you ever notice something isn't right, come and tell Mommy."

"Or if someone goads you into climbing on the roof with a broom," Dad said. "Maybe you should ask a second opinion from an unbiased source. Like one of us. Or another adult."

"Missy told?" I shrieked.

"No. Mrs. Mesker called me when I got home from work," Mom said. I hadn't counted on the elderly neighbor to be the one to tattle on me.

Despite my parents' intervention, I couldn't shake my belief in magic.

On my eleventh birthday, I sat at the window, waiting for my owl to come and tell me I had been accepted to a magical school of witchcraft and wizardry.

My older sister, Missy, bounded into the room, dressed in a cheerleading uniform from spring break camp. She waved a letter around. "Look! They want me to come to drill camp this summer and invited me to try out for the high school squad. They've chosen me!" She ran out of the room, oblivious to my misery.

I wanted someone to tell me I was the chosen one, that I was special too. Maybe it was because my older sister was so good at everything, and I wasn't good at anything. Except drawing, and that didn't count.

No owl came. No letter arrived. I was destined for an ordinary life of non-magic. Or so I thought.

CHAPTER TWO
The Day My Sister Was Abducted by a Witch

I had just celebrated my fourteenth birthday a few days before we went to Oregon Country Fair. Back in the early two thousands it was considered the bohemian Mecca before Burning Man gained notoriety.

"It's one part renaissance fair, one part music festival, and two parts hippieville," Dad said as he parked the minivan. "There's something for everyone at this event."

Even before my family exited the van, I knew it was going to be a magical day. A lady wearing a medieval gown walked toward colorful banners above the entrance, followed by a troupe of teenagers in black and white striped costumes reminiscent of characters from a Tim Burton movie.

Something flitted past the window. The bright colors and rapid wing movement reminded me of a hummingbird. The shimmer was more like the iridescence of a dragonfly. It zipped around the van as my parents unloaded backpacks with water bottles, snacks, and ninety-nine other items my mom thought were essential. The little creature hovered above Dad's bald spot, and that's when I saw the body was shaped like a person's.

"Look, a fairy," I said in wonder. "A real fairy!"

Missy raised an eyebrow. "There's no such thing as fairies. You know that, right, Clarissa?"

I pointed. Mom and Dad were busy talking and didn't see. By the time Missy turned to look, the creature had flown off. I was certain this was a sign anything could happen today. Magic was *real*. Even if no one else thought so.

We passed a jillion cars in the field as we walked to the shady area where the entrance of the woodland fair was located. Dad made us stop in front of a dragon statue to snap a photo with his digital camera.

"Say cheese doodles," Dad said, making a goofy face so we would smile.

He took another photo of Mom, Missy, and me in our matching tie-dyed shirts next to a wall of artwork. The blue and green of our shirts made the auburn of my mom's hair shine more vividly in the summer sunlight. It even made the golden whiskers peppered through Dad's beard appear redder. I could only imagine what it was doing to my own hair. Missy was so lucky to be born blonde. I would have traded my vintage Spock doll collection to get rid of my freckles and red hair.

"Your eyes were closed, Missy," Dad said to my sister. He snapped another pic. "A real smile, this time, Clarissa. I want to see your seven-thousand-dollar smile."

I sealed my lips together so my braces wouldn't be visible. I hated it when he acted like my braces cost a fortune. He was my orthodontist. It didn't cost him anything.

I thought Mr. Documentary was finished with his photo session, but no, not my parental unit. Dad flagged down a man dressed as a human-sized chess piece. White paint covered his face and arms to match his tunic.

"Nice costume." Dad said. "Would you mind taking a photo of me with my family?"

"Sure, dude," the man said.

Mom eyed the stranger warily. He smelled like a skunk, and I wondered if he had encountered wildlife at the woodland forest of the fair. A lady walked by, her bare breasts covered in glitter paint. My sister caught my eye, and we both giggled. This wasn't like the county fair. Dad had warned us there wouldn't be rides, cotton candy, or people showing off cows and pigs. This was the fair he used to go to when he'd been in college at University of Oregon.

Dad hugged us to his sides under a shady tree, looming over the three of us as the stranger snapped photos. We thanked the man and checked the photos in the digital camera's screen. Dad's head was cut off in the first photo. The second one wasn't so bad, but it showed a woman in a bird costume, black plumage ruffled out like a collar as she photobombed behind us.

Mom stared at the photo, her brow furrowing. She glanced around. The woman was long gone.

Dad muttered under his breath about amateur photographers.

"You're an amateur, Dad," I said.

"I'm not just the president of the Amateur Club of Photographers, I'm also a client." His barrel chest heaved up and down as he laughed at his own joke.

"Lame," Missy mouthed.

"Let me get sunblock on you girls." Mom fussed at us and slathered a gob of white goop over my face. "Now, what is the plan if you get lost?"

"Find a staff member who can escort us back to the main entrance," Missy said in an unenthusiastic monotone.

"And if you get hurt?" Mom asked.

I held up the map, pointing at the first aid symbol. "White Bird's Medical Station."

"There's nothing to worry about," Dad said. "We're all going to stay together."

A shadow blotted out the sun and chilled the air. I looked up. A flock of birds swarmed above us like bees, their silhouettes black and ominous. I'd never seen birds circle in a frenzy like that before.

"It isn't too late to go home." Mom bit her lip, looking at me and talking about me as if I wasn't there. "Fourteen is too young for a place like this."

"Resistance is futile. You will have a good time, hon," Dad said, hugging Mom around the shoulders.

Mom made me hold her hand as we walked through the crowd, even though it was uber embarrassing. Missy held my other hand as Dad snapped photos of everything. I stared in wonder at the booths full of clothes that would have been perfect for a woodland fairy to wear. A rainbow of ribbons hung from a tree, wafting in the wind. The fair was unlike any other festival I'd been to. People wore funky costumes, and there were so many stages playing cool music. We stopped and watched a belly dance performance.

"Isn't it absolutely magical?" I said to Missy. I felt like I'd walked into another dimension. These people were my people, and this place was home. I'd finally found somewhere I belonged.

"There you go again." She nudged me. "Everything is always fairyland with you, isn't it?"

I grinned. She knew me better than anyone else.

The festival stretched on for what seemed like miles. Sunlight sparkled off a booth of glass art. Missy held up a pink and white vase with a tube sticking out the side of it, giving it a quizzical look.

"Is that a musical instrument?" I asked. "It's my favorite color!"

Dad took it from Missy and set it back down. "Heh, you don't need one of those. That's for college students."

Mom groaned. "This is why I didn't think we should take them to the Oregon Country Fair."

"What? Why?" I asked.

Mom took my hand as we perused a long line of shops between us and Main Stage where we were headed. Dad and Missy progressed more quickly, the gap between us widening.

A few minutes later, Missy came skipping back, Dad right behind her. His mustache and beard almost hid his little smirk. He raised the camera again, poised to take a photo.

"I bought something for you with my allowance." Missy was practically jumping up and down in her excitement. "Hold out your hand and close your eyes. I have something for you that's a big surprise."

"Okay," I said. I closed my eyes, and held out my hand, smiling in anticipation of whatever it was.

"That isn't the way it goes," Dad said. A camera shutter clicked. "It's open your *mouth* and close your eyes. I have something that's a big surprise. And it's supposed to be a worm you put in her mouth. That's what your Uncle Trevor used to do to me when we were kids."

Missy and I squealed. I covered my face with my hands, icked out. I didn't peek, though.

"Gross!" Missy said.

"Yeah, Dad, gross!" I said.

Mom chuckled.

"I wouldn't ever do that to you," Missy said. She pulled my hand away from my face. "No peeking."

Something tickled against my wrist.

"Open your eyes," Missy said.

It was a friendship bracelet decorated with pink and white stripes, my favorite colors. In the center of the knotwork were three pink beads threaded into the woven strands: BFF. Best friends forever.

"Whoa! Cool," I said.

I threw my arms around my sister's neck and hugged her. "Thank you! I love it!"

She lifted me off my feet with one of her big sister hugs. "I'm glad you like it." She kissed the top of my head.

"I won't ever take it off," I promised. "I want to get a matching one for you."

Our parents walked behind us as Missy showed me where the booth was. She picked out a bracelet with her school colors: red and white. *My* school colors come September. Just thinking about high school filled me with dread.

Dad went up to the artist to pay with me since he was the one holding my allowance.

"Free samples," a creaky voice said behind me.

A hunched-over old woman held a basket of gingerbread men and women. She was dressed in a mixture of mismatched patterns. Her long nose and pointed chin reminded me of the illustrations of Baba Yaga from Mom's fairytale book. She held a cookie out to Missy.

Mom swatted at Missy's hand as if she was still six. I would have died if she'd done that to me.

"We don't know what's in those cookies," Mom whispered, none too quietly. "They might have drugs in them."

"Mom!" Missy said. "You're being rude. It's just a cookie."

"If you're hungry, we'll get you girls real food." Mom turned away from the woman. "Dessert after."

Dad shook with silent laughter. At least someone was enjoying this.

The old woman grinned a toothless smile. "That's right, dearie. Never accept food from strangers." The hint of an accent flavored her creaky voice, though I couldn't place it. "But we aren't strangers, are we, *Abigail?*"

She knew my mom's name? Mom tugged Missy around a flock of teens, joining Dad and me.

"Who was that?" Dad asked.

Mom's spine was stiff, her tone brisk. "No one."

"Abby, how'd she know your name?"

Mom made a motion with her hand that reminded me of sign language, only she did it behind her back like she didn't want anyone to see. The air smelled green, like her herb garden. "Who's hungry for lunch?"

Dad's eyes became unfocused, and he stopped asking questions. "I'm hungry," he said.

The question that had been on my own lips melted away. I couldn't remember what I'd been thinking about a moment before. Mom looked tired. Missy pouted until I brought her the friendship bracelet and tied it on her wrist.

Missy leaned in conspiratorially. "The 'rental units are driving me crazy."

I giggled. "Yeah, I know. Me too."

We stopped at a food booth for lunch and ate Thai food. Mom bought us coconut ice cream for dessert. I sat next to Missy, and she shared a piece of mango in her ice cream with me. My sister was the best. This was the best day ever, and I got to share it with my best friend. I was so happy, I couldn't imagine any moment in my life being better than this.

Missy and I held hands during the acrobatics show at the Daredevil Palace Vaudeville Stage, our bracelets next to each other on our arms.

"I don't feel like I'm ready to go to high school." I said.

"How can you not be ready?" Missy tore her gaze from the juggler riding the unicycle on the stage. "It'll be great. We'll be at the same school. We can eat lunch together."

"What if I don't fit in?"

She bumped my shoulder playfully with hers. "You can hang out with me, but you're going to have to *try* to fit in. Watch some television shows high schoolers like. And don't say you already do. No one watches *Doctor Who* or the *X-Files* or *Buffy*. Those shows are too old. And they're kind of, well, people think they're nerdy."

I made a face at her. Dad and I liked to watch those shows together. Someone a few rows ahead of us lit up a stinky cigarette. I tried not to choke. Missy waved the smoke away. It finally clicked.

I nudged Missy. "Is this what marijuana smells like? I always thought that was skunk."

"That's because you believe everything Mom tells you." She tore her gaze away from the juggling. "That smell on Beavercreek Road is skunk. In the city, it isn't. I heard Dad tell Mom, out here in Eugene you can't walk a block without getting a whiff of someone smoking pot."

I'd had no idea. We lived in a nice neighborhood with half an acre of yard between us and our neighbors. People where we lived in Oregon City didn't do this kind of thing. At least I didn't think they did.

How could my parents have kept me in the dark about this? What would I do if I didn't have Missy around to explain the world to me?

Missy went back to watching the juggling. It was silly and fun, and I wanted to enjoy it, but I couldn't stop thinking about September and the start of school.

I swallowed, afraid to voice the depths of my fears. "What if there are bullies? What if Jonathan happens again?" I glanced at our parents. Dad was engrossed in the show. Mom watched a blackbird in one of the trees.

"What about that loser?" Missy flicked her long hair over her shoulder. "He moved away."

Jonathan talked about a show called *South Park* that we weren't allowed to watch. He said redheads didn't have souls. Kids who normally didn't talk to me suddenly wanted to "play with me" on National Kick a Ginger Day. He'd convinced five different kids in the seventh grade to kick me as I'd been waiting for the bus. Missy had punched him after school the next day and told him it was National Punch a Moron in the Face Day.

"This holiday is going to reoccur regularly if you ever do that to my sister again, poopbrain," she'd threatened.

Missy was petite like me, but that was where the resemblance ended. She was quick and coordinated, an asset to the high school cheer team. More importantly, she wasn't afraid to hit boys bigger than she was. I wished I could be as brave and tough as my sister.

Missy pulled out her phone from her back pocket. It showed there was no service, and she put it away. "If someone does that to you again and I'm not around, you're going to have to tell a teacher. Or tell Mom or Dad."

I nodded. The idea of confessing to a grownup that the other kids thought I didn't have a soul was too humiliating.

Missy looked away from the acrobats on the stage and circled her arm protectively around my shoulder. "And if you can't do that, tell me. I'll take care of anyone who picks on you." She looped a finger under my friendship bracelet and spun it on my wrist.

Warmth spread through my chest. My vision wavered as tears filled my eyes. I was lucky to have a sister who was so good to me.

With her close by, I felt safe and protected. She kept spinning the bracelet. The air smelled like waterfalls and fresh spring water, perfumes out of place in a dry wooded area. With each turn, I felt more of her words sink in, more of their meaning embracing me. She would never let anyone or anything hurt me. That bracelet felt like a promise—or something stronger.

It felt like magic.

"You're my sister, and we'll always be best friends," Missy said.

For the briefest second, I thought I could see her words sparkle out of her mouth and spiral around my arm, tingling where the bracelet met my skin. I blinked and the vision melted away.

Halfway through the show, Dad stood to go use the restroom. "Anyone need to come with me for a potty break?"

"Dad? Do you have to talk to us like we're five?" Missy asked.

"Pretty much," he said.

Missy and Dad left together. Mom and I remained at the show. Mom kept glancing at the crows in the boughs of the trees. They watched us, heads cocked. I knew Mom didn't like blackbirds. She erected a scarecrow every spring and threw rocks at the ravens if she found them pecking her tomatoes. She said she'd adopted our cat specifically to keep the birds away from the garden, but we weren't at home right now. There was no reason to dislike these birds so much. Even so, she kept glancing at them nervously.

Twenty minutes later, the performance ended. Dad and Missy still hadn't come back. Mom examined the map. The bathrooms weren't that far away.

We walked down the dusty path and shuffled through the crowd until we found the row of Porta Potties.

Dad stood outside of one of the units, knocking on the door. "Missy?" From his concerned expression, I could tell something was wrong.

A lady in a tutu came out, scowling at him.

"Have you seen this girl?" Dad asked, holding up the camera to show the woman a photo.

Dad's face was red, and he was sweating buckets. He knocked on the door of the portable toilet next to the first one. "Missy?" he shouted. He even used her real name. "Melissa?"

Mom rushed forward, tugging me with her. "What's going on? Where's Missy?"

"I saw her go in that one," Dad pointed to the second door. "I went in the next bathroom that opened up. I was only in there for a minute. I was sure I'd be out before her."

Mom turned around, scanning the crowd. A blackbird glided through the clear blue sky and landed on a leafy limb above us. On the ground next to the garbage can something caught the light. I stepped forward and picked it up. It was a cell phone.

"This is Missy's," I said. Why she would have thrown it away, I couldn't imagine.

"That could be anyone's phone," Mom said, dismissing me with a glance and asking Dad more questions.

I pulled up the list of recent phone numbers. It included her friends and our home phone. I waved it in front of Mom's face, but she ignored me. This was important. Missy didn't go anywhere without her phone. Something terrible must have happened to her.

"She was supposed to wait for me." Dad's voice came out choked. "Do you think she went back to the stage? Could she have gotten lost?"

My heart thundered. My sister couldn't be missing. This was my worst fear come true. I couldn't have felt more lost if I'd been the one alone.

Mom shook out the map. "We told her to find someone who works here to walk her to the entrance if she got lost."

That was right. Missy was smart. I didn't understand how she'd gotten separated from Dad, but she wouldn't panic.

"Yes!" Dad said. "That's where she'll go. We need to find a volunteer. They have walkie talkies."

Since there was no cell service out here, that was the best bet.

Mom nodded. "Take Clarissa to the entrance. Don't let her out of your sight." She glanced at the blackbird in the tree, eyes narrowing. "Find someone who works here and report Missy as missing. I'll go back to the stage and see if she's there. I'll find a volunteer in this area."

"No, you take Clarissa," Dad said. "I should stick around in case she comes back. I'm easier to see in a crowd."

A lady in a black dress and a collar made of black feathers perched on one of the wooden fences on the path to the vaudeville stage. She balanced on the fence with accurate imitations of bird's feet. Mom's gaze locked on her.

She looked like that lady who had photobombed our snapshot earlier.

"Go. Now," Mom said in a tone that left no room for argument.

Dad opened his mouth like he was about to object, but Mom stomped off. He took my hand. I glanced over my shoulder. Mom headed toward the lady sitting on the fence. A group of young men, all dressed in pink and playing drums, whooped and hollered, heading toward us. Dad tugged me to the side of the path so we could get past them. I kept watching my mom.

"What have you done with my daughter?" Mom demanded.

The woman's voice was raspy, most of her words drowned out by the crowd, the pink marching band, and the music coming from a nearby stage. I focused on her lips, imagining my ear was next to her mouth. A foreign warmth tingled through me, and her words became clear.

"We haven't done anything to anyone," the woman said. "We aren't allowed to collect lost souls until after dark."

I tugged on Dad's hand. "Who is Mom talking to? Look."

Dad glanced over his shoulder and promptly collided with someone in front of him. He apologized to a man dressed as a robot, still not looking at Mom. He showed the man a photo of Missy on his camera, asking if he'd seen her.

The bird woman lifted one of her feet and pointed to me. Shivers ran down my spine. The lady was a real bird. Or some kind of were-bird.

Mom spoke to the bird woman. "She is not a lost soul. She's in my care."

Dad tugged me along the path, completely oblivious. "Hurry up, sport."

"No, Dad, look!" I said, pointing.

"Clarissa, I don't have time for this. I need you to hurry."

Mom pointed accusingly at the woman, her words lost in the rising beat of drumming.

"Dad!" I ground my feet into the dirt and forced him to stop. "Look. Right now."

He turned, but a parade of people, all dressed in pink, ran between us and Mom, singing and playing drums. They cut Mom off from view. When they passed, Mom was gone. So was the lady.

Dad hustled me toward the nearest first aid station. We found a staff member with a walkie talkie.

"My daughter is missing," Dad explained, the panic returning to his voice. "Have you seen my daughter? Have any teenagers come here and reported themselves as missing?"

"No, I'm sorry, no one has." The man wore a volunteer shirt. "Can you tell me what she looks like?"

"She's sixteen and blonde. We're wearing matching shirts." Dad held up his camera. "I have photos of her. Do you want to take my camera? Will that help?"

The man scrolled through the photos and asked questions. He wrote down a description and reported her as missing on his walkie talkie.

A blackbird watched us from a tree, a gleam in its eyes. Soon another bird landed next to the first. It tilted its head to the side. A third one drifted down to the branch. All three followed us with their gaze as the volunteer walked us to a gate in the wooden fence along the path. I had a bad feeling about these birds and that bird woman my mom had been talking to. I kept watching them over my shoulder as Dad and I followed the volunteer to the other path.

"This area is only meant for performers and volunteers," the man said. "You'll be able to meet security at the main gate more quickly if you go this way."

Fewer people traveled on this side of the fence. A moment later a man in a rickshaw rode up. He wore a hot pink fedora that matched his pink spandex pants.

He extended his hand to Dad. "Hi, I'm Bob. I'll get you to the other side of the fair in a jiffy."

Bob took Dad and me on a ride in a rickshaw along the path behind the wooden fence. It would have been fun racing down the path as some guy pulled us in a cart if I hadn't been so worried.

The rickshaw driver got us to the entrance in twenty minutes. He called someone on his walkie talkie. Volunteers wearing security vests escorted us to a building shaped like a dragon's head. We stood outside the mouth of the dragon as they asked us questions. I hugged one of the teeth that protruded from the counter. It grounded me to hold onto something.

"Has anyone seen her?" Dad asked a security guard.

"I'm sorry, sir. No one has found her yet," said a tall lady in a cowboy hat and a badge that said *Deputy*. "We'll keep looking."

"She's only sixteen," Dad said.

"We have volunteers looking for her inside the fair and outside in the campgrounds. If she's walking on foot from Main Stage, it's going to take her an hour to get here with this crowd," she said. "Unless she finds a staff member and asks someone to help her, she might not have a shortcut like you did."

Missy would know to ask for help. Mom had made her recite the plan. Why wasn't she here yet? I glanced at another blackbird and began to cry. One of the volunteers gave me a cherry popsicle, but my belly felt too queasy to eat it.

Dad made me stand beside him in the shade where people gave the attendants their tickets at the gate. He spoke with people exiting the fair and walking toward the bus loading zone and parking lot, trying to stop each person to ask them if they'd seen Missy. I held the stick of my popsicle, the sugary liquid melting in the heat. It dripped down my hand.

A crow swooped down and pecked at the red puddle. I screamed and jumped back into Dad. He sat me down at a bench in the shade. I couldn't stop shaking.

He threw my stick away and wiped my hand on the side of his tie-dye shirt. "It will be okay, honey. We'll find Missy."

He returned to questioning people as they exited the fair. No one recognized Missy from the photo viewer on the camera. I scanned the crowd for my sister. Any moment she was going to walk along the path and wave to us. I kept hoping and praying, but she still didn't appear.

"Have you seen this girl?" Dad asked a mother with her baby strapped to her back.

"I've seen your sister," a raspy voice said close to my ear.

I jumped to my feet. A woman with black feathers for hair roosted on the bench. She was half bird, like the woman my Mom had spoken to earlier. This woman's hair was shorter, but her feather dress was similar. Her eyes were solid black, like a bird's.

I looked her up and down, afraid. "Where is she?"

Something brushed my arm and another bird woman walked up beside me. This one wore an Elizabethan collar made of black feathers. She gouged the dry earth with talon-tipped bird feet that poked from under her dress.

"Do you suppose either of them know what they are?" she asked the first bird.

"Their guardian keeps them in ignorance." She nodded to Dad, his back turned away from me. "The Morty doesn't know what they are either."

"What do you mean? What are we?" I asked. "Who are you? You said you know where my sister is."

They exchanged amused smiles.

"Your mother was right to tell your sister not to eat the gingerbread cookies the witch offered her." The first bird woman smiled, her teeth pointed and sharp. "I can take you to her. For a price." She glided off the bench, her bird-shaped body seamlessly transitioning into a woman's.

"What do you mean by 'a price?'"

She held out her hand. "Come with me." The deep honey of her voice lured me closer.

I wanted to melt into the melody of her words. She waved me closer. Curved black talons grew from the ends of her fingers. I should have felt fear, but instead I felt calm.

"Come with me," she cooed in a sing-song voice.

Something pinched at my wrist. My friendship bracelet caught the sunlight, sparkling pink and dazzling my eyes as though it were covered in glitter. I blinked.

I suddenly remembered my mom wouldn't want me to go with this woman. I hadn't understood what Mom had been talking about to the other bird woman, but I could tell Mom had been angry. She didn't trust the blackbirds or the women dressed as crows, and neither would I. There was no way I was going with this stranger.

"Daaaad!" I yelled. "These women saw where Missy went."

Immediately he was at my side. The women frowned. He held up the digital camera. "Have you seen my daughter? This is what she looks like."

The women shrank back, their gazes riveted on the camera. One hissed.

"You don't have to stay in character. I'm being serious. My daughter is missing." Dad stepped toward one of them, holding up the back of the camera for her to see better.

She scrambled away. Her lips curled back into a sneer. "Get your human-crafted magic away from me."

Human-crafted magic? Dad stared at her as she backed into the crowd. Her friend was already gone.

I was more worried about Missy than ever.

Dad hugged me, and bought me a bag of peanuts, but I wasn't hungry. The sticky heat made me feel sick. I drank the water he gave me.

"This is all my fault. I shouldn't have insisted we come," Dad muttered.

An hour later, Missy still hadn't arrived. Neither had Mom. Volunteers milled around, keeping us updated.

"Have you called the police?" Dad asked one of the volunteers. If his cell phone had reception, I was sure he would have called them himself.

"We don't need to bother the police. This is a fair matter. We have security," a man said with a strained smile.

"My daughter has been gone for hours now and you're telling me we don't need to call the police?" Dad yelled. "I want you to get on your phone. Call them now."

My eyes went wide. I'd never seen my dad shout at anyone before. He was like the Bob Ross of orthodontists, but instead of painting happy little trees, he joked he worked with happy little brackets.

Twenty minutes later, a male and a female police officer pulled up to the bus loading area and walked to the entrance.

Officer McGathy, a man with beefy arms and the frame of a former football player, asked Dad questions. "Does your daughter have any friends at the fair? A boyfriend? Did you see her talking to anyone she might want to meet up with?"

"We live in Oregon City. That's two hours away. We don't know anyone here," Dad said.

The entire time Officer McGathy spoke to Dad, the burly man remained calm, his tone reassuring. Dad looked as if he was going to cry. I'd never seen him so helpless. Mom was the worrywart, not Dad.

Officer Baker asked me the same questions. She was a middle-aged woman with silver in her hair. She smiled in a friendly way that made it easy to tell her about how I'd found Missy's phone. She nodded and listened better than my parents had. I told her about the old woman who had offered Missy the cookie earlier and the bird women who had wanted to lure me away.

Her brow crinkled up in concern. "Can you give me a description of these women?"

I rubbed my forehead, trying to concentrate. "It's hard to think. I can't remember." The best I could do was say that the first woman was old and had a long nose. The other women wore all black.

"Have you been getting enough to drink?" Officer Baker asked.

"I'm not thirsty," I said. She brought me a bottled water anyway.

"We have some plainclothes police on site. They're looking for suspicious activity and checking out the campgrounds," Officer McGathy told us.

Another hour passed. Finally, the people on the walkie talkies gave us good news. An undercover cop had found Mom and Missy. One of the staff was giving them a ride back in a golf cart.

My sister had been missing for over five hours.

The moment I saw Missy I knew something wasn't right. Her blue eyes were dazed and unfocused. Her usually tidy blonde hair was a mess. Mom helped her from the cart and Missy leaned against her.

I ran to Missy and opened my arms to hug her. The addled expression left her face as she focused on me. She twitched back. The horror reflected in her eyes stung worse than a bee sting. She lurched over to Dad and buried her face in his shoulder.

"What's wrong?" I asked. "Are you okay? Missy?"

Dad placed a hand on Missy's head. He looked to Mom.

"She's been through a lot," Mom said. "We can talk about it later."

"Are you hurt?" Officer McGathy asked.

Missy turned her face away. She didn't answer.

"Can you tell us what happened?" Officer Baker asked.

Missy remained silent.

"My daughter is dehydrated. She needs water," Mom said.

I held out my bottled water. My sister ignored me. Volunteers brought us more water. Missy gulped down three bottles. She clutched a fourth to her chest but didn't drink it.

Officer Baker crouched down, asking Missy questions. Missy

didn't answer. She just leaned her head against Dad's shoulder and closed her eyes.

"Talk to them, honey," Dad said. "Tell us what happened."

"I'm tired," Missy said.

"My daughter has suffered quite a shock," Mom said. "She needs some rest."

"She needs medical attention," Dad said. "Can you direct us to the hospital?"

"We've called the paramedics. They're on their way," McGathy said.

Mom spoke quietly to Officer Baker, who nodded as she glanced at Missy. I wanted to know what Mom was saying, but Dad kept me at his side.

Within five minutes an ambulance arrived. The paramedics checked Missy for signs of dehydration and drugs. The police, my mom, and the EMTs crowded around my sister, asking her questions. I waited outside the circle, not wanting to be in the way. Missy still wouldn't look at me.

Dad joined me. He hugged a sweaty arm around me. "How are you holding up?"

"What happened to Missy?" I asked.

"I don't know, champ."

The medics must have found something to be concerned about because they decided to take Missy to the hospital.

"We'll provide your car with an escort," Officer McGathy said to Dad.

At that, Dad lifted Missy into his arms like he used to do when we were little and carried her the short distance to the ambulance. She dropped the water bottle to the ground. It was empty. I hadn't remembered her drinking it. I scooped it up. Mom climbed into the back of the ambulance with her.

The ambulance drove Missy and Mom to the hospital while Dad drove our van behind the police car. I sat in the passenger seat, watching traffic part for us. It took forty-five minutes to get to the nearest emergency room. Dad and I stood outside the exam room in a hallway. Officer Baker sat inside, talking to Missy and Mom.

"Your mom told us someone abducted you. Can you give us a description of that person?" Officer Baker asked.

"No one abducted me," Missy said in a snotty voice I wasn't used to hearing from her. "When I walked out of the Porta Potty, no one was there. The crowd was gone, and so was my dad."

Missy didn't make a lot of sense. How could no one have been outside the bathrooms? It had been crowded.

Missy went on. "Everything looked wrong. I followed the path, and it led to a gingerbread cottage. I saw the old woman from earlier. She gave me cookies and milk and told me she would take me back to my family *if* I wanted.

"But I didn't want to go back after what she showed me."

"What did she show you?" Officer Baker asked.

"My future. She told me she wouldn't let anyone hurt me if I agreed to stay in the Unseen Realm with her. She said I would be hers, and she would raise me as her own daughter. She would train me, she said. She was nice to me."

"What do you mean by Unseen Realm?" Officer Baker asked.

Missy huffed. "I don't know. I didn't get to be trained and learn from her. Obviously."

I couldn't figure out what she'd meant by "Unseen Realm" either.

"Can you tell us more about the woman who gave you cookies? What did she look like?"

"I don't want to get her in trouble," Missy said more quietly. "She was trying to help me."

"She won't get in trouble. We just want to ask her some questions."

Dad made me take a walk with him. I tried not to cry, but I was so sad and scared for my sister. She was suffering from more than dehydration. I couldn't stop thinking about the were-birds and the little old lady with the cookies. It was all so creepy.

The doctor did a blood test and couldn't find any drugs in her system. All he said was that she was dehydrated. Missy drank Gatorade, and he prescribed something to calm her nerves. I think he would have been smarter giving the rest of us sedatives instead.

Missy was calm as the police asked questions. The only sign she wasn't her usual self was her terse answers and crabbiness.

"Look, my daughter was dehydrated and confused," Mom said. "A sixteen-year-old can't spot a con artist. That's all that lady was. No crimes were committed. Let us take her home."

We didn't leave the hospital until after dark. It was a two-and-a-half-hour drive home. No one spoke. Mom sat in the back with

Missy, stroking her hair and trying to hold her hand when Missy wasn't hugging herself. I snuck glances at my sister. She didn't look at me. She stared out the window, her shoulders rounded over herself protectively. This small, broken girl was not the big sister I knew.

She wouldn't get out of the car when we made it home. "I'm not going in there. It isn't safe."

Mom motioned for Dad to take me inside. She remained beside Missy.

"Why did you have to take me away? The witch would have protected me." Missy's voice rose in terror.

"No, honey," Mom said. "That woman was a liar."

Dad placed a hand on my back, guiding me toward the front of the house. Our lawn was a brilliant green compared to the brown and yellow of our neighbors' grass. Mom stroked Missy's hair.

Missy pulled away. "I know what I saw. She showed me my future. She showed me what would happen to me."

Mom closed the car door. Her voice was muffled. "She put something in those cookies. You hallucinated. She was preying on your fears."

"The doctors told you there weren't any drugs."

"It wasn't drugs she put in those cookies," Mom said.

I wondered what else she could have put in the cookies.

"Come on." Dad unlocked the front door. "Let your mom talk to your sister alone."

I lingered in the doorway, not wanting to go in. I wanted to run to my sister and hug her and make her feel better. Mom said something quietly I couldn't hear.

"I can't go in there!" Missy screamed. "She'll kill me. I saw it."

"No one is going to hurt you," Mom said.

"The witch showed me. She said I have to learn to protect myself. If I don't, Clarissa will kill me before my eighteenth birthday."

CHAPTER THREE
Frenemies

I sat in front of the dollhouse castle my dad had built for me. Two weeks had passed since Oregon Country Fair. The summer ticked by with uncharacteristic slowness.

Using a spray bottle, I spritzed the air fern growing on the bark roof. The castle looked like something in between a hobbit hut and a medieval manor, with rustic furniture and Celtic knotwork decorating miniature rugs and tapestries on the walls. If only my parents would decorate our house like this.

I rearranged two My Little Pony unicorns outside the house and the Barbie dolls dressed as fairies in the branches on the outside.

"Don't you think you're a little old to be playing with dolls?" Missy asked from the doorway. Her eyes were dark bruises. Her shirt hung loose on her petite frame.

She didn't come in my room. I was just happy she had said more than two words to me.

I raked a miniature plastic comb through Princess Anastasia's snarls. Ever since I'd used an orange marker to make her hair closer to my hair color, the plastic strands had turned into dreadlocks.

I set the doll on a stand and posed her with the fairy prince. "I'm not playing with dolls. I'm just dressing them and arranging them so I can draw them. You can help me choose an outfit for the prince."

"Not interested." She clenched and unclenched her fists, waves of nervous energy rolling off her.

Missy liked playing dress up, whether it was with our clothes or with our dolls. She still wasn't back to her normal self. I wished we'd never gone to the fair. I kept thinking back to the bird women. Mom attributed what I'd seen to dehydration and second-hand pot smoke. She said the lady who had lured Missy away had been a con artist. I wasn't so sure after those strange raven women.

What if that lady had been right, and I might do something to hurt my sister? I pushed the thought away. Missy couldn't think I was capable of hurting her. Her irritability was trauma induced.

I wanted to help Missy get better and make things the way they once had been between us.

"What's wrong?" I asked. "You can tell me. I won't tell Mom."

"Yeah?" She snorted. "You think you can keep a secret?"

I leaned forward eagerly. "What really happened?"

"I need you to help me with something," Missy said.

"Okay." I stood up. This was the first time Missy had expressed interest in spending time with me in the last couple weeks. There wasn't anything I wouldn't do to make my sister happy.

I followed Missy downstairs. She stopped before the curtained window of the living room and peeked out. Mom's red hair showed over a hydrangea bush as she weeded at the base. Missy heaved a wooden chair from the kitchen table to the stairs.

"Are you going to just stand there or are you going to help me?" she demanded.

I tried not to let my sister's crabby mood get to me. Silently, I grabbed the legs of the chair and helped her haul it upstairs. We'd almost made it to the top before Lucifer, our cat, got underneath our feet. First, he tripped me and then Missy. I stumbled on the stairs and Missy dropped the chair on me.

"Ow!" I said.

Missy yanked the chair off of me and dragged it the rest of the way across the hallway carpet. She kicked at the cat and missed.

"What's the chair for?" I asked.

"I need you to help me find something."

"What are we looking for?" I followed her past her room.

"The truth."

I was intrigued now. "About what?"

She dragged the chair into our parents' room. She placed it next to the closet and slid the door open. Mom's clothes hung from the rack, neat and tidy. Her shoes were arranged on the floor in a wooden frame Dad had made for her. Hat boxes and storage tubs collected dust above and below.

A lump of dread settled in my stomach. "We aren't supposed to be in Mom's closet."

"That's why I need you to help me." She pointed down the hallway. "Go stand at the bottom of the stairs and tell me if Mom comes into the house."

I bit my lip, torn. I wanted Missy to be my best friend again, but this didn't seem right. I shook my head and backed away. "I don't want to do something Mom wouldn't like."

"Don't be such a wimp." She punched me in the arm.

"Ow!" I ran out of my parents' room. "I'm not a wimp. I just don't want to be bad."

Missy chased after me. "Too late for that. It's in your blood."

"What's that supposed to mean?" I ran to my room, away from her.

My sister had never talked to me this way before. I knew she'd been traumatized, but she couldn't believe what the old woman had told her. I'd never done anything mean to her. Not ever.

I tried to push the door closed, but Missy was bigger and stronger. She rammed the door open, knocking me back. "That old lady I met at the fair told me all about you." Her voice turned icy and sharp.

I inched away. This was the first she'd talked about the fair with me. I wanted her to tell me more, but I was afraid of the anger in her eyes. "Mom said that lady put *something* in your cookies. The lady lied to you because she wanted to scare you."

"No. She wanted me to know the truth. She showed me magic." Her lips drew back into a sneer, showing off perfect pearls of teeth. "You like magic, don't you? Want to see a magic trick?"

Missy snatched up one of the dolls. She twisted the head off the fairy prince and threw it down at my feet. I stared in horror. Never had I imagined my older sister would do such a mean thing. She dove forward again. I tried to block her, but she pushed me out of the way and grabbed Princess Anastasia.

"No!" I screamed, reaching for my doll. "Please!"

She leapt back, holding the doll above her head where I couldn't reach. One hand gripped the fairy princess's head. The other held the body. "Go to the bottom of the stairs. You'll be my lookout or

Barbie gets it."

"Fine, just put her down."

Missy tossed my doll on the bed. I trudged down the stairs. Lucifer followed and darted past me into the kitchen. Mom stood at the counter, drinking a glass of iced tea. Dirt caked her skinny jeans. She wiped at the sweat on her neck with a bandana.

Lucifer meowed. Mom looked at me, her brow furrowed.

I glanced up the flight of stairs. I knew I was supposed to call out and warn Missy, but I wasn't sure what I was supposed to say. It would be kind of suspicious if I said, "Mom's back. Get out of her room."

I waited for Mom to finish drinking her tea.

She set the glass down. "Why do you look guilty?"

I shook my head. "No reason."

Lucifer sauntered to the blank place where the chair had been at the table. He meowed. Mom looked from me to the table and back to the stairs. Her eyes narrowed.

"Missy!" I said.

My mom held up her finger and shook her head. As silent as a ghost, Mom climbed up the stairs. Even the creaky step didn't give her away. I floundered after her, scrambling noisily in my haste.

"You'd better not be coming up here, ginger," Missy called.

She stood on the chair, a shoebox under her arm. She held a piece of blue paper with a fancy border in her hands. At the top of the paper in large letters were the words: Certificate of Adoption.

"What are you doing?" Mom asked.

Missy spun, dropping the contents of the box on the tan carpet. She squealed and would have toppled from the chair if Mom hadn't dove forward, caught her, and set her on her feet.

Mom tore the certificate from Missy's hands. I kneeled to pick up the papers on the floor. On thick parchment in fancy cursive was a list: eye of bat, pickled dragon liver, 1 tsp. coriandrum sativum. I was pretty sure that was coriander. Mom grew it in the garden. Those weren't the only ingredients on the list that looked like some kind of witch's brew. At the top of the paper was the title "How to Win Friends and Influence People." I had a feeling this wasn't a page from Dale Carnegie's book that Dad sometimes read to us.

Mom grabbed me by the arm and hauled me to my feet. "Leave it," she said.

She pushed Missy out the door, dragging me along behind her. Our feet crunched over scattered papers. My foot kicked a glass vial across on the floor. The liquid inside shimmered like mercury, shifting in the light. A sea of papers with curving script littered the floor. A satchel of dried herbs had spilled across ancient-looking parchment.

Mom closed the door behind us, obscuring the mess. "Why were you going through my closet? That box is for grownup eyes only." She gestured toward her and Dad's room, the blue paper still clutched in her hand.

"She made me do it." Missy's gaze was riveted by the paper Mom held. "She said if I didn't do it, she'd—"

"I did not!" I said. "You twisted the head off my fairy prince because I told you I didn't want to help you."

"You did that yourself, and now you're blaming me for your clumsiness."

"I am so disappointed with you girls, fighting like children." Mom folded the blue paper, concealing the writing. "You are sisters. Family doesn't act like this."

I hung my head in shame. She always knew the right words to make me feel guilty.

"That's the adoption paper, isn't it?" Missy asked.

Mom's eyes went wide. "What?"

"The woman at the fair. She told me—"

Mom's anger evaporated, leaving in its place a husk of sorrow. "That lady was a bad person. She wanted to abduct you and hurt you. She filled your head with lies."

Guilt churned in my belly as I realized why Missy had made me her accomplice and spy. She was obsessed with what had happened to her. I felt bad for my sister.

"That paper said 'adoption.' I saw it," Missy said. "Tell me the truth. Clarissa and I were both adopt—"

"Shh." Mom held up a finger in stern warning.

Missy silenced. I stared with wide eyes, afraid to breathe.

Mom unfolded the paper and smoothed out the creases against her jeans. "Neither of you were adopted, but both of you know I was." The air shimmered between her fingers, reminding me of waves of heat rising from blacktop on a summer's day. The perfume of sage and basil wafted toward me.

Mom smiled. "And so was Lucy." She meant Lucifer.

Mom held up the paper. It remained blue, but something about it looked different. The fancy border was still there, and the words "adoption" dominated the top, but the writing took up more space on the page. In larger letters halfway down the page was the name: Lucy Lucky Lawrence. Lucy was the name my mom called her cat, not what Dad nicknamed him. Dad's name fit better. Lucifer could be pretty evil when he shredded up Dad's work clothes or peed on Missy's cheer bag.

"These are Lucy's papers from the Humane Society when we adopted him." Mom waved a hand at the cat. He licked one of his paws indifferently.

"Oh." I breathed out all the fear I'd been holding.

Missy stood there, rigid and clenching her fists as Mom hugged her and patted her back. I could tell she didn't believe Mom.

"See, you weren't adopted." I smiled. Everything would be all right. She would stop believing everything she'd seen at the fair.

Only, I didn't think *I* could stop believing. I didn't want to believe any of it had happened, but doubts still wormed their way through my self-resolve. I tried to take Missy's hand.

She stepped back, eyes burning into me. "That lady said *you* were the daughter of an evil witch. I wasn't. She said *you* were just like your mother. She told me my fortune and said I have to protect myself because if I don't you're going to kill me before my—"

"Stop." Mom held up a finger in warning again. The aroma of mint and lavender filled the air this time. Heat wavered around Mom, but the air wasn't hot. Missy mumbled something I couldn't understand. Tears welled up in her eyes.

I didn't know how my mom did it. She could silence anyone with a look.

Mom patted my shoulder, giving me an apologetic smile. "Clarissa, go downstairs."

I walked away as slowly as I could get away with. I listened at the bottom of the stairs.

"We've talked about this before," Mom said. "It hurts Clarissa every time you say that. If you want to talk to me about this, you need to do it when we have privacy."

It was hard to understand Missy through her high-pitched crying. Lucifer watched me from the top of the stairs. I hid around the corner, not wanting him to give me away.

Mom's voice was soothing. "That woman had been watching us. She saw Clarissa and me with our red hair, and your father with the red in his beard. And she saw you with us. She saw that you looked different from us and recognized that you wanted to be like everyone else. She preyed on your fears." Mom lowered her voice so I had to lean into the stairwell to hear. "That's your fear, isn't it? That you aren't like other girls."

"I am like other girls! I'm on the cheer team. I like cool music, and I dress like everyone else. I'm the normal one. It isn't fair!"

"No, it isn't. It isn't fair for either of you," Mom said. "I understand you're afraid Clarissa will hurt you. That witch showed you things that scared you. But you have to understand, that future she showed you in her crystal ball—"

This didn't sound like my mom. She didn't allow us to indulge in the idea that magic existed. I could only imagine she was trying a new tactic since Missy refused to believe the truth. Either that, or my mom did believe in magic.

Missy's voice rose. "She didn't show me a crystal ball. She put me there in the moment it happened. I saw what Clarissa did to me. I felt it."

I hated that Missy still believed what the woman had told her.

"You saw one possibility for the future. That lady showed you what would further her agenda to try to convince you to go with her. That's a future I'm not going to allow. I love you both, and I'm going to protect both of you—from witches and bad people—and each other. You just need to let me help you. Can you believe me when I tell you I'm not an evil witch? Do you believe me when I tell you I'm going to protect you?"

Missy choked on a sob. "I don't know."

What my mother said unsettled me. I knew that conversation wasn't meant for me to hear. Even so, I wished I hadn't eavesdropped. It sounded like they both thought I was capable of hurting Missy.

I twisted the friendship bracelet around my wrist. I would have done anything to get my old sister back. Only, I didn't know how.

CHAPTER FOUR
My Worst Nightmares

The scream woke me from a tranquil sleep. I sat up, my heart racing. I scrambled to turn on the light on my nightstand. The digital clock showed it was one-fifteen in the morning. Maybe I'd dreamed that scream.

It came again.

The source was clear this time. I ran to my sister's room and flipped on the lights. She sat up, drenched in sweat, gaze darting around the room until she fixed on me.

"It's okay," I said. I fought the urge to sit down beside her and console her. I didn't want to make things worse. "It was just a dream."

"Get out!" She threw her pillow at me. "Out! Out! Out!"

I backed away, wanting to help, but not knowing how.

Mom and Dad's feet thundered over the hallway carpet behind me. Mom rushed past me into Missy's room. I slipped farther into the shadows of the hall. Mom's voice cooed at Missy while my sister sobbed hysterically.

Dad's voice was a low rumble. "I know this is hard on you." He squeezed me around the shoulders. "How are you holding up, sport?"

Horrible, I was tempted to say, but I didn't want to make things worse for him and Mom. I shrugged.

Mom's voice came through the wall, singing an Irish lullaby to Missy.

Dad guided me back into my room. "Do you think you'll be able to get back to sleep?"

"Probably." *Not*, I added mentally.

"How about a bedtime story?" Dad selected a novel from my shelf and opened the book at a random place. He read a section from *Lord of the Rings*, giving Gandalf an old man's voice that reminded me of the grandfather from *The Simpsons*. I laughed.

That's how Mom found us, giggling and whispering as we took turns reading. "Does my other baby need a lullaby?" Mom asked.

"I'm fine," I said.

My parents kissed me goodnight. Eventually I fell asleep.

In the morning when the alarm went off, my eyes burned with fatigue. I stumbled out of bed, perking up when I smelled bacon and eggs. Mom must have gotten up early. She didn't usually cook breakfast on weekdays when she had work. Ten minutes later, we all sat in our pajamas around the table as if it was Saturday.

Mom had made us smoothies with produce from the garden to go with our meal. As usual, the smoothies were green and probably contained a whole bunch of healthy ingredients like spinach and kale. I took a sip to be polite and tried not to barf.

"Thank you for making breakfast, Mom," I said.

Missy didn't touch the green concoction in front of her.

"Try your smoothie," Mom said. "It will give you energy."

"You can't make me forget." Missy crossed her arms. "I'm not drinking your witch's brew."

Dad's cheery smile faded. "That's no way to talk to your mother."

Mom's face was calm, more concerned than hurt. "Do you remember what we talked about the other night?"

Missy sighed and rolled her eyes.

"You need to start eating better and taking care of yourself," Dad said around a mouthful of eggs.

Mom went on. "If you aren't going to let me help you, we're going to have to send you somewhere they can."

"Why am I the one who gets punished? Clarissa's the one who should have to leave." Missy glared at me.

"What are you talking about?" I asked.

Missy made a face like she'd swallowed something sour. "Haven't you heard? They're going to send me away."

"What?" They couldn't! How would I survive high school without my sister?

"No," Dad said firmly. "We gave you a choice. It's just one option. And it's up to you if you want to go to a private school or stay here."

Missy huffed. "Why would I choose to go to a reform school?"

Mom took Missy's hand. "Listen to me. Your fixation with death isn't healthy for you or Clarissa. Womby's is a perfectly nice private school. Their headmaster said they even have a cheer program. You wouldn't have to give that up."

"I'm not going to some school for freaks. I'm not the freak." Missy stormed away from the table.

Tears filled my eyes at the jab, but I tried to brush it off. "Why would you send her away?" Didn't my parents understand? Missy needed me. She just didn't know it.

Mom scooted her chair closer to me. "You do understand why she's doing this, don't you? Missy thinks you're going to do something bad to her. We know that's not true, but we thought it might be easier if she lived somewhere else so she could take a break and . . . recharge."

"I don't want her to go away," I said.

"I know, honey." The dark circles sagged under Mom's eyes. "Drink your smoothie for me. It will make you feel better."

I didn't want to drink a smoothie, but I did so anyway, not wanting to be like Missy and hurt Mom's feelings. The drink was cold, but it warmed my belly and made me feel cozy like when my mom cuddled me. My appetite returned, and I ate my eggs and bacon.

Nagging worries about bird women, witches and prophesies melted into nothingness. Oregon Country Fair felt a million years away. Mom was right about the smoothie giving me energy. I was ready to go to the library and learn like nobody's business!

Mom kissed my forehead. "I will protect you, the both of you. I promise." Just like before when Missy had made her promise to protect me, I felt a cool tingle against my skin. Unlike the scent of rain and spring water that had come with Missy's words, I smelled green herbs and sunshine. This promise felt different, but it wasn't any less potent.

That's when it came to me. I knew what I needed to do to help my sister. I needed to make a promise to Missy that *I* would protect her.

CHAPTER FIVE
Resting Witch Face

School would be starting up in a few days. I had just gotten my braces off. I should have been happy. But how could I be excited with my parents whispering about sending Missy away? I had to make my sister want to stay. Life would be unbearable without her.

I used my red pen on pink glitter paper to write the oath I intended to give my sister. Afterward, I decided the red looked like blood. I started over, this time using a purple pen.

Contract of Fealty and Devotion

Dear Melissa Lawrence,

I, Clarissa Lawrence, solemnly swear I shall never harm my older sister or allow harm to come to her. I faithfully promise to be her best friend and do anything I can to help her in any way she needs so that she will want to stay here with our family and not go away.

Sincerely,

Clarissa Lawrence

When Missy came home from cheer camp, I folded the paper into a fancy origami style envelope she had taught me how to make two years before and slipped the paper under the door to her room. I waited for Missy to burst out and throw her arms around me like she used to.

Nothing happened.

I returned to my room. I sat in my wardrobe, leaning against the cushion of winter coats as I read *The Chronicles of Narnia*. Ever since

I'd turned fourteen, everything was getting too small for me, my wardrobe included. But I wasn't ready to give up my sanctuary yet.

From inside, it was easier to ignore the grating valley girl cadence my sister had adopted since starting the newest round of cheer camp. She passed my room, a basket of laundry in one arm, her cell phone in the other as she prattled away.

A moment later Missy stopped in my doorway, her cell phone in her pocket. "What are you doing, ginger?"

"Don't call me that. You know I don't like that name." I didn't look up from my book, but I lost the line I was reading anyway. "So . . . did you get my note?"

She didn't acknowledge the question. "I hope you don't think sitting inside that thing is going to transport you to Mordor."

Maybe she hadn't seen the note. "The wardrobe is in the Narnia books, not *Lord of the Rings*." I didn't bother to explain no one would want to go to Mordor—well, unless they were on an epic quest.

When I was six, I had begged my mom to buy me an armoire from a garage sale because I wanted to be transported to Narnia. If I had communicated why I wanted it so badly, she might have been able to save me from the disappointment of finding out the truth when we got home. No matter how many times I opened it, no matter what hour it was, I still dreamed of being transported to another land. I couldn't shake the belief magic was real.

"Maybe you would have a boyfriend if you weren't reading stupid books all the time," Missy said.

Her gaze raked over the fairies in the potted plants along the windowsill, the tapestry with the unicorn pegasus on the wall, and the crystals on my nightstand. The fairy prince rested in his stand in the dollhouse, his neck bandaged together with superglue and medical tape Dad had used to give him a neck brace.

Every space of my room was filled with magical creatures and Celtic knotwork, creating my own Rivendell since my family couldn't go there on vacation. I imagined I was a fairy princess who gave up immortality for true love. I didn't fit into this world, so I wanted to join another one where magic existed.

"Actually, I can't have a boyfriend because Mom says I'm too young." I was only fourteen.

Missy lifted her nose into the air. "When you're sixteen, it's not as if the world will suddenly change and boys are going to notice you."

"Dad says the only boys worth my while are ones who will like me for who I am on the inside." I surveyed her red lipstick, sprayed-on tan, and the layers of makeup she covered her face with. She wore a red and white jacket with the school colors over a pleated miniskirt like the other cheerleaders wore.

She no longer wore our friendship bracelet. I still wore mine.

"You'll be waiting a looooong time if that's your game plan." She placed a fist on her hip. "There's going to be a point when you're going to have to ask yourself if you want to be yourself and a freak, or do you want to be normal and like everyone else."

I scooted closer to the edge of my wardrobe, letting my feet dangle out. "Do you feel like you have to be like everyone else?" That was what Mom had said she was afraid of. It was only a few weeks ago, but it was hard to remember what else they had talked about after catching Missy sneaking into her closet.

She swallowed and her eyes looked sad, but only for a second. "I *am* like everyone else. I don't live in a fantasy world and believe magic is real like some people I know. I have friends. Plus, I don't wear children's clothes."

I looked down at my Disney princess shirt. I was small for my age. I couldn't fit into clothes from the junior's department like she could. Any day now I would have my growth spurt like she'd had.

"Did you get my note?" I asked again.

No reply.

I ducked my head down and pretended to go back to reading. I tried not to blame Missy for her bad moods. Mom said it was probably hormones. Dad said she would grow out of it with time. I hoped they were right.

Missy called over her shoulder as she walked away, "You should see if Mom will take you out to find something more age appropriate so you don't embarrass yourself when you start high school."

"I could go shopping with you on Saturday," I said. "You can help me pick out clothes."

She froze. "How did you know I was going out on Saturday?"

"I wasn't eavesdropping," I said quickly. "You just talk loud on the phone."

She continued down the hall. "Whatever."

I scrambled out of the wardrobe, dropping my book on my Tinker Bell bedspread as I tailed after her. "You can teach me how to fit in. You can tell me what to wear." She used to help me when we were in middle school together, and before that, in elementary school. "You're better at fashion than I am."

She snorted. "Anyone is better at fashion than you are."

I follow her into her room. "That's why I need your help. I'll do whatever you want."

I spotted the pink paper still folded into its own little envelope on the floor. I nudged it into her line of sight with my foot.

She threw her smelly cheerleading uniform at me. "Get out, dorkbreath, this is private property."

I trudged back to my room and threw myself on my bed. Mom wasn't going to be home until five and Dad wouldn't be home until six. I felt so lonely. All I had were my books to keep me company, and I didn't feel like reading. I wanted someone to hug me. I laid my head on my arms and cried. I wanted my sister back. I didn't know how to help her. I had to think of another way.

Missy sighed from my doorway a moment later, dressed in jeans and a t-shirt now. She held my pink paper in her hands. "Come on, I'll let you help me do laundry."

"Yay!" I said, jumping up and wiping away my tears. I opened my arms to embrace her.

She elbowed me off her. "Don't do that. You act like you're fourteen."

"I am fourteen."

Missy shoved the laundry basket full of her uniforms and practice clothes into my arms.

"So you read my note? Everything is okay now? I can be your protector too? I will, you know. I'll do anything for you." I followed her down the stairs to the main floor and then down the other stairs into the basement.

"I know." She waved her hands through the spider webs on the railing and wiped them on her jeans.

My note had helped her see I wasn't ever going to do anything bad to her. I was so glad I'd thought of it.

The basement was dim, even with the overhead light and the afternoon sun shining in from the grimy windows at the top of the walls, but I wasn't scared of the dark like I used to be. Plus, I had my big sister with me.

Missy showed me how to separate the laundry by fabric type and color. She held up a red sequined top. "This can't be put in with the white clothes or everything will turn pink. And it can't be put on a hot setting or else the plastic will melt." She showed me the different dials.

I nodded and smiled. I liked spending time with my big sister. I helped her sort the clothes. Laundry was one small step for Missy, one giant leap for sissykind. Soon we would be shopping together, and we would be friends again.

She leaned against the railing of the stairs, watching me from a few feet away. "Mom is going to expect you to know how to do your own laundry when you start high school this year. She isn't going to do your school clothes for you. And you're going to have to start making your own lunch. It's part of acting more grownup."

"I can do that. I want to be more grownup like you."

"Right." She smiled. Her eyes remained hard and mirthless. "I'll be back in a minute."

I sorted the rest of her clothes, only putting the white clothes in the wash like she'd shown me. She returned five minutes later, surveying me from the top of the stairs. Lucifer tried to squeeze past her, but she grabbed him by the scruff of the neck and tossed him out. She closed the door so he couldn't get back in. He scratched at the other side of the door and meowed.

"He can't get to the litterbox if you keep him out," I said.

"We have a cat door. He can go outside."

She clomped down the stairs, surveying my handiwork with tepid enthusiasm. Something bulged from the pockets of her jacket, and she carried a book under her arm. I started up the washing machine the way she showed me. I smiled.

She didn't. Her lack of warmth made me uneasy.

"You said you'd be willing to do anything for me. Did you mean it?" she asked.

"Yes, of course. I want to help you."

"Good, because I need your help." The corners of her lips curled upwards. "Do you want to see if magic is real?"

My eyes went wide. I couldn't tell if she was joking. "What do you mean? I thought you didn't believe in magic."

"I don't. Magic is for freaks, and I'm not a freak like you are. But let's just pretend. Let's play a game . . . like we used to."

"Okay," I said, uncertainly. My mom didn't mind the fairies or unicorns, but when it came to witches and spells she got a little weird. Especially after we'd been to Oregon Country Fair and Missy had insisted she'd met a witch.

Missy's request made me uneasy. I didn't see how this would help her, yet if this was what she needed, I'd do it. Maybe she needed to see there was no such thing as magic so she'd know I couldn't ever hurt her.

We sat on the cement floor between two aisles of canning jars stuffed with pickles, tomato sauce, and jam. Missy lit stubs of white candles reserved for power outages she'd pilfered from the kitchen junk drawer. She placed them around me in a circle.

"Why aren't we putting them around you?" I asked.

"You're the one who wants magic in her life."

Missy turned off the light using the switch at the top of the stairs. The flickering flames of candles danced across the shelves of canning jars, making the contents resemble eyeballs and pig fetuses like one might find in a witch's pantry. My heart quickened. I wasn't scared, I told myself.

Missy drew a pentagram on the floor between us with a nub of chalk. She sprinkled herbs around me and in the center of the star. They smelled like mold and dirt. I fought the urge to sneeze. She read from a book titled: *How to Crush Your Enemies and Destroy People*. It reminded me of that paper I'd seen in Mom's shoebox: *How to Win Friends and Influence People*.

"Is this a Dale Carnegie book?" I wanted to believe that was where she'd gotten it. Even as I asked the question, I knew it was unlikely.

"Sure," she said.

"I didn't know he wrote about magic." It seemed like Dad would have read those passages to us, not just the sections about making friends. My suspicion meter was starting to go off. I opened my mouth, about to object.

"Shush," she said.

She kept reading, her voice quiet compared to the rumble of the washing machine on the other side of the basement. The book was written in another language. I'd only taken three years of Spanish, but I could tell this wasn't a romance language. She stumbled over the words, and I suspected her pronunciation was off.

I shifted uncomfortably on the cement floor. This was stupid.

Missy was probably playing a joke on me. She was going to scare me, and say, "Boo!" and tell me this was what I deserved for believing in childish things.

She stopped reading and glanced around. She skimmed the page, looked to me, and then back to the book.

"What?" I spun the friendship bracelet around on my wrist.

"Nothing happened."

Magic had never worked for me all the times I'd tried it either. Disappointment weighed heavily on my soul until I remembered what Missy needed. It was for the best magic wasn't real because that meant the old woman had been a liar, not a witch.

"It's just like Mom says. Magic is make-believe," I said. "It can't hurt you. *I* can't hurt you. Even if I wanted to—which I don't."

She turned a page. "Oh yeah, that's right." She closed the book. "Close your eyes and hold out your hand."

I hesitated. "Why?"

"I have a surprise for you." She extended her hand to me.

For the briefest moment, I slipped back into the memory of her being my best friend about to give me a present she had bought for me with her allowance. I wanted to believe we could be like that again. She smiled, and I placed my hand in hers. She turned my palm face up.

"Close your eyes," she said.

I did so. The washing machine thumped noisily like the clothes inside had lumped together. Dad said we needed a new washer because there was something wrong with the spin cycle.

Two seconds later something sharp stabbed into my palm. I yelped and tried to yank my hand back, but Missy gripped my wrist. She held a knife in her other hand.

"What are you doing?" I asked, smacking at her hand.

"I needed a sacrifice. The witch told me magic doesn't come without a price." She tossed the knife aside.

She jerked my arm over the pentagram. She wasn't that much bigger than I was, but cheerleading had built her muscles and made her strong.

I tried to pull away, but I couldn't. "Why would you listen to that lady? Mom said she wasn't right in the head."

A trickle of blood fell onto the pile of herbs. Missy released her grip on my arm.

I cradled my hand to my chest, probably getting blood on Ariel and Cinderella. "Mom said that lady was mean and a liar. I'm not ever going to do anything bad to you, you know. You're my sister, and I love you. Didn't you read my note?"

She snorted. "I read it."

The washer thudded against the wall, louder, more insistent. My hand throbbed where she'd stabbed me. I wanted to cry, but my eyes felt too dry. All moisture had wicked away from my mouth.

Missy stood and dusted herself off. She laughed, the sound high and nervous. "I'm being a dork, aren't I? You're right. Magic isn't real." She patted my shoulder, the gesture apologetic and exceptionally awkward for my usually gregarious sister.

I wanted to believe this was over for her. I had helped Missy overcome her trauma. I looked down at the red line oozing from my palm. I would allow her to try magic on me again if that's what it took.

She walked up the stairs to turn on the lights.

The bulb flared and popped. She sighed in exasperation, the hiss of air from her lungs lost underneath a louder pop. Metal groaned. It sounded like the washing machine was finally breaking down.

The washer toppled over in a giant crash and a geyser of water shot out of a pipe. Steaming spray arched across the room, knocking over a stack of boxes. It gushed out of the wall and upward, splattering Missy. She slipped and fell onto the stairs, screaming and scrambling to get away. An impossibly large tide showered her. She clung to the posts of the railing to stay on the stairs.

"Missy!" I screamed.

I jumped to my feet to come to her aid. The moment I did so, something popped to my right. Sharp glass shards peppered my arm. A jar to my left burst, spraying me with vinegar, glass and pickles. The fluid doused the candles. I raised my arms to cover my head. Jars exploded with such violence, the force sent me into the other shelf. I crashed to my knees.

I screamed, but my voice was lost in the pops and crashes of glass. My sister's choking and shrieking rose over the roar of water.

I lay on the floor, covering my head with my arms. The storm of water died down. Something dripped in the darkness. Missy coughed. A light flashed across the sticky mess near me. I raised my head.

Mom stood at the top of the stairs. "What are you girls doing?"

49

Light from the kitchen shone down on Missy clinging to the railing.

Missy crawled up the stairs on hands and knees. "It was magic. It was her magic."

Mom heaved her up the stairs to the kitchen.

"No," I called after her. "*Our* magic." I was shaking so hard from cold and fear my voice came out tremulous.

"No, it wasn't. I'm not like you. I don't want to be like you." Missy coughed and blubbered from the kitchen.

Mom's shoes sloshed down the steps and over the concrete floor, a flashlight sweeping over the toppled washing machine. I scrambled to my feet. She frowned at the scattered candles and the soggy herbs and pentagram half washed away by the contents of canning jars.

She picked up the book Missy had dropped and wiped away globs of jam from the cover. "Where did you get this book?"

"I don't know. Missy brought it down here."

"No, I didn't!" Missy yelled. "I was just minding my own business doing laundry when I saw you doing witchcraft down—" Missy broke into a fit of coughing.

"She's lying!" I said.

"No, *she's* lying." Her voice came out a rasp.

I kicked a green bean off one of the candles. The evidence was not in my favor considering I was surrounded by testaments of magic and Missy wasn't.

Mom swept the flashlight over the cuts on my arms. "We need to take you to the hospital." She held out her hand and helped me navigate the mess.

Mom wrapped us up in towels and tried to herd us to her station wagon.

"I'm not getting in the car with her," Missy said between coughs.

"Yes, you are," Mom insisted.

Missy's eyes narrowed. "No, I'm not. She almost killed me. And she'll do it again before I turn eighteen."

Mom called Dad, and then drove me to the hospital without Missy. I tried to explain what had happened, that we hadn't tried to make the washing machine explode, but I couldn't tell if she was listening.

"I was trying to help," I said.

"Uh-huh." Blackbirds flitted across the sky, drawing Mom's attention.

"I wanted to prove to her I would do anything for her. I thought she wanted to see that magic was make-believe. I didn't realize it was a real spell."

Mom kept glancing into her rearview mirror as if she thought we might have been followed.

Dad met Mom and me at the ER fifteen minutes later.

The moment he walked in the door, she gathered up her coat and purse. "Missy needs me at home. I don't want to leave her alone right now." She cast a venomous glance over her shoulder at me like this was all my fault.

I waited for two hours in the lobby before the doctor saw me. Dad stayed by my side the entire time, asking me questions about what had happened. I told him the truth. He listened better than Mom, drumming his fingers against the magazines on the end table. He didn't interrupt.

"Have you considered that maybe, just maybe, it wasn't magic? That washing machine has been on the fritz for a while. The water shooting out might have knocked the canning jars around and caused them to break. You were pretending to use magic and then an accident happened, which confirmed your belief in magic. That's called confirmation bias."

I shook my head. "No, that isn't what happened. It was a spell."

"Hmm," he said, unconvinced. He bought me a granola bar from a vending machine for a snack at dinner time.

At eight-thirty I was home with stitches and butterfly bandages all over my arms and legs. I only had one cut on my face, a little one on my jaw. It was way less cool than Harry Potter's lightning scar.

I found Mom in my room, dropping books and toys into boxes.

I ran forward. "What are you doing?" In the first box I found a candleholder with a pentagram and an unused notebook that was decorated with Celtic knotwork around a star. Several of the Wiccan art books I'd gotten for my birthday were piled in. The deck of tarot cards with fairy art and the Ouija board that I'd never used were scattered in pieces in the box.

"I've tolerated your obsession with magic for far too long." Her nose was pink and her eyes red and swollen as though she'd been crying. "Those books are a bad influence on you. We're getting rid of them." She climbed onto her step ladder and pulled boxes of games and puzzles out of my closet, letting them come crashing to the ground. Pieces from *Harry Potter* Trivial Pursuit fell everywhere.

I snatched up my collection of My Little Ponies from the box on the floor and hugged them to my chest. "No, you can't do this to me. It isn't fair." I burst into tears. Hadn't today already been bad enough?

Dad placed a hand on Mom's shoulder. "Honey, maybe you're taking this a little too far."

"Do you want them to kill each other?" she snapped. She shoved a box of my old toys into his arms. She grabbed a plastic tub with my Gryffindor costume in it.

My eyes went wide. "No, not that! Not Harry Potter," I begged.

Dad held onto her elbow as she stomped down the ladder. "Let's calm down and talk about this. I don't want us to do anything we'll regret."

"No more witchcraft," Mom said. "Never again."

She didn't release my Gryffindor costume as he guided her out of the room. Dad closed the door of my bedroom.

I hid the armful of My Little Ponies under my pillow. I removed the Barbie dolls dressed as fairies from the second box and shoved them under the mattress. I didn't know what to do with all my books or the doll castle. There was no way I could hide everything.

"Abby," Dad said from out in the hall. "She's going to grow tired of those toys in another year, anyway. Let her get rid of them when she's ready. Let her be a kid. If you take everything away from her that she loves, she's going to rebel."

Mom said something too quiet for me to hear.

He went on, "If you do this to them, you're just confirming their fantasies in magic. They'll think they actually caused the washing machine to break. Let's act reasonable about this and they will too."

Half an hour later Mom came back in. "Tomorrow I'm taking the day off. You are going to remove any books, toys, or art related to witchcraft from your room tonight."

My eyes filled with tears, and my breath hitched in my chest.

"You can keep your unicorns and fairies," Dad added. He kneeled at one of the boxes and picked out the porcelain fairy figurines and plastic troll dolls, placing them back in my castle.

"What about the *Chronicles of Narnia*?" I asked in desperation. "The witch is bad in that series."

My mom hesitated.

I could see I had her. "My Anne McCaffrey books take place on other worlds. They're science fiction. And my Mercedes Lackey books are fairytales, not witches."

Dad rubbed a hand over his beard trying to conceal his smile.

Mom waved a hand at the shelves. "Fine, but the non-fiction books about ghosts, witches and psychic phenomena have to go. You are going to get rid of *Lord of the Rings*, *Harry Potter*, and any other book that glorifies witchcraft. You can keep the other books." Mom's cherub lips puckered into a frown.

"How about I take these books to work?" Dad tapped at the box with the *Harry Potter* series. "Brenda's kids would love these." He smiled apologetically at me. Maybe he thought he was helping me feel better when he suggested they were going to give away my things to people we knew.

Mom and Dad carried out the boxes and went to Missy's room next.

I retreated into Narnia and sat in the wardrobe, pretending I was elsewhere. It was fine, I told myself. I could go to the library and read whatever I wanted. I would be like the character from *Matilda* with my untapped potential ready to explode. My anger simmered inside me.

A few minutes later when Missy began to scream at my parents, I closed the doors to my wardrobe to muffle the sound. I watched out the crack between the doors when my parents marched past my room again. They didn't carry anything from Missy's room. And why would they? She didn't like fantasy or witches.

We ate dinner at ten that night, hours later than we usually did. Dad heated up leftover tamale pie. Mom chopped cilantro from the garden and sprinkled it on top. I didn't feel hungry. Maybe it was that granola bar Dad had bought me from the vending machine at the hospital that had ruined my appetite. Or maybe it was my life.

No one spoke as we ate. Missy pushed the food around on her plate, but didn't eat. Her shoulders sagged and her eyes were dark. I didn't know what she was sulking about. Mom hadn't carried boxes of things out of her room.

I tried to make myself eat, but I couldn't manage more than a bite. I was too angry—at my mom for taking away my things, at my dad for letting her, and at Missy for blaming me. Everything about my life sucked.

Halfway through dinner, Lucifer rubbed up against Mom's leg and meowed. She silently rose. I thought she meant to see if Lucifer was out of water or food. A moment later she came back. She held a Ziploc bag of shredded herbs.

Missy's eyes went wide. "I was just holding that for a friend."

"Please say this is tea." Mom said through clenched teeth. She tossed it on the table.

Dad opened the bag and sniffed. He held it away from himself, making a face. "Yuck! That stinks. But it's not marijuana."

"Yeah, Mom, duh. What did you think it was?" Missy asked. "Drugs? Really? I'm on cheer team."

My sister might have turned into a grade A jerkface over the summer, but she didn't use drugs. I didn't think she would ever use drugs after the incident at the fair. But she had sprinkled putrid herbs on the pentagram when we'd been in the basement earlier. Maybe these were the same kind.

Missy leaned back in her chair and crossed her arms.

"Eat your dinner. It will make you feel better," Mom said.

"Why? What did you put in it?" Missy demanded. "Something to make me into a good girl?"

Mom's eyes narrowed.

Dad tried to make a joke out of it. "If only your mother would put something in it. I probably would like tamale pie better if it was more like Uncle Trevor's 'special' brownies." He chuckled.

No one else laughed. Partly out of spite to show everyone I wasn't going to be rude like Missy, and partly because I didn't want to hurt Mom's feelings and not eat dinner, I stopped stirring around the casserole and ate a few tentative bites. For the briefest moment, I thought I saw glitter flash and flicker above my plate, but then it was gone.

Mom smiled and stroked my hair out of my face. Eating did make me feel better. After hours of holding tension in my muscles, it melted away. The anger and hurt that I'd been holding onto faded. My mom's cooking always had that effect on me. I wondered if I would ever be able to cook as well as she did.

It was my job to do dishes that night. I was in such a good mood I didn't mind. I retrieved the rubber gloves from under the counter so the water wouldn't cause problems with all my bandages.

Dad patted me on the shoulder. "It's all right, champ. I'll take one for the team this time."

"Thanks, Dad."

My brain felt dull and sluggish. I couldn't remember why Missy and I had been so set on playing down in the basement. It all seemed so childish and silly now. I yawned.

I thought I would get to go to bed. It was past my bedtime. But no, that would have been what normal teenagers got to do after the basement exploded on them and they'd gotten stitches. My mom took Missy and me out to the garden burn pile where she'd dumped my books and witchcraft paraphernalia. The light from the kitchen window fell on the Halloween decorations of witches and pumpkins from holiday boxes she'd ransacked from the basement.

All the warm and cozy feelings from dinner faded as the reality of my life sank in again. I hugged my arms around myself as she dumped gasoline on my wooden wand, cape, and books titled things like *Witchcraft 101* and *What is Wicca?* I sniffled and wiped the tears from my eyes.

Missy stood on the other side of the burn pile, staring at the ground. She kicked a dandelion.

Mom emptied the baggie of herbs onto the lawn. I wondered why she didn't burn them along with everything of mine.

"I need you to understand why magic is bad," Mom said. "When you tinker with forces you don't understand, someone can get hurt. You can't play with magic."

I stared at her incredulously. "What?" I asked. Surely she couldn't be saying what I thought she was. Mom didn't believe in magic.

"It wouldn't be *playing* if you taught us what you know," Missy said. "You could show us how—"

"I can't," Mom said sharply.

Missy bawled up her fists. "Can't or won't?"

Mom was always saying magic wasn't real. When we watched reruns of *Bewitched* with Dad, she'd always say things like, "You know people can't do that. Right, girls? You can't solve problems in the real world with magic."

When she complained about me reading *Lord of the Rings*, I assumed it was because she didn't want me to believe in fanciful daydreams. It hadn't occurred to me she might be making me get rid of everything I liked because she was afraid of magic.

Until now.

"Are you saying magic is real?" My voice came out a squeak.

"No." Mom hesitated. "There are people out there—bad people—who will tell you they can cast spells," Mom said. "They might even think they can make things happen. But they're deluding themselves and you. They want to use you, to take advantage of you. Those are people you should stay away from."

This sounded more like my mother, reasoning that there was no such thing as magic. Her voice trembled and rose as she spoke. "I've met people like that. And so has Missy."

Mom rolled up her sleeve and held out her arm. She pointed to the scar that ran up the length of her forearm. I'd seen the scar lots of times, but she stood in shadows, so it was hard to see the white line in the dark. "I told you my foster mother hit me with a shovel when I was seven. What I didn't tell you was why." She drew in a shaky breath. "My adopted mother "collected" children to use. She did this to me because she wanted to harness my pain for her magic. Energy has to come from somewhere, she said. So she intended to take mine." Mom didn't talk about her foster parents much. Now I knew why.

Mom glanced at my bandaged hand. I wondered if she'd gotten the truth out of Missy or she had guessed.

"My foster mother was crazy," Mom said. "There are a lot of people out there who will hurt you and want to use you, especially if they think you're naive and trusting. I will not let these witches—these *monsters*—hurt my girls." She lit the match and tossed it on the pile. Golden flames whooshed upward, painting my mom's face in the flickering light. Her red hair wafted from her face, and she glowed like a fire sprite.

"And I am not going to let you two fight with each other and blame it on witchcraft. You are family." She took my good hand in her right and Missy's in her left. "Missy, you need to understand that your sister loves you, and she isn't going to hurt you. Try to forget about what you saw at the fair."

Didn't Mom see I felt the same way? I didn't want Missy to hate me and be afraid of me because of some story a stranger had told her about me. I stared across the fire at Missy. She still wouldn't meet my eyes.

Mom turned to me. "Clarissa, you need to understand how your obsession with magic is driving your sister away. She is afraid of you, and you aren't helping with your—"

"I am not!" Missy shouted. "I'm not afraid of her. I'm bigger and stronger. She can't hurt me. I won't let her."

That was the moment I saw through my sister's façade. All her ridiculing me about acting like a child and believing in magic—it was because she believed in magic. She still bought what that old woman at the fair had told her. My heart broke at the idea of who she had become. Hot tears burned down my cheeks, and not because of losing my stupid toys. My anger crumbled away and was replaced by pining for my sister's friendship and affection. If only I had realized what she needed sooner. I would have traded all my toys to regain my sister's love and comradery.

I sniffled. "I'm sorry, Mom. I'm sorry, Missy. I love you. I'll try harder not to do things that will make you hate me."

Missy looked away. "I don't hate you. I just. . . ." She sighed.

That was all the encouragement I needed. My sister still loved me. I closed the distance between us and hugged her. She didn't push me away, but she didn't hug me back either. Awkwardly, she patted my shoulder.

"I want you to stay here and not have to go to another school," I said. "I'll do anything. Really."

She nodded.

"You're a good person, Clarissa. I know you'll try to make your sister more comfortable." Mom squeezed both of us to her. "You both have it in you to be good human beings." She looked from Missy to me. "If you want to fit into this world, you need to be like everyone else. You need to leave these fantasies behind. Both of you."

I nodded emphatically. "I promise." Magic was a fantasy. I didn't believe in it anymore. Not if it hurt Missy.

Tomorrow I was going to voluntarily pile my Narnia, Mercedes Lackey and Anne McCaffrey books in the boxes for Dad to take. I still had Star Trek, My Little Ponies and my fairy Barbies I could enjoy.

Mom tucked me into bed that night. She smoothed a hand over my forehead and sang an Irish lullaby to me in Gaelic like she used to when I was little. The song was called "Blessings" or something along those lines.

When I'd been five, I used to think she was wrapping me up in blessings when she sang that song. Even now I felt as though she was rocking me in a cradle and keeping me safe and warm. When I closed my eyes, I could see green blankets of light hugging around me and protecting me. Mom kissed my temple and went to Missy's room next.

When I woke up in the morning, something poked my shoulder from under my pillow. I slid out a hardback of *Harry Potter and the Sorcerer's Stone.*

Someone hadn't wanted me to give up all my dreams of magic. I just didn't know who.

CHAPTER SIX
Far from Hogwarts

My first day of school as a freshman at Oregon City High School wasn't the magical experience I'd hoped for. Of course, it wasn't hard to fall short when I had been hoping for Hogwarts and got Mordor instead. Not that I still believed in real magic—that stuff was for little kids—but a small part of me wanted to be transported to a secret world where fantastical things might happen. I wanted to find a place where I would feel like I belonged.

High school was the first day of my new life, I told myself. Things would be different from middle school. I was more grown-up. Mom said I could eat hot lunch. The people I'd gone to middle school with would be more mature. No one was going to pull my hair—I wasn't wearing it in pigtails. Over the weekend I'd bleached it blonde like Missy's. That would probably help. I had grown taller over the summer and gotten my braces off. People weren't going to call me nerd or reject.

I wore a blue and bronze striped scarf that happened to be Ravenclaw colors. Not that I was trying to flaunt a love for *Harry Potter*—my family would have disapproved.

I made it through the morning without problem until lunch. The jungle of the cafeteria was daunting, the noise overwhelming. Everyone looked like they were six feet tall. The hot lunch line stretched on endlessly. It took twenty minutes to get a pizza, tater tots and a scoop of fruit cocktail. All the while, I scanned the sea of faces, searching for someone I knew.

My friend, Becky, had moved to Nevada. I didn't see my friends Garret or Melanie. There were so many people. Tables were crowded with teenagers I didn't know. I made my way over to a group of laughing freshman. A few of them I knew from middle school, not well, but at least they weren't scary-cool seniors looking down at me as I passed. Before I could sit in the only empty seat at the table, a girl in a mini-skirt swooped in from the right and got the spot. One seat was vacant next to Karen Walker, but I didn't feel like being made fun of.

I didn't know where to sit.

My older sister loitered with her cheerleading friends at a table halfway across the cafeteria. They were all so pretty and popular. Missy was easy to spot with her red and white uniform and the sparkly red bow in her platinum hair. She'd never had a problem fitting in wherever she went. I waved, but she didn't see me.

I skipped over to her. Now that I was older and didn't dress like a baby, she would see me as an equal. I'd given up most of my witch-related art and toys, and hidden anything else that was obvious so I wouldn't make her uncomfortable. We could be friends again. This would be just like when we were in elementary school and sat at the same table and were best friends. She would show me around the school like she had when I was in middle school, only now it would be juniors she introduced me to instead of eighth graders. Her aura of coolness would rub off on me just like it had then.

She would help me fit in.

Missy's lips pressed into a flat line and she shook her head at me as I approached. Maybe it was the scarf. I shouldn't have worn it. She probably knew it was Ravenclaw colors.

I tried to sit down next to her, but she blocked me from taking the empty seat. "This table is for cheer." She lowered her voice. "Don't embarrass me."

Embarrass her? The words stung. Why was she being like this? Didn't she understand how overwhelming the first day of school was? I just wanted to sit with her.

Sarah, the captain of the squad, lifted her nose in the air. "Who's this?"

"No one," Missy said quickly. She waved me away, but I stood, rooted to the spot. My feet didn't want to move. I looked around. I didn't know where to go.

Last year during one of the games when Missy had still been new on cheer team, I'd seen Sarah chew out my sister behind the bleachers for not being peppy enough. Sarah was a life-sized blonde Barbie doll—only prettier. And scarier.

Sarah looked me up and down. "I can't believe they're letting children onto campus these days."

My sister's face turned as red as a beet. She laughed along with the other girls. She turned to one of her friends and pretended not to know me. With envy, I watched Missy surrounded by her friends.

"I thought maybe I could sit here," I said in such a quiet voice I could hardly hear myself over the commotion of the cafeteria.

Sarah stood up, glaring down at me. "Are you sure you're ready for the adult table?"

She had to be six feet tall and all legs. I was the shortest person in my family at four foot ten. I hadn't hit my growth spurt yet, but I was in high school. I was sure it would happen any day now.

Missy pointed at me. "Did Snow White lose one of the dwarves?"

I gripped my tray so tightly my fingers turned white. It wasn't like Missy was considered tall herself. She was only five-three, perfect for being thrown up into the air from the top of pyramids. They never failed to catch her when she came down, but at the moment, I hoped they'd miss one of those times.

Immediately after the thought crossed my mind, I felt guilty. If Mom knew I'd hoped for something bad to happen, she would say this was just the kind of thing that alienated me from my sister.

Missy whispered something to the tall brunette next to her.

"Which one are you?" the brunette asked. "Dopey, Smelly or *Gingy*?"

Gingy? My face burned with shame. My sister had told her friend my darkest secret. Now everyone would know I wasn't a natural blonde.

The cheerleader tittered. My sister, my new nemesis, laughed the loudest of them all.

Tears filled my eyes. I regained use of my feet. Sort of. I stumbled backward.

"Watch it, midget!" some boy in a letterman jacket snarled.

My tray teetered and fruit cocktail spilled to the floor.

A lanky teenager strode past me, pointing a bony finger at Sarah.

His mop of hair was neon blue, and he was almost as tall as she was. He glared at the cheerleader from hell. "Is that your face or did your shoulders vomit?"

She put her palm in his face. "Talk to the hand, dweeb."

His eyes cut over to the two teachers standing in the corner, too engrossed in conversation to notice the teenage drama unfolding. With a mischievous smile, he hawked a loogie and spit onto her palm.

"Eew!" Sarah waved her hand like the spit was radioactive. She flicked the phlegm onto my sister's face.

I was glad. Missy deserved it. She squealed.

The boy with blue hair turned to me. "Hi, I'm Derrick. Do you want to sit with us?" He waved a hand at the next table over.

The gnawing panic in my chest faded. I smiled. "Thank you." I was so relieved I didn't think about introducing myself.

"No problemo." He leaned closer, lowering his voice conspiratorially. "No one should accidentally wander into a pack of feral cheerleaders. They're like sharks in a feeding frenzy."

I followed him to the table. There were six teens sitting on the benches. They looked older than freshman, but they weren't the intimidating kind of high school students who gave me the evil eye for getting too close to their table.

A girl with a lip ring and short black hair pulled back with a funky headband introduced herself first. "I'm Mandy. Welcome to the nerd herd," she said in an easy, self-deprecating way that made me smile.

"I like your lunch box," I said, pointing to the Power Rangers picture. She'd drawn horns on the pink ranger.

A boy with a snake tattoo on his neck nodded to me. He scooted over and made room on the bench.

"This is Isaac," Derrick said, waving a hand at the boy with the tattoo.

"Call me Ace," the boy said.

Everyone laughed. Mandy rolled her eyes. "He's just going through a phase. Last week he wanted us to call him Chlamydia."

He punched her in the shoulder. "Shut up! No, I didn't."

She punched him back.

"Isn't a chlamydia a kind of flower?" I asked. My mom grew all sorts of flowers in the garden.

Ace/Isaac doubled over laughing. Mandy choked on a potato chip. I suspected I'd said something wrong, but I couldn't figure out what. Maybe my mom grew clematises, not chlamydias.

"I like this one." A girl with a green streak in her hair looked up from a sketchpad. "Can we keep her?" I later found out the girl's name was Jessica.

I craned my neck to see the girl's drawing. It was an anime character. Three more of the students had sketchpads out, though their books were closed.

"Are you all artists too?" I asked.

Mandy poked her tongue against her lip ring, making the stud protrude from her lip. "For sure. You should join the art club."

Derrick stole a tater tot off my tray. "So, come here often?"

I fumbled with my chocolate milk, trying to open it without spilling any. "I'm a freshman. It's my first day at the high school."

"Yeah, I know. I could tell."

"Thanks for, um, saving my life back there."

The infectious music of Derrick's laugh had me laughing too. "No problem." He took out a deck of playing cards from his pocket and shuffled them before spreading them out. "Pick a card, any card. Just don't let me see it."

I selected a card. It was the two of hearts.

"Now put it in the deck. Anywhere."

I replaced it in the stack. He shuffled the cards, his hands moving with the skill of a professional poker player. He allowed me to shuffle the deck after he was done and hand it back to him. It took him ten seconds before he found the two of hearts.

"How'd you do that?" I asked.

"Magic." He winked.

"I want to learn how to do magic!" I said excitedly. I knew it wasn't real magic, but it was as close as I would ever come to it.

"Just don't ask him to share his secrets with you," Mandy said. "Magicians are touchy about that." She made a face at him like they'd had this discussion before.

"Oh," I said.

He leaned closer. "Well, maybe just one. An easy one."

By the end of lunch, I'd laughed chocolate milk out of my nose twice. I learned a magic trick and made friends.

It turned out Derrick and I had a lot in common. We both liked watching *Buffy the Vampire Slayer* and *Star Trek: The Next Generation* reruns, we both identified as bookish Ravenclaws, and we wore striped socks. Derrick and I shared sixth period art class.

These were all promising signs we'd be bosom buddies, but more importantly, it was Derrick who introduced me to the possibility of *real* magic.

CHAPTER SEVEN
Making Fiends—And Friends

"My name is Mr. Topolewski, but you can call me Mr. T," the old man at the head of the art classroom said. "I pity the fool . . . who doesn't know the joys of watercolors." He laughed at his own joke. A few students chuckled along with him.

Mr. T's art class was a kaleidoscope of colors. A poster of a bright optical illusion was nestled between a painting of a woman with calla lilies by Diego Rivera and one with melting clocks by Salvador Dali. Art decorated every wall, mobiles hung from the ceiling, and the tables and chairs were painted with student art. The moment I walked in I knew it was going to be my favorite place in the world.

Derrick and I worked next to each other on our first art assignment in companionable silence. Occasionally I looked up to study Derrick's art. He finished the line and shape exercise Mr. T gave the class in a fraction of the time it took me to do the same work. He doodled in his sketchbook for the rest of the period.

Near the end of class I noticed him studying me. The moment I realized he was drawing me, I fidgeted, self-consciously.

"Stay still," he said. He looked from me to his sketch pad and added more detail to his drawing using quick, confident lines with colored markers.

"That's really good," I said.

He tore it out of his sketchpad and handed it to me. "It isn't perfect. I should draw another."

The girl in the drawing had my upturned nose, freckles and bleached blonde hair. The long lashes and big eyes reminded me of a cartoon. She didn't have any pimples on her nose or forehead either.

"It doesn't look like me." After I said it, I realized how insulting that sounded. "I mean that in a good way. What I mean is, it looks more like my sister." Still not helping. I struggled to express what I was trying to say. "It's like what I'm supposed to look like, not what I actually look like. Prettier."

He shrugged. "I don't know about that, but I'll keep trying until I get it right."

He drew another portrait, skipping the pencil and starting with pens. This version of me had nicer hair, and was even cuter than the first drawing. His hand moved over the paper confidently, without hesitation. He added color and shading. After seeing him work with Copic Markers, I knew what art supplies I would ask for as a Christmas gift from my parents.

High school wasn't all bad, I decided. I'd made friends, even if my sister wasn't one of them. I almost felt like I fit in. I just hoped I wouldn't mess it up.

Each day at lunch I sat with the nerd herd in the cafeteria jungle. Even after a week of joining them, I didn't feel like I belonged with the group of older students. I said little, afraid if I made a mistake, and they'd reject me like my sister had.

Mandy sat on the table, swinging her legs, her black mesh hose torn, but it didn't seem to bother her. She told us a story from third period health class. "Then the teacher showed the video. Afterward, Amy Smith raised her hand and was like, 'What about oral sex? Can you get HIV from that too?' And the teacher said, 'Yes.' And she said, 'Oh no! I'm screwed!' And I was like, 'Literally.' She pretty much admitted her sex life to the entire class."

Jessica made a face. "Ick. I just barfed in my mouth a little." Her hands and arms were covered with 666 markings and anarchy symbols.

Mandy poked her lip ring with her tongue. "I didn't know about the oral sex and HIV, though, so I was glad she asked the question. It makes me wish I'd washed my mouth out with soap, too."

Isaac laughed loudly, drawing stares from the table of jocks eating lunch next to us. "That isn't all you can get from oral sex, you moron."

She made a face at him.

I'd been following this conversation, or trying to, anyway. I asked, "Are you being serious? You can get AIDS from kissing?"

All my friends laughed like they thought I was being funny. I tried to laugh along with them, but I didn't get it.

"I guess it just depends where you kiss someone!" Mandy squealed.

Derrick leaned in closer, his breath warm against my ear. It made my stomach flutter pleasantly. I tried to push away the thought of us being so close. We were just friends.

"You do know what the difference is between oral sex and kissing, right?" He didn't say it in a snotty way like Missy would have, but I still felt self-conscious.

Heat flushed to my face and my words came out in a rush. "Of course, I do." Or I thought I did. But everyone's reactions had thrown me off.

I left lunch early to look it up in a book in the library. When I found out oral sex wasn't French kissing, I felt sick with humiliation. All my friends knew how stupid I was.

This was all because my mother had insisted the school waive my sex education class in middle school. She had said she didn't approve of what they taught Missy. She'd let Missy take health in high school last year, but she had said I wouldn't be in it this year.

I could hardly imagine having to face Derrick in art class. I went home early. The next day I ate lunch alone in the art room.

Derrick found me there in the quiet sanctuary while Mr. T dozed at his desk. Derrick sat down beside me. I glanced up at him briefly before returning my gaze to my anime drawing. I didn't know what to say. I probably should have started with "hi" but I only thought about things like that five minutes later.

He bumped my arm with his elbow, making my pencil jump across the page. "Are you mad at me?"

"No," I said quickly.

"What's wrong?" he asked.

"Nothing." I tried to come up with some excuse that wouldn't sound lame, but I didn't have one. I realized I was hugging my sketchbook to my chest, crumpling the top sheet of paper. The concern in his eyes made me feel worse. I didn't want him to know how ignorant I was if he hadn't already figured it out.

"Do you want to see a new trick I learned?" He asked with enough bubbling enthusiasm to make up for my lack of it.

He pulled three golf balls from his pocket and threw them up in the air. He juggled them for a minute until one flew off and hit Mr. T's desk. The old teacher sat up with a start, his nap interrupted.

He looked around confused. "Was that the bell? Where is everyone?"

"No, Mr. T. It's still lunch. Sorry," Derrick said.

I covered my mouth, trying not to giggle. Mr. T leaned back in his chair again and closed his eyes. Derrick tiptoed around the teacher's desk and retrieved the golf ball that had rolled behind our teacher.

"Will you teach me to juggle?" I whispered.

"Sure. We could practice together." He tugged me to the far side of the room and showed me how to juggle.

He broke juggling down into basic steps. He tossed one ball up into the air and caught it in the other hand. The ball looked like it floated from one hand to the other. When it was my turn to try, I missed. The ball hit the floor and flew off under one of the desks. Mostly my juggling lesson consisted of chasing golf balls around the room every time I dropped them. By the end of lunch, though, I could catch a ball. I doubted Missy could do that.

I was relieved Derrick hadn't pressed the topic of why I'd been avoiding everyone. He made it easy to want to be around him. While he taught me to juggle, I didn't have to think about what a clueless dork I was.

The next day we worked on juggling again, this time with the nerd herd as our audience in the cafeteria. I could only catch one ball at a time. Introducing a second ball brought it to a whole new level of difficulty. Derrick brought out a fourth ball and kept all of them in the air at once.

Some jerk built like a mountain on steroids walked past Derrick. He whacked one of the balls with his palm, making it fly off under a table.

"Freak," the boy muttered. He and his friends laughed as they paraded away.

"That was rude," I said.

Derrick frowned. "Some people don't understand brilliance when they see it." He said it in a playfully huffy way, but I could see the true hurt in his eyes underneath the façade.

I retrieved the stray golf ball. When I came back, I heard the tail end of conversation between my friends.

"Why are you teaching *her*?" Isaac crossed his arms, grumbling. "You've never showed me how to juggle."

Derrick rolled his eyes. "You asked me to teach you how to juggle knives. When I said we had to start with balls, you declined."

"Heh, you said balls," Mandy snickered. "I want to juggle balls."

"No wonder you said no, with these two horndogs." Jessica twirled her finger through the green streak in her hair.

By the end of the week I could juggle three balls. Most of the time I didn't drop them. I wasn't as good as Derrick, but I didn't expect I would be. I hadn't been practicing as long.

I showed my family at home with mandarin oranges. Missy plastered a great big fake smile on her face. "Wow. You should join the circus."

Mom cast a warning look at her before turning to me. "How nice that you're making friends this year. Good for you."

"Show me how to juggle," Dad said. "This is cool. Maybe I could learn to juggle knives."

That made me laugh, and I lost my concentration. I broke juggling down into steps like Derrick had for me. All weekend I practiced with Dad, improving my skills along the way. I couldn't wait to show Derrick how good I'd gotten.

On Monday at lunch, Derrick said he'd forgotten his golf balls.

"Oh shucks," I said.

"Oh shucks," Isaac imitated in a goofy voice. "Who even says that these days?"

"Shut up," Mandy said, placing an arm around me and squishing me to her side. "Clarissa says it, and I say she's cool, so screw you."

Isaac's scowl was replaced with a mischievous smirk. "You wish I would screw you."

"Not even. You're soooo not my type." Mandy stroked my shoulder in a sisterly way.

"Um," I said, uncomfortable with all the profanity being thrown around. The more Mandy hugged me and stroked my back, the weirder that made me feel too.

Derrick shook his head at her. "Mandy, stop groping."

Mandy chuckled and let me go.

During art class, Derrick presented me with three wadded up balls of gum erasers he'd pressed together. They were sticky and heavier than golf balls, but I didn't think it would be too different. We huddled in the corner next to the supply table, a poster of Vincent van Gogh's *Starry Night* painting on the wall above us. Mr. T was turned away from our corner of the room, showing a student her grade at his desk.

"Show me what you've got," Derrick said.

I threw the balls up into the air and demonstrated how much I'd improved. Derrick smiled and offered words of encouragement. He pulled a fourth gob of erasers from his pocket as I juggled.

I shook my head. "No way. I'm not ready for more."

He placed his hands next to mine and tossed the ball up into the air. I could already see I was going to miss it. With warp speed reflexes, he grabbed my hands and shifted them into the right places.

My stomach clenched at the warmth of his touch. I allowed him to lead me and to position my hands. I could barely concentrate on the balls with him standing so close. Never had a boy held my hands before. Not that this was holding my hands exactly, but it did seem forward. All I could think about was him touching me. The air shimmered and my skin tingled where Derrick's hands held mine. One of the balls flew off, but I didn't see where it went. I didn't hear it drop.

There were only three balls, but Derrick continued to guide my hands. He laughed, and I laughed with him. He moved my hands more quickly. Another ball flew off. Two balls were easy the juggle, but a few seconds later they disappeared too.

I looked up. They weren't on the ceiling. We didn't find them on the floor. The *Starry Night* painting on the wall behind the desk looked different, but I didn't pay much attention to it looking for the erasers.

"Weird," Derrick said. "They disappeared into thin air."

Mr. T grumbled from his desk. "I pity the fool who goofs off in this class instead of working on their assignment." He eyed us over his bifocals. "Such students might earn fewer participation points."

We sat down at our table. I should have worked on my shading still life, but instead I gazed at the Vincent van Gogh poster. The colors didn't look right. The stars were supposed to be yellow in an indigo sky, but the stars looked dull. Coincidentally, there were four large stars. I returned to the supply desk, gazing at the poster. Brush strokes made with gray dashes radiated from the sources of light. In the center, they looked like they were made of textured globs like the eraser. I stretched across the desk to feel the poster on the wall. It was smooth.

I went back to my assignment, completing a charcoal drawing. I moved on to the next task in my packet. I set up a still life from the plastic fruit Mr. T kept in the trunk in the corner and sketched that.

Halfway through class, the principal entered the room, followed by another man with dark shoulder-length hair. I'd only seen the principal once, at Freshman Orientation Night. He wore the same American flag necktie. The man with him wore a tweed suit, the charcoal gray fabric matching the hue of his eyes. An indigo neckerchief peeked out from under the high collar of his shirt. Something about his suit reminded me of the Victorian era, but I couldn't quite place my finger on why. He wore a badge on his jacket that said: school district psychologist.

"Check it out," someone whispered behind us. "What a freak."

I glared at the boy behind me who had said that. I had little patience for the immaturity and intolerance of my classmates.

The man carried a notebook. He spoke quietly with the principal and Mr. T. The principal left. The man's cool gaze fell on me.

Chills ran up my spine. I'd seen his face somewhere before. I had the strangest sensation of déjà vu. He was handsome—or would have been if he'd been smiling. The fluorescent lights shone blue on his midnight hair. He scribbled in a black book, walking up and down the aisles.

No one in the class spoke. The air felt electric around the man, as if invisible storm clouds followed him everywhere he went. He lingered at *Starry Night*, making another note in his book.

He resumed walked up and down the aisles, stopping to look at Derrick's drawing.

He snorted. "Derivative."

That didn't seem like the kind of thing a school psychologist would say.

Derrick said nothing. For once he wasn't smiling. The man eyed my drawing with even more disdain, but he didn't say anything about it. He left shortly after.

The air still felt strange, tense. All somberness dissipated when some boy in the front row made a farting noise, and the class laughed. People started talking again.

"Who was that guy?" I asked Derrick.

He shook his head. "I don't know. I've never seen him before."

I wanted to ask Mr. T, but I always felt apprehensive talking to adults I didn't know well. Finally, my curiosity outweighed my shyness, and I went over to his desk.

"Who was that man who came in a minute ago?" I asked.

He looked up from his sketch of a lion. "The principal, Mr. Dowdy."

"No, who was that guy with him?"

Mr. T scratched his silver hair. "No one was with him."

"Yes, there was. That man in all. . . ." I couldn't remember what color he'd been wearing. The image of him was hazy in my mind. "I think he was in all black." I twisted my friendship bracelet around on my wrist. No, I was sure he wore all gray. He'd had black hair. I just couldn't picture his face.

Mr. T stared at me perplexed. "Are you talking about that runner from the office who brought me a box of supplies earlier?"

I shook my head.

A girl stood behind me, probably wanting to ask a question about her art.

I turned to her. "Did you see that man who came in with the principal?"

"No." She looked me up and down in a snobby way like she couldn't believe I was talking to her. From the red bow in her hair, I guessed she was on the cheer team and probably friends with my sister.

I returned to my seat. Derrick had finished his assignment, early as usual. He worked on a drawing with his Copic Markers. All the lines were quick hatches, spiraling across the page like wind.

"A minute ago, that guy came in here," I started. "Do you remember him?"

"Yeah, what a jerk. He called my art. . . ." His brow furrowed. "Didn't he say something rude about my art? I can't remember now."

"Do you remember what he looked like?"

"He was short and old, wearing a business suit."

"No, that was the principal."

"Huh." He shrugged. "I don't remember."

Neither did I. Weird.

I twisted the friendship bracelet around on my wrist. I felt grounded when I touched it. Safe. The string was starting to grow gray and dull compared to the vivid colors it once had been, but I didn't want to remove it. As I spun it around on my arm, I remembered the man's disdainful sneer more clearly.

He'd called Derrick's art derivative.

"I like your art. I think it's creative and original," I said.

He smiled.

The four balls of erasers that had disappeared earlier came thudding down onto the table in front of Derrick and me. He leapt back with a start, falling out of his chair. I glanced around. Everyone sat, quietly working. No one had the sneaky smirk of someone who had just thrown wadded up erasers at us.

"Where did they come from?" I asked.

"Huh," Derrick scratched his head, looking around too. "Another dimension, I guess."

He smiled when he said it, but there was an uneasiness in his eyes, as if he might actually be afraid that was the truth.

CHAPTER EIGHT
A Taste of Magic

Mr. T must have been seventy. Perhaps that's why he was asleep at his desk again. I didn't want to wake him to ask his advice with the face I was sketching, even if it was class time. I asked Derrick to help me instead. In the three weeks we'd been in art together, I'd been wowed by his art skills.

Derrick tried to erase the heavy pencil lines, but I'd etched them into the page. "First of all, you have to learn how to sketch lightly, otherwise you'll make it impossible to correct your mistakes."

"You sketch with a pen," I said.

He used his Yoda voice. "Young Padawan, Jedi yet you are not." He flipped the page in my art journal and found a clean sheet.

He placed a hand over my hand to show me where to make the marks with my pencil. He started with the oval and a line of symmetry, and then made dashes where the placement of the eyes, nose and lips would be. His fingers were warm against mine. He moved my hand lightly across the page, the pencil caressing the paper with the lightest of strokes.

I blushed at the intimacy of the moment. I knew Derrick didn't mean anything by it. He was just showing me how to hold my pencil to sketch lightly. He was seventeen, and I was fourteen. There was no way he would be interested in a lowly freshman.

I watched the faint lines come together to make the proportions of a face. He helped me place the eyes, mouth and nose, and marked where the eyebrows and hairline would go. At first it was a normal drawing, no different from any other time Derrick had helped me. But this time it *felt* different.

I couldn't concentrate on the artwork. I could only think about his arm pressed against my arm and his hand on mine. He sat close, like a boyfriend would, and I didn't mind the idea of a boy liking me. Warmth flushed through my body. The room shimmered, and the air wavered like a mirage through the heat of a desert.

The lines shifted under our fingers, the face changing from one expression to another like an animation, not a drawing. Derrick removed his hand from mine. I set the pencil aside. We both watched the paper. Neither of us were drawing, but the pencil lines shifted as if we still worked on it together. The sketch flickered into a more detailed face, into a finished drawing with shading and expression. It settled into the elf face I'd seen in my head and tried to draw. I stared transfixed, too much in awe to move.

Derrick sat rigidly in his chair, eyes wide. He wasn't screaming or majorly freaking out, but he wasn't his usual, relaxed and laughing self either. I couldn't tell if he'd seen what I'd seen. I couldn't tell if *I'd* seen what I'd seen or it had been my imagination playing tricks on me.

Derrick cleared his throat. The silence was unbearable.

"Um," I said, using the extent of my vocabulary for awkward social situations.

He still sat stiffly in his chair, not looking at me. Maybe it wasn't because he'd just seen something magical. Not that I believed in magic.

I fell back on the only logical conclusion for Derrick's sudden lack of friendliness. It must have been obvious I secretly had a crush on him. When he'd placed his hand on mine, I'd probably just acted like a middle schooler and drooled on him or something without realizing it, and he now thought I was an immature child. My heart ached at the idea of losing Derrick as a friend. It was bad enough I would never achieve the easy social status of Missy with all her popular friends, but for the friends I did have to think I was a freak was unbearable.

Something flicked into my shoulder, making me jump. A folded piece of paper landed on the floor. I scooted away from Derrick to pick up the paper, unfolded it, and read the note.

Does the carpet match the curtains?

A group of boys snickered two tables back. I crumpled up the paper.

"What?" Derrick asked. He glared at the group of students.

"Nothing. They're just being idiots." I threw the paper back at them. "I wish my mom would let me dye my hair blue like yours," I said. No one would ask if that was real.

"This isn't dye. It's natural." He pretended to flick his hair over his shoulder like Missy did when she was being snotty, but his hair was too short for the same effect.

"I probably would go with hot pink or purple," I said.

I glanced back at the sketch in my book. It was just an unfinished sketch. I could see the potential for more, but the drawing wasn't anything special. It wasn't magic. Whatever I thought I'd seen must have been my imagination. I'd been daydreaming about what I wanted the finished product to look like.

Derrick bumped me with his shoulder. "Auburn would be a good color on you."

"I hate my natural hair color," I said.

"Why?" He tugged on my braid.

I slapped his hand away.

He grinned, and it was hard not to grin with him. His smile was full of so much sunshine it brightened each moment. "Hey, do you want to come over and LARP sometime?"

That sounded like something I'd heard teenagers whispering about in the cafeteria. "Um, is that supposed to be some kind of innuendo?"

This was only my third week in high school. I didn't want to say anything stupid. Already I felt self-conscious about not being in sex education class. Every time one of my friends brought up something sexual, I had no idea what they were talking about.

Derrick's brows furrowed. "Are you serious? You've never LARPed before? We've got to remedy that!"

I glanced around to be sure no one had overheard. I wasn't like Mandy and some of my other friends, comfortable saying the words "sex" or "get laid" or "French kissing" out loud, even if I was in high school and that practically made me an adult.

Avoiding the topic wasn't going to help me. I didn't see any way around discussing LARP. Still, I didn't want to admit I was a LARP virgin, so I played it cool. "Just kidding. Sure, I've LARPed bunches of times. I just think, um, maybe I need to, you know, do something more . . . less. . . . I really should cut back."

"We could play *Magic: The Gathering* instead. It's a card game. Are you into that?"

Oh, I got it now. He was talking about games. Maybe he wasn't trying to be sexual. When I actually thought about it, I realized how ridiculous the idea was. Derrick didn't even like me like that.

I giggled in embarrassment. "I'd be willing to try *Magic: The Gathering.*"

I doubted my mom would approve of anything with the word "magic" in it, which made me want to play even more. Then I thought about Missy. I didn't want to make her uncomfortable.

"What other games do you play?" I asked.

"*Dungeon and Dragons.* Some online games like *World of Warcraft, Diablo II,* and *Fallout.* Do you play?"

I shook my head. There was no way to ask about LARP now without putting my foot in my mouth. "If we play with magic," I whispered. "We have to do it in secret. My mom wouldn't approve."

"You mean, *Magic: The Gathering?*"

I nodded. That was what I had meant.

"No problem. Is your family churchy?"

"No," I said quickly. It was the truth. There was more to it than that, but I was afraid of what Derrick might say if I told him about what had happened at Oregon Country Fair and how Missy had changed.

That night I asked my parents if I could go to Derrick's house after school and play board games. Mom asked me five jillion questions and ultimately concluded I would not be going to Derrick's house because no adults would be home to supervise us.

"I don't know this boy, and we've never met him. I don't want you alone with him," Mom said. "It might not be safe."

Dad suggested, "Why don't you invite him over here? That way your mom can ask him for his driver's license and social security number." He nudged her when he said it to show he was teasing.

If Derrick came over and we did anything that even remotely sounded like witchcraft, we would have to be extra secretive.

Derrick came over on a Wednesday after school. The moment he stepped into our house, my mom's eyes went wide. Her gaze lingered on his blue hair. She was polite as she introduced herself and welcomed him, but her smile didn't reach her eyes.

We went upstairs to my bedroom in the hope that my mom wouldn't see what we were up to and think our games were too closely related to witchcraft. I'd researched LARP and decided that was the safest game in my family's house, but Derrick didn't remove the book from his backpack right away.

He gazed at the pink carpet and flower wallpaper. My stuffed unicorns and teddy bears were piled into one corner of the bed. Barbies were displayed across a shelf, clad in medieval gown replicas Mom had made for me. The way Derrick studied every detail of the room made me see it anew: my Tinker Bell bedspread, the fairy statues I'd stuck into the potted plants on my windowsill, the My Little Ponies lined up on my armoire-style wardrobe, and the doll castle Dad had made me for my fairies to live in.

Derrick didn't say it, but I could see it in his eyes.

I swept a hand over the expanse of my small kingdom. "You think my room is too . . . childish?"

He shook his head. "I have Teenage Mutant Ninja Turtles on my dresser."

Missy stuck her head in the door, making a tsking noise. "He thinks you're a loser."

Her hair was streaked with orange. The food dye in her Herbal Essences shampoo had been Derrick's idea. The follow-through had been my doing.

After the way she'd treated me the first week at school, revenge had felt sweet. She'd ranted for the last two days that someone had slipped it into her shampoo in the locker room at cheer practice, but the truth was, I'd snuck into her duffle bag and added the dye to the shampoo at home.

Derrick shook his head at me. "You know that isn't true. Don't give up what you like because someone else says it's uncool."

Our black cat, Lucifer, sauntered between Missy and the door, flicking his tail at her in his aloof way.

"Don't encourage my sister," Missy said. "She'll never grow up if someone doesn't peer pressure her into acting normal. Speaking of things that are probably abnormal, what are you two lowlifes doing anyway?"

A smile tugged at my lips. "None of your business, *ginger.*"

"Shut up! You're the ginger, not me." She clenched her fists. A vein throbbed in her temple. "I have a soul."

The dreaded *South Park* allusion. She knew which wounds still hadn't healed from my childhood and exploited them mercilessly.

I stood up. "Are you sure ginger-vitis isn't contagious? I've learned to accept my condition. Maybe you should too."

Derrick fell on the floor laughing.

"It was you, wasn't it?" Her pupils looked as though they flashed red like they did in her school photos. But it must have been a trick of light—maybe the chandelier crystal in my window flashing rainbows across her face.

Lucifer jumped away and hissed. The scaredy-cat dashed across the room and darted under my bed.

"What was me?" I feigned innocence.

Before she could answer, I slammed the door in Missy's face.

Lucifer peeked out from under the bed. Gray dust coated his midnight fur. I pulled him into my arms and stroked the dust bunnies from his back. He extended his claws in warning, and I stopped petting him. Dad didn't call him Lucifer for his cuddly personality. The cat tolerated me holding him on my lap as he gave himself a tongue bath.

Derrick sneezed from all the dust.

Mom burst in on us a minute later. Her auburn hair was as wild as a witch's, and she had a smudge of dirt on her cheek from working outside. Her soiled garden gloves hung out of her jeans pocket. She had that crazy look in her eyes. The mom look. Missy appeared behind her, peeking in, a smug smile on her face.

"The door needs to stay open," Mom said.

I hugged Lucifer to my chest. "Mom! You're embarrassing me."

Lucifer squirmed out of my arms and made a bee-line for my mom. I was lucky he hadn't clawed my face off. The little traitor rubbed up against Mom's leg and purred.

"If you have a guest, this stays open." She pushed the door all the way against the wall before leaving us. Out in the hall she told Missy, "Keep an eye on your sister."

I groaned.

"Oh, I will," Missy said with an evil older sister cackle that rivalled the Wicked Witch of the West.

Derrick mouthed the words, "Your sister is such a bitch."

That was an understatement. Even so, I felt compelled to stick up for her. "Don't say that about her. You don't know what her life has been like."

I didn't want him to hate her. I now wished I hadn't squirted orange food dye in Missy's shampoo. It hadn't been a nice thing to do. Why did I always drive my sister away?

I looked to Derrick apologetically. "I'm sorry my family is being like this. Missy isn't always this crabby." Only, she was, but I didn't think it was right to tell him about her personal issues. She still hated me because of that woman from Oregon Country Fair. And now she was going to hate me because I'd made her into a redhead.

Derrick drew his LARP bible out of his bag. "She's just jealous."

I looked away, flattered but embarrassed.

"No, I'm not!" Missy said from the hallway. "You don't have anything I would want. You're stupid and ugly and uncoordinated. You aren't special in any way."

I sighed. This was so humiliating. I wished Missy would go paint her nails or listen to her latest boy band heartthrobs—anything else that didn't involve telling the world about my every flaw. I slid Derrick's book underneath his bag so she wouldn't see it.

Derrick leaned in closer. "Who has a 5.0 GPA?"

I managed a weak smile. "I do." It was the honors classes and two online college credit classes that had boosted it past a 4.0.

"Who did Mr. T say was an incredibly gifted artist who he selected for the art show?"

Heat flushed to my cheeks. "Me."

He squeezed my hand. "Who are boys always writing notes to because she's so cute?"

I rolled my eyes. He hadn't read those notes. They weren't flattering. I would have explained, but I suddenly felt tongue-tied. I couldn't stop thinking of his hand on mine.

Missy poked her head in my room. "What are you whispering about?"

"Your mediocre backflips at state," Derrick said.

I drew my hand away before Missy noticed. Not that we were doing anything. We were friends. I just didn't want *her* to think we were doing anything.

Missy howled, kicked the wall, and stomped off.

"My mom listens to every stupid thing she says." I lowered my voice. "My parents keep making all these dumb rules they didn't have when she was a freshman. They said I can't have a boyfriend, and I can't date until I'm sixteen."

He shrugged. "My grandparents have some lame rules too. They say their rules mean they love me. Lucky me, right?"

Derrick was always talking about his grandparents. He'd never come right out and told me why he didn't live with his parents. My parents said prying was rude, but we were friends, and it was worse to say something unintentionally stupid like I always seemed to be doing.

I paused, uncertain. "Where are your parents?"

He opened his LARP bible, eyes on the text. "I've never met my dad. My mom died when I was a baby."

"I'm sorry."

"No biggie." He shrugged with one shoulder and tried to smile. His blue eyes were so sad, I could see it was a big deal.

In that moment, I forgot about my sister. I threw my arms around him and hugged him. He flinched like he was afraid I was attacking him, but after a second, he placed his arms around me and patted my shoulder. It was uber awkward, and I wondered if he felt as uncomfortable as I did. I drew back, crashing my butt into my fairy castle and knocking over a bunch of doll furniture. Ugh! Why did I have to do clumsy things all the time?

"Moooooom!" Missy leaned against the doorway, a vicious smile on her face. "They're making out. And they're reading some kind of devil book."

Considering there was a grim-looking demon engulfed in flames on the cover, it did look a smidge satanic. Still, I wasn't going to let Missy get away with that.

"Is that Devil's Red lipstick?" I asked. I'd seen the label on it in the makeup drawer in the bathroom. I knew it was.

Even with the seven layers of foundation and power on her skin, her face turned crimson. "I don't know what you're talking about."

"Stay out of my room or I'll tell Mom about your makeup," I said.

"Stay out of my makeup or I'll make your life a living hell. *More* of a living hell. I'll tell Mom to have another come-to-Jesus talk with you. Do you want her to burn the rest of your toys?"

I grimaced. Now she was just being sadistic. Derrick was probably going to think we were one of those cultishly religious families. Mom celebrated Yule and went to her hippie-dippy harvest moon circles, or whatever they were. We only went to church once or twice a year with Dad.

I shouted, hoping my mom would hear downstairs. "We are not making out! Missy is lying. She keeps peeking in, and she's being annoying." I rose and closed the door again. I was probably going to get in trouble, but I was too angry to care. I should have waited until Missy was at a practice before inviting Derrick over.

"Sorry," I said to Derrick. "My family is driving me crazy."

"We don't have to play a game right now. We can catch the bus and go to the movies or something." He leaned back against my bed. "We'd be alone there."

I rolled my eyes. "How would we be alone? We'd be surrounded by a bunch of people." Sure, they would be less annoying than my family, but not by much.

"Yeah, forget it. It was a dumb idea."

"Wait? Were you asking me on a date?"

"No." He blushed. "Didn't you say you aren't allowed to date?"

The door burst open to reveal my dad this time. He still wore his white orthodontist jacket over his slacks and button up shirt. He held up a cordless drill from the garage. It whirred loudly as he pressed the trigger.

"It's time for a cavity check," he said ominously.

Derrick jerked away and crab-walked backward.

"Dad! Stop! You're being a jerk!" If it wasn't one parent, it was the other.

Dad's barrel chest and broad shoulders took up most of the doorway, giving off an ominous appearance. Or as much of an ominous appearance as a balding middle-aged guy with a bad comb-over could give off.

He laughed. "I'm just messing with you, Derrick."

Derrick gave a half-hearted laugh. "Heh. Good one, Mr. Lawrence."

"How about a game of Monopoly in the kitchen? We'll see if Missy wants to play with us." Dad glanced down the hall and lowered his voice to a whisper. "You know how much your sister hates board games. She'll run away faster than Lucifer from a bathtub full of water."

"Thanks, Dad." I smiled in gratitude.

I shouldn't have. I had to endure hours of my parents ganging up on me and Derrick and evicting us from Park Place and the Boardwalk.

After that, I confirmed Missy wasn't home before inviting Derrick over. I was only allowed to do things with him outside the house if Jessica, Mandy or other girls accompanied us. No dates were allowed.

Derrick came over after school on Friday when Missy was at a game. We practiced juggling together, and he demonstrated magic tricks. When I begged him to show my mom his latest card trick, her eyes narrowed in suspicion.

"That's an illusion," she said. "Sleight of hand?"

Dad just laughed. the entire barrel of his body bounced like Santa's belly. "What else would it be, honey? Magic?" Dad slapped Derrick on the back.

Mom made us sit at the kitchen table as Derrick showed me his sleight of hand. He was banned from my bedroom, but at least he was allowed to come over. Mom chopped dinner at the counter, her eyes more focused on Derrick's tricks than on the sharp knife she used.

"How do you do it?" I asked.

"Magicians aren't supposed to give away their tricks," he said with a wink.

"Please," I begged. "You showed me that one trick."

"You know this isn't real magic," Mom said. "There's no such thing as real magic." Her eyes were troubled.

"Right. I know," I said. "It's not witchcraft."

"That's right." Derrick glanced from me to Mom. "These are illusions, Mrs. Lawrence."

She went on, completely oblivious to my embarrassment. "I just don't want you to get it in your head that fairies and wizards are real like you used to think. Remember that movie we watched? That's what happened to Harry Houdini—he thought he could do magic—and he locked himself up in chains in a tank of water and drowned on stage. All because he let *illusions* go to his head."

Derrick started to object. "That wasn't what happened to—Ow!"

I kicked him under the table and shook my head. That movie was a Hollywood fabrication. I'd done a book report on Harry Houdini in the fifth grade. I was sure Derrick knew how he actually died as well. But I didn't correct my mother. There would be no end to it if I did. He didn't know how my mom could be.

"I know, Mom," I said. "This is just pretend magic. Stage magic. We won't let it go to our heads."

I watched Derrick's sleight of hand, making a card appear and then disappear. I tried to imitate the gesture, but my hands were clumsy and awkward.

"It takes time," he said. "Plus, misdirection helps." He snapped his fingers. With the other hand, he flipped a card seemingly out of thin air.

I clapped my hands.

"This is why a stage magician has a pretty assistant. It distracts the audience. See, if you were my assistant, we could do all sorts of tricks." He winked when he said it. "You already distract half the boys in class. Think of how you could use that on a stage."

I rolled my eyes. "Tripping over my shoelaces is not distracting the class." That was my latest fiasco. Before that it had been the toilet paper stuck in the back of my pants that had made the class bust up laughing at me.

Derrick shuffled the deck again. "Plus, you're small enough we could put you in a box to cut you in half. You could walk on stilt legs or something so everyone would think you're tall and it would misdirect them. It would be a great trick."

I grimaced. "I don't want to be an assistant. I want to be the magician. You can be *my* assistant. We'll cut you in half."

"I'm too goofy-looking to be the assistant. I'd have to wear something really crazy, like a bright yellow banana costume to distract people."

"Sexy," I whispered. I glanced at my mom. Her gaze remained fixed on the celery she chopped.

Derrick lowered his voice. "Bananas are considered phallic, so someone probably thinks so, right?"

"Yeah, monkeys," I said.

Mom's knife thudded loud against the cutting board. I guessed we hadn't been as quiet as we'd thought.

"I'll show you my best trick." Derrick rose from the table and leaned against the kitchen counter. His lanky build made my mom look like a hobbit. "Mrs. Lawrence, do you mind if I borrow a slice of carrot for my next trick?"

Her tone was gloomy, resigned. "Go ahead." I wished she would be nicer to Derrick.

He swiped a slice from her cutting board. He placed it in my palm and curled my fingers around it.

"You should have a top hat," I said.

"Concentrate. Imagine the carrot disappearing and reappearing somewhere else. Where should we choose? My math book?"

"No, mine," I said. I didn't want to make it easy for him. My math book was in my backpack on the linoleum floor behind me.

Mom waved her knife at us. "That reminds me, don't you kids have algebra to be working on?"

"Calculus," I said. "I'll do it just as soon as Derrick shows me this last illusion."

Derrick closed his hands around mine. Past him, Mom frowned.

Outside, Lucifer hissed and yowled. Dad yelled, "No, Lucifer! Get down! Abby, I need your help out here!"

"That damned cat," Mom muttered. She dropped her knife, flung open the kitchen door that led to the backyard, and ran out.

"Don't open your hand," Derrick said. "Keep concentrating. Visualize the carrot between the pages of your calculus book."

I tried not to imagine which neighbors' dog our cat was attacking. Or if he had launched himself at someone's face again. He could be as vicious as a Rottweiler. I kept finding dead squirrels in our yard. Mom insisted they weren't Lucifer's doing.

Derrick's hands sandwiched mine. My fingers tingled where he brushed his calloused thumb against the back of my hand. A chill rushed up my arm and sank into my spine. A breeze blustered in through the open door, rustling Derrick's bright blue hair. Goosebumps rose on my arms.

He wasn't goofy looking when he wasn't making funny faces. He was cute, and his skin was flawlessly smooth. The blue of his eyes seemed to grow brighter, as vivid as his hair. It reminded me of a cloudless sky. I could sink into that color and float away. He leaned closer and blew on my fingers. A thrill rushed through me.

"Open your hand," he said.

The carrot pressed against my palm. I turned my hand over and opened my fingers. The slice of carrot was gone.

I stared, transfixed. This couldn't be real. I leapt to my feet and pried his hands open, but he didn't have anything in his hands. He laughed. There was nothing in his sleeve or pockets.

"Look in your math book," he said.

I scooped up my bag and dumped the books on the table. The pages of the book parted naturally around a lump. When it fell open, I found the slice of carrot. He picked it up and bit into it.

"How. . . ?" I asked.

"Magic." He lowered his voice to a whisper and looked over his shoulder toward the back door where Mom had exited. "Real magic."

"No way! How does it work?"

"I don't know." He lifted one shoulder and dropped it. "I just believe and sometimes it happens. It isn't a science. It's more like an art."

I'd always hoped—dreamed—magic could be real. I held my breath, afraid to move, afraid anything I did would break the thrall. At any moment Derrick might laugh and tell me it had been a joke. But he didn't.

"Do it again," I begged.

This time we used a pencil. It worked a second time.

I jumped up and down in excitement. "Teach me how to do that. Please!"

"I can't. It doesn't always work." He leaned back in his chair, a tired smile on his face.

"But you will *try* to show me?" I asked. "Pretty please with a cherry on top!"

Mom came back in, cradling Lucifer in her arms. He licked his paw, giving off an air of indifference. Mom's gaze flickered from me to Derrick. "Dinner will be ready in a minute. Isn't it time for you to go home, Derrick?" She smiled, but her tone had turned icy.

I prayed she didn't know what we'd been doing. She would be angry. She would accuse us of believing in witchcraft or tell me I was alienating myself from my sister. Just the thought of what I was risking made me want to kick myself. It was one thing for Missy to act grumpy and mean for a while, but I didn't want her to hate me for the rest of our lives. I didn't want to reinforce her fears of magic.

Derrick picked up his bag. "See you tomorrow, ginger."

"I'm blonde, that doesn't even make sense." I tried to punch him, but he ducked out of the way.

I walked him to the front door. I stared after him as he headed down the street toward his house. More than anything in the world I wanted to believe magic was real. But I was afraid later he would laugh and tell me it had been a joke.

Mom came up behind me, hands on her hips. "That boy is a bad influence on you."

I didn't answer. She could be such a hypocrite. She went to her women's spirituality circles with friends who were different religions. Wasn't that pagan and more witchy than stage magic?

"He's teasing you and taking advantage of your naiveté. Think about it, Clarissa. Why would any boy three years older than you want to hang out? He's just using you. Why don't you make friends with some girls your age?"

"Sure. Why don't I just join the cheer team like Missy?" I asked. "And instantly become popular while I'm at it too?" I stomped off.

My mom didn't understand me at all. I doubted she'd ever been nerdy and unpopular. She didn't get how hard it was to make friends. Derrick accepted me for who I was, instead of who he wanted me to be. She didn't have any idea what it was like to want something so badly you could almost taste it.

Magic. It was like cotton candy: fluffy and sweet and melting away to nothing on my tongue before I ever had a chance to sink my teeth into it. It was illogical to believe in magic. Even so, she couldn't make me give up the hope that it was possible.

CHAPTER NINE
The Sorcerer's Apprentice

Derrick said he would have taught me real magic if he could have, but it was elusive and mysterious. We practiced at lunch and after school in art club on days when no one else showed up.

Even then, I was afraid Missy might walk into my classroom at any moment and accuse me of witchcraft. I didn't want her to think I was a bad person who would harm her. But I also didn't want to give up being me and doing the things I loved. After I had cleaned out all the magic paraphernalia from my room and sacrificed my books to the bonfire, I'd expected some reward for my efforts. I was tired of waiting for her to accept me again.

There were random moments I sat with Derrick, not even trying to make magic happen, when a feeling tingled in my core. It was almost always when Derrick leaned in close and repositioned my hand as I was doing trick magic or if I was drawing and he placed his hand on mine to help me with a technique. In those moments, I felt something click into place, and the world no longer existed. It was only Derrick and me—and a bundle of nervous energy inside me fighting to break free.

It was never perfect or even intentional. There was never a repeatable scientific method. I couldn't tell if I was making it happen or it was him pushing magic into me.

I could only imagine what my mother would say if she knew. She would tell us we were being silly, impractical, and all this was fanciful and childish. She would say I wasn't making an effort to help Missy feel more comfortable around me. But it wasn't like we did it when Missy was around. We only practiced at school and in secret. My family couldn't know.

One quiet day in January, no one else showed up for our literary magazine meeting in Mrs. Kelly's room during lunch. The teacher ate in the staff room, and this was the third time no one had showed up to the meeting. Derrick sat close to me, showing me the magic he'd been practicing. No matter how many times I tried, I couldn't make the card materialize in his pocket. I could use sleight of hand to make it appear to have come from somewhere else, but never by magic. The air didn't shift and swirl around the classroom for me like it did for him.

"I know you can do it," he said. "I can feel the magic inside you."

My stomach gurgled. The only thing I felt was lunch digesting.

I had to believe Derrick was right. I could do this. I wanted this so badly.

Derrick set his half-eaten sandwich aside and showed me the trick again. The room tingled with electricity as he gestured with his hands. Air shifted around us. The world moved into place for him. Wind gusted against the windows and a breeze swept through the room, bringing with it the scents of like faraway places. The perfumes of cut grass and spring flowers washed over me, even though it was winter.

I could tell each time when magic was going to happen.

He nodded to me. "Check your back pocket."

I blushed at the intimacy of where he'd placed the card. I reminded myself it wasn't like he was magically groping me. I hadn't even felt it appear.

I shoved my hand into my jean's pocket. There was no playing card this time. Instead, I found one of his Cheetos from his Ziploc baggy. I held it out to him.

"Oops. Um, yeah, I meant to do that." He laughed and crunched into it. His eyelids drooped with fatigue.

I suspected he wasn't going to be able to keep this up much longer.

He nodded at me. "Your turn."

I tried again and again, but I couldn't do it.

"How did you learn this?" I asked.

"I don't know. I sort of taught myself. Grandma says my mom

used to do little tricks. She could go through a deck of cards and guess whether they were red or black, and she was right about ninety percent of the time. She couldn't see the suits of the cards, but she was good at poker. Too good. People accused her of cheating in Las Vegas. She was kicked out of a casino." His brow crinkled, and he grimaced. "I wish I'd had a chance to meet her."

"I'm sorry."

He raked a hand through his blue hair. "My grandparents can't do anything like that, but every once in a while Gramps finds something, an old watch, a set of tools, or a piece of jewelry—always something metal—usually from the thrift store or an antique shop. He'll pick it up and put it down real quick and say he doesn't like the way it feels. There's bad energy or something, he says. Sometimes he can even tell you details, like the person who used to own it died, or was a drug addict, or beat his children. It's kind of freaky."

"That's psychometry." It had been listed in the big book of psychic phenomena I used to own.

"That's right. It isn't very useful, though. And it doesn't run in the family. I tried it."

"So, people in your family have this . . . gift. Do you think it's genetic?" I thought about my sister and my mom. I would swear Missy and I had cast a spell in the basement. Mom had a sixth sense when Missy and I had been children and we'd been up to something we weren't supposed to. But maybe all mothers had that.

"It would make sense," Derrick said. "You got red hair and green eyes from your mom, right?"

"And you got blue hair from one of your parents?"

He chuckled. "That's what Gramps says."

"That day with the drawing. . . ." I waved a hand at my sketchpad. "There was that day my drawing came to life. Did you see that?"

He nodded somberly. "I don't know what that was."

"Maybe art is some kind of magical talent for me."

"You draw all the time. It hasn't happened since then, has it?"

He hadn't placed his hand on mine while I'd been drawing for a while. I swallowed. "Maybe we could try again, like we had that day? Together?"

He drummed his fingers against the table, thinking it over. "Sure, there's no harm in trying."

I opened the book to a blank page and held a pencil. Derrick scooted closer. The angle was wrong. He'd been sitting to my right before, and it had been easier for him to help me. His palm was clammy against my skin. He wet his lips. I wondered what it would be like to kiss him. I pushed the thought away and returned my gaze to our hands.

We waited. Nothing happened.

"Try drawing something," he said.

I sketched the oval of a face. Still nothing.

I nodded to the pencil lines. "Maybe you have to correct me." There were so many variables that could have caused that moment before, but I didn't know which served as the catalyst. We were alone now instead of in a crowded classroom. My drawing previously had been farther along.

Derrick guided my hand over the page, sketching a line of symmetry and the line to show the proportions where the eyes would be placed, followed by guidelines where the nose, mouth and eyebrows would go.

Suddenly my hand jerked to the left, gouging a dark line into the paper. Our hands wrote the letter "D."

"Are you doing this?" I asked. "You, are, aren't you?"

He didn't say anything. He stared at the letters unfolding as our hands wrote. D-O-R-

My heart thundered against my ribcage. This was like the Ouija board. My mom would say this was bad. I tried to let go of the pencil, but Derrick held onto my hand. I started to hyperventilate.

"Derrick," I said. "We should—"

The mischievous smile on his face halted my panic. I turned my gaze back to the page. D-O-R-K-F-A-C—

Dorkface? Really? I wrenched my hand out from under his. "You were playing a trick on me?"

He sat back in his chair, laughing. "I'm sorry. I couldn't help it. I saw an opportunity, and I took it."

My mom had been right about Derrick. I was young and naïve, and he took advantage of that.

"You think I'm stupid, don't you?"

The smile slipped from his face. "No, that isn't it."

I stormed out. I would practice without him.

CHAPTER TEN
Adorkable Derrick

I opened my locker, jumping back as two dozen origami cranes spilled out. I picked one up from the gritty tile floor. Scribbled across one side of the pale pink paper were two words: *I'm sorry.*

Another crane said: *Forgive me?*

Another said: *I'm the dorkface, not you.*

More messages covered other birds. It had been a week since Derrick had played that trick on me. I'd chosen to sit at a different table during art class. At lunch I ate alone. I practiced magic by myself, not that I could get it to work. After school I avoided Derrick so I didn't have to walk home with him.

I didn't want to be mad at Derrick. He was my closest friend. It just hurt so much that I trusted him, and he had made fun of me. I wanted to talk to him, but I didn't know what to say. As the days stretched on, the distance between us grew, and I didn't know how to fix what had happened.

The origami cranes were the invitation I needed.

Five minutes before sixth period art class, I found him sketching in his journal at his usual table. Other students shuffled into the room, grabbing the daily warm up and chatting with friends. I plopped down next to Derrick, dumping the paper birds on the desk. I waved a hand over the flock of origami birds, trying to vocalize the thoughts in my head, but I was never very good at getting a conversation started. I wanted to thank him, apologize, and say so much more all at once.

He pushed his two-point perspective project aside. "In Japan, you need to make a thousand cranes for your wish to come true," he said. "But I only had twenty pieces of paper."

He was so eccentric, it was hard not to laugh. I did the math in my head. "You get two percent of a wish."

He swallowed. "Please don't be mad at me." His eyes were serious, earnest.

More students hurried into the classroom, trying to beat the bell. The noise level grew, but I lowered my voice so no one would hear. "I'm not mad. I just . . . my mom doesn't like that you're so much older than me. She thinks you want to take advantage of that. She said you would try to fool me, to make me believe magic was real, and then laugh at me. I thought maybe. . . ."

"No, I'm not like that! I wasn't trying to trick you." He shook his head, his blue hair flopping around. "I was just teasing because you're my friend. My best friend."

Tears filled my eyes. I hadn't had a best friend other than my sister. I tried to smile. I felt so happy and sad at the same time. My breath hitched in my chest.

"Don't cry," Derrick said. He ran to the corner of the classroom and snatched up the tissue box for me. "I didn't want to make you cry."

I blew my nose and wiped my eyes. "You aren't making me cry. I'm fine."

The bell rang. Mr. T yelled above the chaos of the class, telling people to do their one-point perspective warm up. People milled around, getting what they needed from the supply table, sharpening their pencils, or wandering across the room to select a new worksheet of exercises.

Derrick squeezed me around the shoulder. "I know you're younger. I wouldn't take advantage of you." He paused. "You're like a little sister." He cleared his throat.

A little sister? That was almost worse than being called dorkface! My mom would have been relieved he didn't like me romantically, but I wasn't.

"Hey! You two!" Mr. T shouted at us from across the expanse of the students starting their assignment. "Stop flirting and get to work."

My classmates laughed.

"We aren't flirting," I said.

Mr. T snorted.

Derrick and I started our perspective exercise, talking quietly.

"It isn't a trick. You know that, right?" Derrick said. "I can do real magic. I showed Isaac what I could do once. He didn't believe me and accused me of being a liar. Jessica, well, she freaked out. I don't know if you've noticed, but she doesn't want to be alone with me. She's still nice and polite, but . . . not the same."

I hadn't noticed. Maybe it was his imagination. Or maybe I wasn't observant.

He kept his head bowed, not looking me in the eye. "They think it's weird, but you don't. I feel like you're the only one who understands."

"I wish I could do what you do." I drew a horizon line and vanishing point. I ducked my chin and fixed my gaze on my paper as if that would hide my guilt. "My mom thinks magic is bad, that it's witchcraft. It's because of what happened to Missy at Oregon Country Fair. I know I shouldn't still want to make things happen with magic. If I pretend to be normal, Missy might like me some day again." I twisted the friendship bracelet around my wrist. The pink embroidery floss had become frayed. Even where Jessica had wrapped more pink around it days ago, it looked fragile and thin, like my relationship with my sister.

Derrick placed a hand on mine. My stomach fluttered. "What happened to Missy?"

The truth spilled out of me. Whispering so no one else in the class would hear, I told him how close Missy and I had been, what had happened at the fair, and what Missy had said about me trying to kill her someday. I told him about the time in the basement. Derrick nodded as I told him. We did more talking than drawing that period.

Telling someone lifted the burden from my conscience.

"You aren't a bad person. You know that, right?" Derrick said. "Just because you want to learn magic doesn't make you evil. It doesn't mean you would ever hurt Missy."

"I know," I said quickly.

"Do you? Being a good sister and being a witch aren't mutually exclusive. You can be both."

I nodded. I almost believed that.

CHAPTER ELEVEN
The Cost of Magic

I wasn't sure what woke me up at three a.m. on a Friday night. I listened for a scream or some other sign Missy had been having a nightmare. The house was eerily quiet. My mouth was dry like I'd eaten a pepperoni pizza, but I hadn't consumed anything overly salty that day. The plastic cup on my nightstand was empty, even though I'd filled it before bed.

The bathroom water tasted like rusty pipes, so I tiptoed down the stairs in the dark to the kitchen to refill my cup. The stairs creaked, and I hoped I didn't awaken anyone. I paused at the bottom of the stairs, hearing whispers. It could have been the sound of rain rustling the leaves of trees in our yard, or the music of gurgling water down a drain, but there were words.

I inched toward the kitchen, hesitating when I saw the glow of light from around the corner. I tried to swallow, but my mouth felt like the Sahara. Missy stood at the stove, stirring a bubbling mixture in one of Mom's copper-bottomed pans.

The air smelled putrid, sour, and sulfurous. It was worse than that time I'd gotten a perm. I covered my nose.

The glow came from a circle of candles. Missy read from a book. She said a lot of words I didn't understand, but I made out the phrase, "Put a pox on my enemies."

I backed away, majorly creeped out. This could not be real. Missy hated witchcraft. I hurried out and used the bathroom to fill my cup of water.

In the morning, I hoped it had all been a bad dream.

It was an unusually warm spring afternoon, a perfect day for hanging out with my friends and making *Doctor Who* cosplay costumes. Missy was at an all-day cheerleading competition two hours away. I had an entire Saturday without her.

I tried not to think about the weird scene I'd come across the night before. That couldn't have been real, I kept telling myself. There was no evidence to imply it had happened. The house smelled like flowers and spring. The kitchen was clean. Mom's pots and pans were neatly stacked in the cupboards.

My friends and I would have sat inside sewing and crafting, but Mom kicked us out into the sunshine. Mandy, Madison, Jessica, Isaac, Derrick and I crowded around the table on the deck.

Mandy insisted she was going to be the eleventh doctor, so she was sewing a bow tie and painting a yogurt tub to look like a fez. Jessica upcycled a blue dress into a police booth, adding extra fabric and a grid of white ribbon to look like windows. I made a Dalek costume out of tin foil, duct tape, and cardboard boxes. Madison, a girl who'd just switched to our school at the start of second semester and was the newest addition to the nerd herd, helped Mandy. She hadn't decided what kind of costume to make yet.

Mom weeded under her rose bushes along the fence, quiet and almost invisible in the shrubbery as my friends chatted away. Almost. She didn't say anything, but she kept glancing at Jessica's green hair, Madison's black nail polish and death metal shirt, and Isaac's dragon tattoo. I was acutely aware of every bad word that came out of Mandy's mouth and how my mom might think she was a bad influence.

Isaac nodded to my pile of cardboard, tinfoil and duct tape. "You're making those bumps in the wrong places."

The convex half circles I'd formed with duct tape over wads of newspaper to look like the rivets on a Dalek's body were lumpy and asymmetrical, not how they looked on the show.

"What do you mean?" I asked. They looked like they were the wrong shape, not incorrectly placed.

Isaac grabbed his chest like he was cupping breasts. "That's where I'd put some bumps."

Mandy laughed. "That's what I'm talking about! Yeah, let's make some sexy robots."

My face flushed with heat. I glanced down at my flat chest. I was embarrassed how near my mom was, listening to them.

Jessica threw a wad of blue fabric at Isaac. "Shut up, you perv." She threw a piece at Mandy too, and it stuck in her short, spiky hair.

Derrick rolled his eyes at them. "Don't be like that. You're going to make Clarissa uncomfortable."

I glanced at my mom. She didn't act as though she'd heard. She waved a blackbird away from the bulbs she'd planted at the base of her bushes. She stood up next to the fence, sniffing the air.

I smelled it too, that tangy, metallic odor. When Lucifer brought her dead birds, they smelled sickly sweet like old blood. Lucifer stalked the fence line, prowling back and forth, watching another crow perched in the oak tree in the neighbor's yard.

Occasionally the buzzing of an electric saw from the garage roared above our conversation. Dad worked indoors, cutting boards. He'd claimed he was working on a home improvement project. Because he wouldn't let anyone see what he was making, Derrick and I had spied on him through the window earlier. He was making the TARDIS from *Doctor Who*.

Mom took a break around two and brought out milk and homemade chocolate chip cookies.

"Thanks, Mom! You're the best!" I said.

"Thank you, Mrs. Lawrence." Derrick set his knitting aside. He planned on being the fourth doctor. After three hours, his scarf was four inches long.

The girls chimed thank yous. Derrick kicked Isaac who sewed pouches on his pleather thrift store belt. Isaac refused to watch *Doctor Who*. He made himself a Jedi costume instead.

Isaac looked up. "Food! Yes! Thank you, Mrs. L!" He grabbed the entire plate, placing it on top of the brown robes in front of him.

"Didn't you learn how to share in kindergarten?" Jessica asked.

He snatched up a cookie in each hand and crammed one into his mouth.

I set the plate back in the center of the table.

Mom shook her head, laughing. She tucked a dog bone chew toy in the pocket of her gardening apron and walked toward the side of the house where the gate to the white picket fence was situated between our house and the neighbor's.

"If your dad asks, I'm at Mrs. Wilson's house playing with Buddy," she said to me. "I think he's depressed. This morning I saw he hadn't eaten any of the dogfood I set out."

"Okay. I can walk him later," I called after her. I dipped a cookie in milk and bit in. My mom was such a good cook.

"Who's Buddy?" Isaac asked around a mouthful.

I jerked a thumb at the five-foot wooden fence that divided Mrs. Wilsons's yard from ours. My mouth was full of cookie, and no one understood me as I mumbled an explanation.

"The neighbor's dog." Derrick said. "The one that's always barking."

Buddy was the biggest Saint Bernard ever. Mrs. Wilson had let me ride him when I was ten.

I swallowed. "We're looking after Mrs. Wilson's dog while she's in France."

The dog wasn't barking today. Mom was probably right about him being depressed.

Isaac gazed after my mom walking down the path to the gate, her slender hips swaying with her usual spry and cheerful energy. "Your mom is hot."

"Um. . . ." I said, trying to think of something to change the direction of this conversation.

"Yeah, redheads are sexy." Mandy waggled her eyebrows. "Your mom is every teenage boy's MILF. And mine too."

"What's a MILF?" I asked.

Madison covered her mouth and giggled.

"Nothing." Derrick glowered at Mandy. "Watch your filthy mouth, young lady. That's Clarissa's mother. She just made you cookies." Between the knitting on his lap and his admonishment, he reminded me of an old lady. It made me smile.

"Yeah, I know," Mandy said. "That makes her even hotter. She's sexy and she knows how to cook. I want a wife like that someday."

"I'm good at making brownies," Madison said.

Another screech of the saw thundered from the garage. As the vibration died down, a scream rose from the neighbor's yard. It sounded like my mom.

I jumped toward the side of the yard where the gate was, but I tripped on Jessica's blue dress. I kicked a foot through the cardboard box I'd intended to be a Dalek. Mandy and I collided. We both toppled to the ground. Madison and Isaac ran toward the gate. Derrick charged toward the wooden fence, grabbed onto the post, and vaulted over like a parkour acrobat.

"Oh God," he said.

The sound of him retching came from the neighbor's yard. Mandy scrambled over to the fence. She tried to hoist herself up, but she wasn't tall enough or strong enough.

"What's going on?" I asked. I ran toward the fence.

"Don't!" Derrick called from the other side. "Clarissa, stay in your yard."

"Why? What is it? Is my mom okay?"

"She's fine. Just don't come over here."

A few seconds later Madison and Isaac came back a few paces ahead of my mom. Derrick had his arm around Mom's shoulder. She was crying.

I ran to her. "What's wrong? Are you hurt? Do you want me to get Dad?"

Mom wiped her eyes. "No, I'm fine. There's no need to bother your father." She sniffled. "I just had a little fright."

"It's the neighbor's dog," Derrick's face was pale against the neon blue of his hair. "It's . . ." He swallowed.

Oh, no! Something had happened to Buddy. He dog was the gentlest dog I'd ever met. He even got along with Lucifer, which is to say, he ignored our cat. Lucifer had never clawed him.

"Hon, do you think you could make me a cup of tea?" Mom asked me. She looked to Derrick. "And one for your friend, too."

I started toward the house. "Sure."

She waved a hand toward the clusters of bushes. "Use the fresh mint from the garden. Please."

Madison and Mandy helped me collect mint. Mandy grabbed a handful of the wrong plant.

"No, not that one. That's lemon balm," I said. "She wants mint. It helps with upset stomachs."

"Oh, cool. I didn't know that," Mandy reached toward another bush.

"Not that one. That's oregano." I pointed to the peppermint. I couldn't believe she didn't know the difference.

Madison flicked a ladybug off a leaf. "Wow. You know a lot about herbs, Clarissa."

"I guess. I'm still learning. My mom knows what every plant is good for."

Jessica stayed with my mom at the outside table as I went into the house to prepare tea. She wet a strip of blue fabric from her police box dress and held it to my mom's wrists. "My dad is a nurse. He says this helps with nausea."

I didn't know where Isaac and Derrick had gone off to. As Mandy, Madison, and I ground up the herbs with my mom's mortar and pestle in the kitchen, I saw Derrick and Isaac walk with my dad to the patio where my mother sat. Dad crouched next to Mom. His soundproof earmuffs were around his neck and his eye guard on top of his head. Mom brushed sawdust from his beard and flannel shirt as he kneeled beside her chair. He looked at her with such concern and tenderness in his eyes, I had to look away. I felt like I was watching something intimate and personal, even though they weren't doing anything. I wondered if any man would ever look at me with so much love in his eyes.

I wasn't the only one who noticed their chemistry. Madison and Mandy nudged each other and smiled. I went back to pulverizing herbs. I added dried lavender and chamomile because those herbs were supposed to be calming. We made a giant batch of tea in my mom's porcelain teapot.

"Your family knows a lot about herbs. Is your mom, you know, like New Age or Wiccan or something?" Madison asked.

"Dad says she's a hippie." I glanced at Mandy's pentagram necklace. "She doesn't like witchcraft."

"Oh." Mandy fidgeted with the necklace and tucked it under her t-shirt.

I carried the teapot on a tray to the table outside. My friends carried cups and our honey pot. I pushed our costumes aside and set Jessica's dress on her chair.

Dad remained at Mom's side.

"Really, I'm fine," Mom said. "I just wasn't prepared for . . . a dead dog."

Dad stood up. "I'll go over and take care of Buddy."

"No!" Mom jumped up, knocking my pile of cardboard from the table. "I don't want you to see."

"If Derrick can handle seeing a dead dog, so can I," Dad said.

"I'm a doctor." Dad straightened and tugged at the bottom of his flannel shirt, looking proud of himself. As if being an orthodontist was the same thing as a medical doctor.

"Derrick." Mom looked around. "Where's Derrick?"

Jessica handed a shovel over the fence to a pair of hands, probably Derrick's. Mom spotted her too.

"Oh, no! He shouldn't be over there," Mom said. "He shouldn't have to see that."

"He's a big boy. Sit and drink your tea. We'll take care of it." He kissed her cheek and strolled off toward the neighbor's yard.

She bit her lip. I hugged her and patted her shoulder. I'd never seen her look so fragile and vulnerable. She was so small.

A moment later I heard Derrick. "Dr. Lawrence, you might not want to—"

The unmistakable sound of vomiting came from the other side of the fence.

"Dad?" I asked, stepping toward the fence.

"Stay over here," Mom said. "I don't want you exposed to that mess over there."

Mandy and Madison tried to peek over the fence.

"Girls, come over here. Drink some tea with me," Mom said.

"I'll have some tea." Isaac sat next to her, devouring the last cookies.

I couldn't imagine what Derrick and Dad had seen that would make them sick. Maybe the dog had diarrhea, or maybe Lucifer had clawed Buddy's face. I glanced at the cat. He didn't have any blood on him, but that didn't mean much considering his tongue bath tendencies. He snuggled against Mom's leg.

My friends stayed for another hour. As soon as they left, Mom gathered a bundle of herbs. Derrick and Dad continued to work next door. I heard them spraying down Mrs. Wilson's deck. I tried to peek through the boards of the fence, but all I could see was grass.

"Clarissa, don't go by that fence." Mom waved me over to the sage bush.

I trudged back to her, feeling like a dog on a leash. "Why? It sounds like it's all cleaned up. I won't see any blood."

"That's not what I'm afraid of. There's bad energy over there." She bundled her sprigs of sage together with a length of twine.

I eyed the herbs. It looked a lot like a smudging stick. I'd read in a book at the library how Native Americans used sage for cleansing. "I thought you didn't believe in magic."

"I don't. But energy isn't magic." She shoved the bundle into her pocket.

Sometimes she could be so contradictory, but I let the comment slide. She still looked shaken from what she'd seen.

Dad and Derrick came back, sweaty, and their clothes dripping from power washing. Dark stains were splattered across Derrick's jeans.

"How about I get you a change of clothes? We can wash these for you," Mom offered. I'd never seen her treat Derrick so nicely.

Dad gave Derrick a spare set of his clothes that were ten sizes too big for him, and Derrick showered in the downstairs bathroom. Mom washed both their clothes in the new machine in the basement.

She waved me off. "You go clean up after your friends outside. I'll check things over next door. I don't want Mrs. Wilson to come home to a mess. It will be hard enough breaking the news to her." She shoved a salt shaker into her pocket.

Mom left with her magic sage wand poking out of her other pocket. She probably didn't think I knew what smudging was, but I wasn't stupid. Though, I didn't know what the salt was for.

Mom was gone for a long time. As soon as Derrick came out of the bathroom, I peppered him with questions.

"What did you see next door? Why did you and Dad barf? What were you and Dad doing for so long?"

He toed the floor with a sock. "I don't want to talk about it."

"No way. We don't keep secrets from each other."

He crossed his arms and looked away.

"Please, tell me."

He looked into my eyes and moistened his lips. "It's hard to say no to you." For a moment, I thought he was going to tell me. Instead he gathered up his four-inch scarf and shoved it into his backpack. "I should go home."

"What about your clothes?"

"You can bring them to me on Monday, ginger."

I rolled my eyes at his insult.

My mom stood in the doorway to the patio. "Stay a moment longer, Derrick." She beckoned him toward the doorway. He trudged after her. I followed them out.

"That was nice of you to help out today," she said.

"No biggie." He shoved his hands in the pockets of the oversized jeans.

She looked to me. "Clarissa, go inside the house. I would like a private word with your friend."

She was going to say something unkind to him, I just knew it. "Mom!"

"Now."

I hated it when she treated me like a little kid. I went inside. The window was open above the kitchen sink. I ducked down and listened.

Mom asked, "Do you understand what you saw today?"

"It looked like that dog had been attacked by something, you know, like a coyote or a wolf. Or some kind of predator."

"We don't have wolves or coyotes in Oregon City, do we?"

"No."

Mom's voice was cool and collected. She didn't sound shaken anymore. "An animal wouldn't have arranged the dog's entrails into such an . . . *artful* pentagram. So, what kind of predator do you suppose did that?"

I gasped. No wonder Derrick hadn't wanted to talk about it. What a horrible thing to find. Poor Buddy.

"A person," Derrick said. "A really sick and twisted person."

He and my mom must have been walking away because it was harder to hear them.

Mom said, "I know Clarissa wants you to teach her magic."

"Mrs. Lawrence, I didn't do that. I wouldn't ever do something like that."

"I know you wouldn't. You're a good kid. But there are other people out there who aren't."

I peeked through the window at them. Mom had her hand on Derrick's arm, guiding him farther from the house.

Mom went on. "What you saw is the reason we don't do magic in this family. People who try to do witchcraft do things like that. They think there has to be a sacrifice—that some creature's suffering has to be the cost."

"That isn't how it works," Derrick said so quietly I had to lean over the sink to hear.

"But you don't understand how it works, and that's why you're

SARINA DORIE

dangerous to yourself and others. I will not allow you to teach Clarissa magic."

Was my mom admitting magic was real? I couldn't tell.

"I need to protect my girls from witches—and supposed witches. If you ever try to do something like that, if you ever expose my daughter to those kind of people, if you ever try to hurt—"

I leaned farther over the sink to hear, pushing myself up onto my elbows and practically burying my face in the windowsill herb garden to hear them.

"I wouldn't! I don't want anything bad to happen to anyone. I don't want Clarissa to get hurt either."

A voice behind me made me jump. "What are you doing, pumpkin?"

I lost my balance and fell headfirst into the sink. I knocked over a stack of tea cups and plates. The clatter drowned out whatever they'd been saying outside. The counter dug uncomfortably into my stomach and ribs.

"Clarissa?" Mom asked. "Were you eavesdropping on us?"

I didn't move from my perch. I twisted my head to stare up at Dad, begging him with my eyes not to give me away.

He waved out the window and ran the water in the sink, splattering the side of my face. "Eavesdropping? Would one of your daughters do that? I was just minding my own business, washing dishes." He held up a dish sponge on a stick and scrubbed it against the back of my neck. That was Dad, thinking he was funny. He slid the window closed and then the curtains.

He gave me the stink eye. "Don't spy on your mother."

"Yes, Dad." I wiggled my way backward until my feet touched the ground and stood.

His stern expression faded. "You owe me big time, Clarissa."

"I know. Thanks, Dad."

He chuckled to himself. "Your mom is probably just having the birds and the bees talk with your boyfriend."

"He isn't my boyfriend!"

He patted my head. "Of course not."

I headed toward the laundry in the basement to check on Derrick's clothes. I paused in the doorway, watching Dad open the dishwasher and slide out the tray. "You were the one who put *Harry Potter and the Sorcerer's Stone* under my pillow, weren't you?"

104

Dad's eyebrows shot upward. "When was this?"

I lowered my voice. "You know, when Mom took it away. I found it under my pillow the next morning."

He shook his head. "Your mother banned that book. I put the entire series in the box to give to Uncle Trevor and Aunt Linda to give to their kids." His brow furrowed.

Was he pulling my leg? I couldn't tell. Mom wouldn't have slid it under my pillow, not after making me burn everything else related to witches. There was only one other person in the house who might have given me that small gift of hope for magic, and that was almost more unbelievable than the idea of magic itself.

Missy trudged in at quarter after nine. Mom had already gone to bed. Dad and I sat in the living room. He quickly changed the channel from an old rerun of *Bewitched* to a sappy Hallmark channel movie. He wasn't fooling anyone. Only Mom watched those movies.

Missy's eyes were dark, and her frame lacked her usual energy. She didn't even glance at the television.

"How was your day, honey?" Dad asked.

She shrugged and passed us. I set aside the Dalek costume on my lap and followed her to the kitchen.

"Hi, Missy. How was your competition?" I asked.

"Mind your own beeswax." She headed straight to the fridge and chugged milk from the gallon jug, even though Dad hated it when she did that.

I fidgeted with my friendship bracelet. "Did you have a good time?"

She returned the empty milk carton to the fridge and grabbed a pitcher of orange juice. "Where's Mom?" Her voice was rough and scratchy. She coughed.

"Upstairs, asleep. Buddy died. She had a rough day." Understatement of the year.

"Who's Buddy?"

I waved a hand at the neighbor's house. "Mrs. Wilson's dog that Mom was watching."

Missy plopped down on a kitchen chair, hugging the pitcher of orange juice to herself. "Oh."

"Mom found the dog." I decided not to describe the state he'd been left in. I didn't want her to think *I* had something to do with it.

"That's . . . that sucks."

My mind flickered to the dream I'd had of Missy in the kitchen the night before. It had looked a lot like witchcraft. Mom thought Buddy's death was the work of witches. I considered telling Mom about what I'd seen, but I didn't even know if it was real. And if I did tell Mom, it would only cause more problems between Missy and me.

Missy folded her arms across the table and laid down her head. She sniffled.

"Are you okay?"

"Get lost, loser."

I got Dad. All she said to him was, "I feel like I'm going to puke."

In the two seconds it had taken me to get him, she'd drained the pitcher of orange juice. No wonder she felt sick.

Missy stayed in bed for the next two days. On Monday at school, I heard the rumors. Missy's rival cheerleading team had come down with a case of herpes right before the big competition. Another team would have won, but a girl on that team broke her neck when they threw her up in the air from the top of a pyramid and failed to catch her. Her death was the talk of the school.

It was also first time the Oregon City cheer team had ever won a regional competition.

Missy remained quiet and sullen. She stayed home sick from school until Tuesday. I kept wondering if she had cast a spell or it was a dream. There was a cost to magic, my mom had said.

I didn't want to think poorly of my sister. She was a nice person deep down, even if I didn't see that side to her often. She wouldn't hurt anyone. After all she'd been through, she wouldn't ever want anything to do with witchcraft.

People probably convinced themselves of things like that when their older sisters were involved with drugs and gangs, too. I couldn't allow my sister to spiral out of control. She had promised to protect me, and I had promised to protect her. I knew *I* wasn't going to hurt her.

I just didn't know how to save her from herself.

CHAPTER TWELVE
The Road to the Dark Arts and Crafts

Mom was too far gone down the river of deNile to be much use. I enlisted Dad's help instead. I waited until Missy was at cheerleading practice after school. He was working in the garage on the TARDIS.

"Dad, we need to have a grown-up talk," I said.

"Sure, champ. What's on your mind?" He set the power tools aside. He pulled out a bench for me to sit and clasped his hands in front of him. From his somber expression, I was afraid he thought I was going to say something like, "I'm pregnant."

"It's Missy," I whispered, afraid she had the power to hear me talk about her from miles away. "She's changed since we went to Oregon Country Fair. I'm concerned about her."

Dad nodded. "She has. I can only imagine how hard that is on you."

"I'm afraid she's getting involved with. . . ." I cleared my throat. In my head I'd practiced what I would tell him. I would describe what I'd seen in the kitchen the night before the dog had been mutilated, cite how she'd been sick the day after, and then describe what had happened to her rival team. But now that I was telling him, I realized how fanciful it sounded. He'd tell me this was confirmation bias.

Dad waited patiently.

I changed my tactic. "I heard Mom talking to Derrick about people she was trying to protect us from. Bad people who would use us. I think Missy is involved with the wrong crowd. Maybe you and Mom should check her room for drugs or other things she shouldn't have."

"Why would you think Missy would have drugs? Have you heard Missy talk about drugs?"

"I don't want to say. . . . I just want to help her."

He nodded. "I'll talk to your mother about it when she gets home."

Drugs must have been the right word to get Dad's attention. Before Missy was even home, Mom scoured Missy's room. I doubted she would find any drugs. I walked by Missy's room, pretending to mind my own business as Mom piled books, candles and baggies of herbs into a box.

Dad shook his head. "Abby, is that truly necessary? A book of spells isn't heroin."

For some it was.

Missy came home after dinner. She stormed into my room. "You told Mom, didn't you?" She grabbed me by the front of my shirt.

I tried to push her away, but her grip was too firm. "I didn't want you to hurt yourself," I said.

"No, you don't want me protecting myself from *you*." She shook me.

"I'm trying to help you. I'm not going to hurt you."

"You'll regret this."

I definitely regretted it when I later found all my Barbies decapitated.

I decided not to tell the 'rental units about what she'd done. I needed to find another way. Only, I had no idea how. I felt further from helping her than ever. Even so, I knew I had to save my sister from herself.

I trusted Derrick more than anyone else. It was natural he would be the one I'd confide in. We sat together, alone in Mr. T's room at lunch.

"First we need to identify the real problem before we brainstorm solutions." Derrick selected a silver Sharpie and drew an oval in his notebook.

"I know the problem. My sister thinks I'm the daughter of a wicked witch, and it's my destiny to kill her before her eighteenth birthday. But really she's the one—

"Slow down." Derrick scribbled an annotated version of what I'd said in the center of the oval. "When does she turn eighteen?"

"February seventeenth. Next year."

"Great! A ticking clock." He sounded too enthusiastic for the direness of the situation.

"No, not great. That means I have ten months before I kill her or she does something horrible—more horrible than killing a dog. What if she kills a person?"

He held up his palms in a placating gesture. "I didn't mean 'great' in that sense. I meant, we can use this to our advantage. Scenario one: this prophesy is bunk. When Missy turns eighteen, she'll see that. Problem solved." He drew an alarm clock on the page coming from the brainstorming bubble.

I appropriated his pen and the sketchbook. "Yeah, but we need damage control until that moment."

"Right. So let's entertain scenario two for just a moment: you're Voldemort's daughter—or whatever. It's prophesized you're going to kill your sister. Do you believe in fate or freewill? If this is predestined, nothing you do will stop it, and everything you try to do to help will cause it. So like the Dalai Lama says—"

"You aren't helping. I need solutions here. I need to find some kind of magic to protect Missy from me until after she's eighteen. I need blessings and wards."

Derrick leaned back in his chair, a nimbus of confidence surrounding him. "We need to use your superpower."

"I don't have any superpowers." Still, I leaned in, hoping he would reveal the magical ability I had that I didn't know about.

He raised an eyebrow. "What do you do better than anyone in your Honors English class, social studies and advanced biology combined?"

"Juggle?"

"Besides that."

I drew a blank.

"You're good at research and studying!"

What a letdown. "I've already read all the books in our school library and the Oregon City Library on spells. Mom checks our internet browser history, and she'll confiscate anything about Wicca or witchcraft."

"I'll use my computer at home. Plus we can use the computers at the public library and do a county library search for books. We'll use my library card. If we can't find what we need, we'll go to one of those New Age shops in Portland."

"Portland? But that's the big city. Every time we drive there, my mom says, 'It's a bad neighborhood, girls. Lock your doors.'"

Derrick laughed. "Don't worry. I'll protect you from the big, bad city."

We followed our plan, starting at the library. I used my super research skills every day after school. We read ancient myths and took notes on tactics people used to protect themselves in fantasy novels. During the second week of research, Madison joined us. The third week, the entire nerd herd took notes and helped us. By that point, it was almost June and school would be out soon.

"You should totally hide garlic flowers under your sister's bed," Isaac said in his typically unhelpful way.

Mandy punched him in the arm. "Shut up. Clarissa's sister isn't a vampire. She's a witch."

"More like a bitch," he said.

I shushed them. Their loud voices and foul language drew the stares of other library patrons.

I whispered, "She's not a witch. Or a witch with a b. I'm just trying to make sure she doesn't become one." I'd only told them enough of my concerns to make them interested in helping, not enough that they knew how scary Missy could be.

I glanced over my shoulder. A young lady on a computer stared at us. She looked familiar. I hoped she wasn't a student at our school. If she was, she might repeat our conversation to Missy.

At the end of May, we decided we needed to go to a pagan shop downtown. It took the city bus an hour and a half to get from Oregon City to downtown Portland. I would never have gone to the city without my parents if hadn't been for Missy's sake.

In the first shop we perused books, and I bought a smoky quartz crystal to draw away negative energies. Derrick wrote out a spell to protect a house from bad juju. The second shop was more of a New Age bookstore than a witch shop. The six of us each took an aisle to peruse.

The owner wore flowing hemp robes. She smiled at me and asked if I needed help.

"I need to find a book to prevent something bad from happening. A protection spell," I said.

An orange tabby cat sidled up to her and rubbed against her leg. She picked up the cat and cuddled her. "This is Princess," she said.

The woman placed a hand on my shoulder and guided me over to the section on guardian angels the next aisle over. Another cat slunk out from between shelves and meowed at the woman. The air smelled intensely musky, like wet cat food and Lucifer's litterbox.

"Well, that's odd," the woman said. "This is Gandalf. We haven't seen him for a while." As she continued to show me books, more cats came out from under tables and skulked up to us. One sat in a gap on the shelf between books. The woman scooped him up. He purred and nuzzled her. Two Siamese nudged my legs with their heads.

The owner stared. "Who are these?"

A large spotted cat dove past us, chasing a smaller white cat.

"Look, kittens!" Madison squealed. She carried two in her arms. Mandy carried three more.

"Is this some kind of joke?" the owner asked. "Did you bring these cats in here?" She pointed an accusing finger at me.

I shook my head. "I didn't do it."

"Help!" Isaac stood with back pressed up against a wall. A half circle of ten cats surrounded him. "They're going to eat me!"

The woman shooed them away. "Nonsense. They're harmless. But where did they come from?"

A black cat purred at my feet. Two more napped on the counter by the register. More sauntered down the aisles. There had to be twenty in the shop. Mandy sneezed. I felt like I was in the Tribble episode from Star Trek. We had to wade through a sea of cats to the get to the door. I reassessed my initial number. This was closer to fifty cats.

Outside it was easier to breath.

Isaac's usual tough guy act was gone. He hugged himself, shivering. "That was like the *Twilight Zone* in there."

Mandy sneezed again.

"That was real magic," I said.

"Maybe we should go back in," Derrick said. "There might be something useful inside. The cat lady might know something to help us."

Jessica snorted. "Like what? How to start a cattery?"

"Cool trick back there." Someone behind us spoke. "Which of you is the witch? Untrained, I'm guessing." A man leaned against a long staff under a tree along the sidewalk, smoking a clove cigarette. He was short, almost my height, but he was probably in his thirties. The tips of his white frosted hair and long goatee were dyed cherry red.

"Um. . . ." I said with my typical social gregariousness.

Derrick stuck out his hand and introduced himself and then the rest of us.

"Hunter Lebow, also known as the Sorcerer of Goose Hollow," the man said with a superior affect. "You've probably heard of me."

"We're not from Portland," Derrick said.

The sorcerer dressed in a trendy punk style like my friends, but something about him wasn't right. His smile came too quickly, but it didn't touch his eyes. When my mom had talked to Derrick about the bad crowd she didn't want me falling into, I had a feeling she meant someone like him.

His gaze raked over me. "You want magic. I can give you magic."

The nerd herd looked to each other excitedly, as if this man was our savior.

I was afraid to sound ungrateful, but I forced myself to ask, "What's the price?"

His eyes narrowed. "Aren't you the shrewd one? You've made deals with Witchkin?"

I didn't answer.

"Witchkin?" Mandy asked. My friends looked at each other in confusion. They'd never heard that word before.

I had, I just didn't recall which book it had come from.

"The price depends on what you're after," he said. "Simple hexes and curses are twenty bucks per victim. Complex curses and love potions start at forty."

"What about, um. . . ?" I couldn't remember what we were there for. He kept staring into my eyes. It was hypnotic.

"We need a protection spell." Derrick said. "To keep magical harm from coming to her sister. How much would you charge for that?"

"Is that all you need? I can do that for the low price of . . . your immortal soul."

I crossed my arms.

"Just kidding." He barked out a laugh. "How about for a taste of your blood?"

"Me! Pick me. It's my turn to give blood." Isaac raised his hand, as if he had just been called on in class. He laughed like it was a joke.

I suspected otherwise.

"Sorry, you aren't my type." Hunter stared at me.

I looped my arm through Jessica's. Her skin was cold and clammy.

"Don't do it," she whispered.

"I'm not going to. Duh," I said.

"What do you say?" Hunter Lebow asked me.

I shook my head. "How about twenty dollars?"

"Forty. And you're going to have to pay for all the herbs and items needed for the spell."

That was better than giving him anyone's blood. I just hoped he wouldn't change his mind later.

The sky was a dark azure as the sun set behind the housing development past the field.

Hunter poured a line of salt along the flattened grass around the nerd herd and myself. "First we need to cast a protective circle around ourselves so we don't accidentally summon any lower level beings," he said.

"Like demons?" Derrick asked.

"Fae," Hunter corrected. "Though you might consider what they do to be demonic."

A bird flitted across the darkening sky. Worry wormed its way under my skin. I'd always thought of fairies as being nice and happy. A memory as distant as a dream fought its way to the surface. Something about ravens.

My thoughts were interrupted as Hunter went on. "All of you need to turn off your phones and any other electronics so you don't drain the powers from my spell."

I turned off my phone. Derrick turned off his iPod. Hunter made us form a circle as he incanted a spell. He held a staff in his hand, waving it around and drawing symbols in the air.

During the week that had passed since we'd ventured into Portland on our witch-seeking expedition, I hadn't felt comfortable

SARINA DORIE

with the idea of going to this stranger's apartment to cast the spell. It was a blessing he needed to come to my neighborhood to get closer to Missy for the casting.

My family's home was within eyesight of the field where the nerd herd had gathered with the sorcerer. He'd allowed me to make a copy of his spell to collect the ingredients ahead of time. The chamomile, lavender and wormwood were painless to gather since my mom grew all kinds of herbs. The pig's feet and red wine were surprisingly easy due to Mandy's mom's culinary preferences.

It was a personal item from Missy's room that had been the hardest to collect. First, I tried to steal one of her glittery red bows from her cheerleading uniform, but she tore the house apart looking for it and found it in my underwear drawer. The second item I'd attempted to appropriate was one of her socks—but she'd come home early from practice and caught me in her room. She'd screamed at me until Dad came upstairs and insisted she calm down. The third item I'd stolen had been her Devil's Red lipstick from the shared drawer of makeup in the bathroom.

As Hunter waved his wand in the air, Isaac sighed, as if bored. Jessica nudged him. She silently scolded him by shaking her head. Mandy and Madison mouthed something to each other. Derrick's eyes were riveted by the staff. As Hunter worked, a purple halo sparkled around the wooden stick.

Hunter arranged the items around himself and lit white candles. He made us all join hands as he mixed ingredients.

"It would be better if I held hands with the circle, but I need one hand for my staff to focus my powers, and I need the other for mixing," he explained. "You can always tell the professionals from the amateurs by the kind of staff they—What are you doing?" He slapped Isaac's phone from his knee and it fell into the grass.

"What was that for?" Isaac picked up his phone and wiped it off.

"I already told you. No electronics. Magic is sensitive, and I don't need you messing it up." Hunter scowled. "We need to start the chant over. This time without interruptions."

Derrick sat to my right. I was supposed to be chanting along with everyone else, but I had a hard time concentrating on anything other than the warmth of Derrick's palm against mine. I watched his lips as he chanted, imagining what it would feel like if he kissed me. He caught me staring and squeezed my hand reassuringly.

The wind blew, making the flames of the candles flicker. The perfume of jasmine and cardamom overpowered the scent of grass and wildflowers. Derrick's hand tingled against mine. Hunter looked up from his spell. He twirled his goatee around his finger, watching us.

Hunter didn't ask for a sacrifice or blood. I wasn't sure if that meant not all magic needed a sacrifice or it meant the spell wasn't going to work. Maybe the pig's foot counted as the sacrifice.

Hunter mixed all the ingredients in a cauldron, blessed it in some other language, and then strained it as he poured it back into the wine bottle. I wasn't even sure why he'd needed the lipstick.

He handed the bottle to me. "You need her to drink this in the next twenty-four hours."

"Oh, it's a potion," I said, disappointed.

This was going to be more difficult than I'd expected.

CHAPTER THIRTEEN
The Brew Master

Hunter didn't say how much potion Missy had to drink. I should have asked. My plan to get some of the potion into my sister's drinks involved waiting until everyone went to bed that night.

By the light of my cell phone, I poured out a fourth of her fruit punch-flavored Gatorade because it was red. I hoped the addition wouldn't be obvious. I hesitated before pouring in the potion. What if the raw pig's foot Hunter had stirred the ingredients around in had botulism or trichinosis? I might make Missy sick. What if the prophesy was real, and I killed my sister this way?

"Clarissa?" Dad called from the top of the stairs.

"Just getting a drink of water," I said.

I hurriedly poured the potion into the sports drink. As I placed it on the shelf, I could see the liquid was still red, but now cloudy. I didn't know if she would notice. I hid the blue and green Gatorades in the garage so she would be forced to choose the red one.

The following morning Missy eyed the drink dubiously. "Mooom! Can Gatorade spoil?"

Missy poured it down the drain and refilled the container with water and Kool-Aid.

"Do you want me to help so you won't be late?" I asked her.

"Get lost, loser," she said with her usual churlishness.

This required a more serious strategy. I considered my options. I hated lying to my parents, but it was the only way. I went to my mother where she was braiding her hair in the upstairs bathroom.

"Mom, I want to do something nice for everyone. Can I make dinner tonight? But I don't want you to tell Dad or Missy until afterward because I want it to be a surprise. After they're done, and we ask them if they liked it, then we'll say I made it."

Mom shrugged. "Sure. But you have to use a recipe this time. After you and your father 'invented' that Top Ramen casserole, I don't think anyone is going to be able to stomach another experiment for a while."

I'd executed stage one of the new plan. All I needed was to follow up with the next two steps: cooking and serving dinner without anyone suspecting what I was up to.

Derrick came home with me to help me start dinner. I directed him to cut the potatoes and carrots while I defrosted the lamb from the freezer. Everyone loved Mom's Irish lamb stew. The recipe used bacon and wine, among other ingredients. I collected herbs from the garden.

"You don't think cooking the potion will make it less potent, do you?" I asked Derrick as I dumped the bottle of wine/potion in a large sauce pan. The recipe only called for one cup, but I wanted to ensure Missy got enough.

"Peach pie doesn't contain fewer peaches if it's baked, right?" he asked.

"But there will be less alcohol if it's cooked off," I said.

Derrick looked up from his chopping. "Wait, are you going to be eating the potion too?"

"I'm going to have to. It will look suspicious if I pour the potion in one bowl and serve it to Missy."

Derrick made a face. "You'll have to tell me if you feel more protected tomorrow."

I started the bacon sizzling in a pan. Grease hissed and sputtered at me. I flipped the bacon over, trying to dodge hot missiles of oil. Derrick inhaled the aroma over my shoulder. My stomach grumbled.

The very first piece I set aside, Derrick snatched up. "And for our next magic trick, watch this bacon disappear."

"You can't eat the bacon. It's for the stew."

"Just one or two or five pieces."

"Two pieces."

He set two perfectly crisp pieces aside and resumed chopping herbs. The moment they were cool enough he practically inhaled the first one. I placed a new row of bacon strips in the pan.

He waved the second piece back and forth in front of my face. "It's calling to you. Will you give in to temptation?" He waggled his eyebrows in an exaggerated gesture of flirtatiousness.

"I'll be more tempted when I don't have raw meat on my hands."

He held it closer to my mouth. "My hands are as clean as a baby's bottom."

I laughed. "Is that supposed to make me confident of your hygiene?"

"For real. I just washed my hands for the third time." He held the bacon under my nose so I was forced to breathe in the tantalizing smoky aroma. My mouth watered.

I bit in. A burst of savory heaven exploded on my tongue. He held it out for me to nibble on. His eyes sparkled with mischief when I came to the last bite. He pulled the bacon away and made as if he intended to eat the last morsel.

"No way, dorkbreath. You can't tease me like that!" I said.

"Yes, I can, baconbreath." He nodded to the pan. "Oh, look I'm distracting you. You take care of that, while I finish off your last bite."

The bacon in the pan had turned dark. I quickly moved the pan to a different burner and transferred the strips onto a plate. I set out more to fry. The moment I turned back to him, he held up my last piece.

He grinned. "You didn't really think I'd steal your bacon, did you?"

"Yes," I said.

He shoved the last bite into my mouth, both of us laughing as I bit his finger.

He poked me in the side. "You did that on purpose."

I squirmed back. "It's not magic without a sacrifice."

He planted his hands on my arms, his eyes twinkling at me. The grin on his face faded. He rubbed his hands down my arms.

He leaned closer. My heart drummed in my ribcage. My face felt hot. I suspected his lips tasted like bacon. The flavor of Derrick and bacon sounded like a good combination.

"Do you know what I just did?" His fingers kneaded circles in my arms.

Electricity danced under my skin. "Make magic happen?"

"Wipe bacon grease on you." His grin returned.

"You're impossible."

"That's why you love me, right?"

A hot splatter of grease struck my arm, and I winced. He replaced the lid on the pan. He smiled, shy and boyish. I leaned closer, not ready for this moment between us to end. I wished I could have told him how right he was. I did love him—or at least have a crush on him—because he was funny and smart and he fed me bacon.

"Clarissa," he said. He dipped his head down.

Across the house, the front door opened. Derrick leapt away. He fumbled with the empty wine bottle, shoved it in his bookbag, and slipped out the backdoor.

"Hey, there pumpkin," Dad said, coming in and giving me a kiss on the cheek. "Do I smell bacon?"

"You aren't supposed to be in here." I shooed him away with the spatula. "It's supposed to be a surprise."

"Sorry, I'll get out of your hair."

Mom arrived home shortly after. She tried to sneak a taste, but I had to shoo her away too. Missy was late at cheerleading. I was afraid she might not make it in time and the spell would no longer be effective. I only had twenty-four hours before the potion stopped working.

Missy came home at eight. Mom served dinner.

"My favorite, honey," Dad said to Mom. He gave me a conspiratorial wink. "This smells great."

Mom beamed, looking everywhere but me, trying not to give me away. She radiated with pride.

"I love it when you make Irish stew," Missy said.

Mom blew on a spoonful, a sneaky smile on her face. Dad dug in. He choked and coughed. I feared it was the magic.

Mom wacked him on the back. She tasted her stew a moment later. Her eyes went wide, but she said nothing. Missy spit her stew out. I was afraid to taste mine.

The soup was sour and burned. The lamb didn't taste right. I looked to Mom.

"I think the meat was rancid," she said.

That wasn't possible. I'd gotten it from the freezer.

I forced myself to swallow a mouthful of bacon. Even that didn't taste right. "It's not that bad," I lied. "Try the bacon," I said to Missy.

She shoved her bowl away from herself. "No thanks. Mom said it's rancid. I'm not eating it."

Was it the spell? Or was it my cooking?

Mom patted my shoulder. "I'm sorry. I know you worked so hard on this."

"What?" Missy asked. "You made this? Ugh. No wonder it—"

"Stop," Dad said. "Don't make this any worse."

Mom stood and cleared the plates. "We have some leftover lasagna in the fridge. How about that instead?"

It was bad enough I had failed at magic and hadn't succeeded in covertly protecting my sister, but I also couldn't cook. One thing was for certain, I wasn't a kitchen witch like my mom.

CHAPTER FOURTEEN
Visitations from the School District Psychologist

The school year was almost out. Sunshine filled the courtyard where students loitered. I ate with the nerd herd at one of the picnic tables. Not that I was doing much eating yet.

Derrick and I demonstrated our juggling skills for our friends, tossing items to each other from our lunches. It was difficult to compensate for the variations in size and weight: a mozzarella cheese stick, a package of Chips Ahoy, mandarin oranges, and cartons of milk. Students eating at the other benches watched and clapped.

"You go, girl!" Mandy said, punching the air with a fist.

"Hey, what about me?" Derrick asked. His brow furrowed in concentration. "Why don't you ever say, 'You go, boy'?"

Madison, sitting next to Mandy, shouted, "You go, boy!"

They giggled and leaned toward each other, whispering conspiratorially.

Isaac slouched back on the bench. "You should try fire next."

"We aren't going to juggle fire. Ever," I said. For starters, my mom would freak. Second of all, I would freak.

Derrick shrugged. "Never say never."

All this conversation stole my concentration. I dropped the mozzarella stick. My aim was off as I tossed the cookie package at Derrick, and it struck him in the face. He fumbled to catch the carton of milk. His throw went wide, too far to the right for me to catch, and landed next to a couple making out on another bench.

Isaac scratched at the dragon tattoo on his neck. "Yeah, maybe fire isn't such a good idea after all."

Derrick tossed a package of cheese sticks in his face. We all cracked up. I retrieved the items I'd dropped, trying not to look at the teenagers sucking on each other's faces, and returned the lunch snacks to the bench. Isaac snatched up Jessica's mozzarella stick, but she stole it from him and hit him with it. They shoved at each other playfully, and we all laughed. I'd never imagined I would have so many friends or enjoy high school this much. I still wished my sister could have been one of my friends, but this wasn't bad.

Madison stood up fifteen minutes before lunch was over. "I have to go to my locker and carry five tons of books for my afternoon classes all the way over to the math wing. I'll see you guys later."

Mandy jumped to her feet. "I'll go with you. I can help you carry again. I work out." She flexed her bicep. "Check out these guns."

"You call that muscle?" Isaac rolled his eyes. "You're a shrimp."

"I don't mind the company." Madison bit her lip, smearing black lipstick on her teeth.

Jessica nudged me. I caught it too. Mandy had been volunteering to help Madison more and more. She kept contriving opportunities to spend time alone with her. It was cute the way they smiled shyly at each other. I suspected Madison liked Mandy as much Mandy liked her, but Madison had never come out and said she liked girls.

Mandy draped an arm around Madison's shoulder as they skipped away. They passed the "hall humpers" as we called them, the couple kissing on the other bench. Mandy made a vomiting sound and then giggled.

Seeing other people's public displays of affection was majorly disgusting. I wouldn't ever want to make out in public like that. Not that I had anyone to make out with. I glanced at Derrick. He ate his sandwich. He smiled when he caught me looking at him. I wondered what it was like to kiss a boy. To kiss Derrick. Not that I thought he would kiss me.

"We make a great juggling team," Derrick said. "We could make money at it. We should go to a fair or something and see if we can get tips."

I nodded. I doubted my mom would let me go to any fair after what had happened to Missy. I sighed, thinking about my sister. I wondered if she would ever be friends with me again.

"Why so serious?" He hugged me around the shoulder, probably like he would with a kid sister.

Even if that was how he thought of me, I couldn't stop wanting for more. Fluttery feelings rose in my belly. The air shimmered. It felt as though electricity sparked under my skin. Whenever I felt that tingling, something happened.

Derrick tilted his head to the side, studying me. Did he feel it too?

One of the hall humpers moaned. The girl cried out. I turned to look. They still held onto each other, but something wasn't right. It looked like they were trying to pull away from each other. They twisted, and I could see their profiles.

Their faces had melted into each other. They resembled some kind of hideous genetic experiment from a science fiction film.

Jessica screamed. Isaac stumbled back from the bench. I sat frozen, my eyes wide with horror as I took in the scene. Others in the courtyard screamed. People ran away.

The couple that had melted together flailed and cried out. They snorted and choked, sounding like a congested Pitbull.

Derrick staggered forward, stopped, and kept walking toward them. His breath was ragged and scared.

No, I wanted to say. *Don't get any closer to them.*

If this were a movie, he would be the one to get sucked into the genetic experiment next.

Derrick's brow furrowed. He spoke calmly, only the tremor in his voice giving his fear away. "Stay calm. Can you breathe? Keep breathing." He placed a hand on the girl's shoulder. "Don't try to move. We'll get help."

"Help!" Isaac said. "Someone call 9-1-1."

Yeah, real helpful.

I fumbled to get my cell phone out of my bag. I didn't think paramedics were going to be able to do anything about this. Even so, I dumped out my books, searching for my phone.

A shadow passed over me and stole across the courtyard. Another swept over Derrick and the couple before ebbing away. The sunshine in the courtyard became dappled in a patchwork of shadows. A flock of crows—Or ravens?—circled above like vultures about to swoop in for a meal. More birds joined the others. They glided lower, blotting out the light of the sun.

I hadn't seen birds react this way since Oregon Country Fair. An almost memory tickled my mind. Goosebumps prickled my arms.

There was something about those birds and what I'd seen that day, only I couldn't remember what it was.

A man strolled into the courtyard. He looked up into the sky and made a gesture with his hand. The birds dispersed.

The man's tailored suit hugged his slender frame. His shoulder length hair was glossy black and beautiful, his eyes as dark as storm clouds. I knew I'd seen him at school before. I just couldn't recall when. Between his height and striking features, he didn't seem like someone I would be able to forget easily. Yet, I only remembered who he was when I saw the badge on his chest said: school district psychologist.

"Bloody hell," he muttered under his breath, marching toward Derrick and the hall humpers.

Derrick stumbled back.

The man made a gesture with his hand. The air shimmered and wavered like heat rising from blacktop on a summer's day. The hall humpers fell apart and scrambled away from each other. The girl was crying. The boy fell off the bench, gasping and wheezing.

"Disgusting," the man said in a British accent. "Let that be a lesson to you. Next time, get a room instead." He waved his hand in the air, green shimmers sparkling from his fingertips.

"Do you see that?" I whispered to Jessica.

Her eyes remained wide, unfocused. She looked like she was on drugs. "He just broke up the, um, the fight?"

That hadn't been a fight, and she knew it. The man turned away from the students. His cool gaze raked over me.

He strode over to our bench with quick confident steps. He frowned down at me as if I'd done something wrong. I had a feeling I had. What if I'd somehow caused those students' faces to become glued together? I wasn't sure how I could have done such a thing, but weird things had been happening all year long—ever since we'd gone to Oregon Country Fair.

I still wanted magic to be real, but what if my mom was right? What if someone had to get hurt for it to work? Queasiness churned in my belly as I remembered Buddy.

"Miss Lawrence," the man said. "I am to escort you to the office. You have a test to take."

"A test?" The hairs on my arms prickled, and I shivered despite the warmth of the sunlight shining down on us. "I'm caught up in all my classes. I haven't missed any tests."

Derrick returned to my side. "What kind of test?"

The man didn't look at Derrick. He stared into my eyes. "You are being tested for a learning disability. Follow me."

It was hard to look away from the gray storm clouds in his irises. I twisted my friendship bracelet, and some of the haze in my brain cleared.

A learning disability? No way! I glanced at my friends, afraid they would think something was wrong with me. Jessica sat mutely beside me. Isaac stood against the wall, the big chicken. He stared at the couple who had been making out.

Derrick crossed his arms. "You've got to be kidding. Clarissa is an A student. She takes honors classes and gets college credit."

The man tried to catch my eye, but I wouldn't look at him. "Your teachers filled out an evaluation. You've been flagged for autism. We need to test you further."

Derrick placed himself between me and the man. "Clarissa doesn't have autism. She's just shy."

The stranger removed a piece of paper from his notebook. "Let's see if any of these fit: difficulties with social interaction, trouble with communication, inability to know how to react appropriately to others' emotions, repetitive behaviors or fixations, and hypersensitivity to sounds or . . . touch. The list goes on." He held the form out for me to see. Mrs. Waters, my English teacher had signed the evaluation. It looked pretty official.

All those descriptions fit me. But I didn't have autism. This man was lying.

The friendship bracelet around my wrist grew tight and constricting.

I didn't want to contradict an adult, but I didn't like the way the man stared at me so intensely. I stammered, "I-I-I don't want to go with you."

He pointed toward the door that led back into the interior of the school. "You will accompany me to the office for the test."

I shrank back.

Derrick circled an arm around my shoulders. "She isn't going with you."

I was so relieved he was there.

"How quaint. A chivalrous knight." The man arched an eyebrow.

"We can do this the easy way or the hard way."

"What's that supposed to mean?" Derrick asked.

"I will be forced to have your campus security guard escort you to the office."

"Fine. Go ahead. Get security. Get the principal. I don't think you're a psychologist at all," Derrick said.

"Teenagers. You're more trouble than you're worth." The man untucked something from his sleeve. It looked like a stick. Maybe it was a pencil. I didn't get a good look.

The next thing I knew, I was following the man down the hallway toward the office. My feet moved, one step after the next. I tried to turn around but couldn't. My gaze fixed on the texture of his tweed jacket. I tried to memorize the way he walked, his lean build, and how his hair wafted behind him like black water as he strode forward.

Students loitered in the hallway at their lockers and moved through the halls in cliques. No one looked at me. Not that this was anything new.

"Where are you really taking me?" I asked, my voice coming out small and shaky.

"I'm not going to hurt you. We're simply going to the office. I need to test you."

He walked one step ahead of me, the crowd parting, but never looking his way. I found myself staring at his shoulder-length hair, watching the fluorescent lights reflect cobalt on individual strands. Even Missy would have been hypnotized by the beauty and bounce in that mane of dark locks.

No one in the office looked my way. The secretary sat behind her desk, typing at her keyboard. The bookkeeper spoke with a student at the counter. I followed the man around the counter to the principal's office. Through the glass walls, I could see Mr. Dowdy on the phone.

The moment we entered, the principal said something into the receiver and hung up. He stood. "Pardon me. May I help you?"

"Yes," the school district psychologist said. "I need you to leave."

Mr. Dowdy's brow furrowed. He looked to me in confusion. The stranger removed a stick from his sleeve and muttered something under his breath. It looked like a wand. Without another word, the principal vacated the office.

I watched in wonder.

The stranger took the principal's chair and tucked the wand back into his sleeve. He motioned for me to sit.

"How did you do that?" I asked.

"You already know the answer to that. The question you should be asking is why am I here."

I shifted uneasily in my seat. I wanted to ask, but the disdain in his eyes kept me silent. I was afraid he was a lower level being, a Fae I had summoned. That was why Hunter had cast a protective ward before he'd made the potion. I didn't know how to do that.

The supposed school district psychologist handed me a yellow form. "Fill out this self-assessment. It won't take long."

It was a questionnaire with options for: "Yes," "No," and "Sometimes," and a place for comments.

Question 1: Do unexpected and unusual things happen around you that you can't explain?

Question 2: Do you feel a close connection to an element such as fire, water, wind or earth?

Question 3: Have you ever wished for something bad to happen to someone and later found out he or she had mysteriously taken ill?

The rest of the questions were just as bizarre as the first three. One thing was certain. It wasn't a test for autism.

"Is this for real?" I asked. It looked like it was a questionnaire for magical abilities. I'd always dreamed of being admitted to a magical school.

"Indeed." The man tossed back his hair.

The bottom footer of the form was labelled: *Intake Form/Womby's School for Wayward Witches.* I had heard that name before. It was the private school my mom thought Missy should go to that she'd refused. That meant my mom had known about this school. Missy was magical?

A thrill rushed through me. "So, it's like Hogwarts? If I pass the test I might be admitted to a special school?" This was my dream come true!

The man crossed his arms. "You won't be going to the school. I'm simply using their form."

Sure, he was.

I didn't have a pencil. I'd left my bag behind me in the courtyard. Reluctantly, I took a pen from the cup of pencils and pens on the principal's desk. The man didn't chide me. He watched with narrowed eyes.

Halfway through taking the survey, the flicker of the fluorescent lights above drew my attention. The man leaned against the armrest of the principal's cushy chair, his wand stretched toward the wall. He had shoved it into the outlet. Blue arcs of electricity crackled around the stick. He didn't seem fazed.

"Um, you shouldn't do that," I said. "It's dangerous."

Besides the fact that he might get electrocuted, I thought electricity was bad for witches—or Witchkin—as Hunter had called them. Maybe the Sorcerer of Goose Hollow didn't know what he was talking about.

"Never you mind. Finish your test." The man closed his eyes and leaned his head against the headrest.

I examined his face, trying to memorize the way his wavy hair flowed over his shoulders like dark currents. His features were elegant and refined. He used a wand, not a staff. Hunter had said professionals used staffs.

"Hurry up. I haven't got all day," he barked.

I jumped and went back to my evaluation. The bell rang, signaling lunch was over. Outside the principal's office, the secretary spoke to a student, everything normal and ordinary. Inside the room, nothing felt normal.

A second later, Derrick burst through the door. "Clarissa, are you all right?" He carried his backpack on one shoulder, mine on the other.

"You again," the man said.

I nodded to the form. "Yeah. He just gave me a test."

"I told you that's all I had in mind today." The man waved a hand toward the door. "The bell rang. Go to class."

Derrick sat in the chair beside me, dumping my bag on the floor. "I think I might need to take the test too. I've been feeling a little under the weather lately. I might have caught a learning disability." He coughed.

I tried not to laugh. I expected the man to yell at him for being a smart-ass, but he just eyed him reproachfully. "Can you do anything interesting?"

"What do you mean?" Derrick asked.

The man steepled his fingers in front of him. "How about some magic?"

"Oh boy, can I!" Derrick took his deck of cards from his pocket.

He shuffled them and held them out. "Pick a card, any card. Just don't let me see it."

The man selected a card. I was surprised he indulged Derrick. He allowed Derrick to show him his best magic tricks. The wind blew inside the little office and papers fluttered off the principal's desk. Derrick used real magic, not stage magic. The card appeared in the man's breast pocket.

The psychologist snorted and handed the card back to Derrick. He studied him more thoughtfully now. "Bollocks. Two Witchkin at the same school. It's unprecedented. Bloody hell." His tone remained the same monotone as before. "And of course you'd have to know each other. I'm surprised you haven't done anything worse than what you did today."

Derrick and I exchanged sidelong glances. If we were witches, or the kin of witches, I wondered about my sister. I decided not to mention her late night potion brewing. He already seemed displeased enough.

The man's frown lines deepened as he glared at Derrick. "Son of a succubus. I can't bring you to the school. Merlin's balls."

I stared with wide eyes. It sounded like he was using potty language.

Derrick leaned back in his chair, arms crossed. "I don't see what the problem is. Neither of us are going with you."

"Are you only allowed to bring one witch back?" I asked.

"No," he said. "The problem is, I can only bring Witchkin back who aren't going to destroy the school and kill the other students. You," he pointed to Derrick, "may or may not be harmless, but there's no way I'm bringing you to the school if you know about this one." He pointed at me. "You're something else. And the two of you together. . . ." He stood up, leaning on the desk and looming over us. "Which one of you performed magic today in the courtyard?"

I glanced at Derrick. I wanted this man to know I had magic so he might admit me into the special school, but if I had been responsible for the two students whose faces had gotten stuck together, I had a feeling I would be in trouble.

"Did you *intend* to perform magic today?" the man asked.

Derrick and I both answered at once. "No."

"Did you see the results of your *accident*? The results of *playing* with magic."

"We weren't playing—" Derrick began.

"Don't do it again. Magic isn't something to toy with. It has consequences. Do you understand me? You could have killed someone."

I nodded. The man's eyes smoldered when he looked at me. I fixed my gaze on the form I clutched in my hands.

The man snatched up the paper. "Hasn't your mother taught you how dangerous it is to use magic? The only reason you were permitted to stay in the care of Abigail Lawrence at all is because she promised she would keep you away from witchcraft. Something needs to be done with that awful woman. She's an unfit mother."

I shook my head. I didn't want anything to happen to my family. Tears filled my eyes. "Please don't hurt my mom. She's trying her best. She just doesn't know what to do with me. I'm bad. I disobey her, and I don't listen. She threw out all my pentagrams and tried to make me give up magic. I'll be good. I'm sorry," I blubbered.

The man scanned the form I'd filled out. He sighed in exasperation and dropped it to the desk.

He waved a hand at the door. "You may leave. I have no further need of you."

I jumped to my feet, knocking over the cup of pencils and pens on the principal's desk. I bolted out of the room. Derrick ran after me. I didn't stop until I reached my English classroom. I didn't even have English next period; I had chemistry. I stopped abruptly, Derrick colliding into me.

Aside from a few loiterers, the halls were empty.

I looked around frantically "I'm late for class!"

"For the first time ever. So what?" Derrick held out my backpack.

I was lucky he was more attentive to details like remembering our bags than I had been. As I took it, I nearly fell over with how heavy it was. I dropped the pen in my hand. I hadn't realized I'd still been holding onto it.

"Oh no!" I picked up the principal's pen. "I forgot to put this back on Mr. Dowdy's desk. I stole a pen."

Derrick laughed. "Seriously? After all that, you're worried about taking a pen?"

"I'm a thief." I didn't want anyone to think I was a bad person.

Derrick laughed harder. "You're the most honest person I know. This is why I love you!" He mussed my hair good-naturedly.

Ugh. He acted like a brother would have. I smoothed out my hair.

"I'm way less honest than you are." His smile was mischievous. From his pocket he withdrew a crumpled sheet of yellow paper. He smoothed it out. It was the self-assessment the man had made me fill out.

"Derrick!" I shouted. "You stole that?"

He snickered. "He didn't need it. He'd already decided he wasn't taking you for his school."

A teacher stuck her head out into the hallway. "You kids need to get to class."

I backed away from the teacher. I didn't want to get in trouble. I whispered, "Stealing is wrong."

"So is erasing people's memories." Derrick walked with me toward my next class. "We need evidence to remember this." He waved the form in front of me.

"I don't know if I'll remember today even with the paper." Already the man's face had grown hazy. His message wasn't fading, though. He wanted us to remember not to use magic. "Can you imagine what it would be like to be accepted into a magical school?"

Derrick smiled. "Especially if both of us got to go there?"

"It would be the best thing ever," I said dreamily.

"Do you think we should stop practicing magic?" Derrick asked. "What he said—about that school—it just makes me want to learn it even more!"

I considered what the man had said. Witchkin—the children of witches. Was that what my mom was? A witch? He'd said she was supposed to keep me from magic. All my life she had tried and failed. Now I wondered what would happen if I became a witch. The man thought I was dangerous. That woman at the fair had prophesied I would kill my sister. What if they were right?

I didn't want my mom to know about that man. I didn't want her to know he'd threatened to—I wasn't even sure what he would do if he thought she wasn't controlling me. I didn't want to do anything that might cause him to return. I didn't want to summon him.

I grabbed Derrick's arm. "We can't play with magic. Someone might get hurt." The idea I might harm my sister made my stomach cramp. I corrected myself. "*You* can do magic if you want, but if you do, you have to learn how to protect yourself from calling Fae."

"Sure, we can do more research."

I bit my lip. "I can help you with research, but I can't do any more magic."

"This is about Missy?"

I nodded.

"She doesn't deserve such loyalty."

I glanced down at my friendship bracelet. He didn't know what it was like to have a sister. I had to protect her.

He mussed my hair again. "Well, I wouldn't want to go to some special school anyway. That guy was a creep. Do you think he's the principal or something?"

"Headmaster," I said. He was British after all. "Or a professor."

"Maybe he was just a recruiter. Yeah, I bet he was a crappy recruiting agent. He didn't sound official, like someone in charge of the school and the rules. Can you imagine how much it would suck to have him as a teacher?"

"Whoever he is, one thing's for sure. He's not our school district psychologist."

We both laughed at that.

CHAPTER FIFTEEN
Return to Oz

I had planned on using every day of summer vacation doing magical research at the library, but my mom insisted I do something more active with my summer break than hanging out with friends and reading books. Maybe she knew I was up to something, and that was why she encouraged me to take a condensed track of Biology 101, 102 and 103 at Clackamas Community College, Monday through Thursday for the entire summer to earn college credit that could be applied to my high school diploma and future college degree. I volunteered at the Oregon City library a couple hours a week, mostly as an excuse so I could spend more time there, and did filing and vacuuming at my dad's office during the weekend to earn more allowance.

I didn't want to do any magic myself, but I did want to purchase another protective potion for my sister, and that would cost me money. Derrick and I composed an email from his account to Hunter while we were at the library, asking if the sorcerer would show us how to protect ourselves from Fae.

Hunter's responses were infrequent because he only checked his email twice a week; he didn't like how electronics effected his aura. His response:

Hey there, nerd herd,

I would be happy to show you how to do magic on your own, but none of these potions are going to work unless you know how to infuse magic into them. The easiest ways to do that for untrained Witchkin is by using sex magic, a pain tithe, or a handy combo that uses both at the same time. Let me know if you want to come over to my place. I'll teach you at no charge.

Your magical guide,

Hunter

"Ick," I said.

Derrick made a barfing sound. "I know you want to help your sister, but please don't say you're going to consider his offer to teach you S & M."

"Of course not. He's old. He must be thirty."

I composed a letter back.

Hunter,

Thanks for the offer, but all of us are minors and you aren't, so that would be illegal. If there are other ways to harness magical powers that don't involve breaking the law, we'd be up for that, even if it is more challenging. Or if you have an hourly rate for training, let us know.

Thank you,

Clarissa, Derrick and the nerd herd

"You're more polite than he deserves," Derrick said.

A few days later Derrick told me Hunter had replied, asking for more information about why we wanted to protect my sister and shield ourselves from Fae. Derrick had written back while I'd been at my biology class, explaining Missy's situation and how she'd learned I was destined to kill her.

"You shouldn't have told him," I said.

"Why? You can't expect a doctor to diagnose a disease without knowing all the symptoms. He needed to know."

Maybe he did, but it made me uneasy. I didn't like Hunter, and I didn't trust him, but Derrick was right. Hunter needed all the facts.

"I'm glad I told him," Derrick said. "Hunter had a few suggestions. He thinks the best way to find out if the prophesy is true is to go to Oregon Country Fair and find the witch who originally kidnapped your sister."

I would be in so much trouble if I went to Oregon Country Fair. Or I would be, if I was caught.

The fair was the first weekend of July. I immediately started making plans and saving up for the trip. We wrangled Isaac into borrowing his parent's station to drive us since that was the only vehicle with at least six seat belts. I enlisted Jessica and Mandy to help me create an elaborate alibi so I could say I had spent the day shopping and going to the movies with them.

It took over two hours to get there. Because the trip was my idea, I paid for gas and parking out of my earnings from work. We each paid for our own tickets.

Even before we stepped past the admission gate, my friends stared in wonder. A parade of silent clowns dressed in white ruffled clothes skulked by.

"Cool!" Mandy said.

Isaac snapped a picture of a family dressed as garden gnomes, their heads topped with red pointed caps.

"I wish I'd worn my Jedi costume," he said. "I feel way underdressed."

Already I felt uneasy. Any of these people dressed in eccentric costumes could be a Fae for all I knew. I directed our party toward the eating area. Getting them not to stop at every stage and watch circus plate spinners or jug bands was a trial.

"We are on a mission, people," I said. "We need to go to find the booth with friendship bracelets and see if anyone has seen a woman giving away cookies."

We couldn't find the friendship bracelet booth in the program or while walking. I asked directions, but no one had heard of it. Next, we went to the Daredevil Vaudeville Palace and found the nearest restrooms in the hope that I could find the old woman from there.

The heat was oppressive out in the open.

"I'm tired of walking," Mandy said.

"Yeah, let's sit in the shade and get some lunch," Madison said.

I was too hot and anxious to be hungry, but I bought a burrito. I could only eat half of it. Derrick devoured the rest in addition to his own.

"Let's go back to that Daredevil stage and watch the show," Isaac said.

Jessica jumped up and down. "Yeah! Let's see a show."

Didn't they understand? I wasn't here to enjoy the fair. This was a matter of life or death for my sister.

Derrick leaned in to conspire with me. "How about we go investigating without them? We can meet back at the Daredevil

Vaudeville Palace in two hours."

I agreed to the compromise. No sooner had we left the nerd herd at the stage and journeyed back to the crowded path than someone hip-checked me, making me stumble into Derrick.

"Well, fancy bumping into you here," a man said.

Even before I saw him, I recognized the cloud of clove smoke drifting my way. Hunter smiled, his teeth looking sharper than I remembered.

"Oh, hi," Derrick said.

Hunter leaned against his staff. "Found your witch yet?"

"No," I said. "Thanks for asking. We should get going." His smile made my skin crawl.

I wondered what he was doing here. Had he followed us? Of course, that was silly. How would he know we'd be here on Saturday at this time? We hadn't told him. There had to be thousands of people here. He couldn't have found us. It was a coincidence, I told myself.

"I've been asking around on your behalf," Hunter said. "You're looking for a specific witch. A woman who sells shortbread cookies, right? I think I've found her."

"Gingerbread cookies," I corrected.

"Yeah, that's what I meant. I can take you to her."

I bit my lip and looked to Derrick. He was frowning. I could tell he didn't like this anymore than I did.

I tried to think of an excuse. I pointed to a wooden shack selling bottled water. "Derrick and I are going to get a drink first. Would you mind waiting here?"

Hunter looked at his watch. "I'm in a hurry. There's a show I want to see. Don't take too long." He leaned against his staff.

I headed over to the line of people, keeping my voice low as I leaned toward Derrick. "I don't trust him."

"Neither do I. We should go back to the nerd herd."

He was probably right. Even so, I didn't know what other chance I had for finding the witch.

"Will you be mad if I go with him?" I asked.

"I'll be mad if you don't take me with you. We're in this together." He bumped me with his shoulder, playfully.

I smiled, reassured by his loyalty. "Okay, here's the plan. If he does anything creepy, let's hold up our electronics and threaten to zap his powers with them."

Derrick laughed. "We can try."

After we got our waters, Hunter escorted us along a path away from the crowds of people. He chattered away about witches and folklore, half his words drowned out by the music from a nearby stage. As we traveled along the path of shady trees, the heat of the day melted away. He stopped at a fork, examining an oak before starting along a path to the right.

We stepped through a ring of toadstools and he hesitated, examining a tree covered in a rainbow of ribbons. The sky darkened with clouds. Windchimes played in the distance. It was quieter here, the sound of the fair gone. I wondered if we had stepped through a fairy ring to another realm. I didn't ask, afraid it was childish to believe in fairies. I didn't know what was real magic and what was fairytales anymore.

Hunter sat us down on a mossy patch next to a stream. "I need to perform a spell. It won't take long."

He poured dried herbs in his hand from a pouch at his belt and rubbed them between his palms before caressing the green bits onto his staff. Immediately, he started to chant. He drew symbols in the air with his staff, a glowing afterimage remaining in the air.

I tried to catch Derrick's eye. Hunter hadn't used any salt or made a circle of protection around us. Derrick nodded, almost imperceptibly. He'd caught it to.

Hunter set his staff across his lap and smiled. "All done."

"What about that protection spell?" I asked.

"Huh?"

"The one you do to keep from summoning Fae?"

"That would have been counterproductive. I just summoned a Fae for you." He ran his tongue across the sharp edge of his teeth. "You're welcome."

CHAPTER SIXTEEN
Putting the Fairies Back into Fairytales

My stomach churned. I glanced around. Something rustled in the trees around us.

"Why would you summon a Fae?" Derrick asked. "I thought you said before—"

"You wanted magic. Now you'll get it." Hunter chuckled.

The dappled light peeking in through the canopy of leaves overhead grew darker. Black wings fluttered through the boughs of the trees. I didn't understand what was happening, but I knew enough to be afraid.

I jumped to my feet, clutching at the sleeve of Derrick's shirt, ready to run. A woman blocked the path. Her short hair was black and spikey like the feathers of her wings. The fitted bodice and black tutu she wore was made of down, glistening like an oil slick. Birds drifted from the sky and settled themselves lower in the forest. It took me a moment to notice the woman's thin legs ended in pointed talons like a bird of prey.

"What have we here?" she asked in a raspy voice. "Did someone perform magic?"

Hunter lifted his chin. "Yes. I have brought you two sacrifices. Now you owe me a boon."

Derrick stood beside me now. He clasped my hand. "Is this real?" he whispered to me.

Discretely, I tried to remove my phone from my back pocket,

hiding it between us.

"A boon?" the woman said. "Only the Raven Queen has the power to grant such a request, though in this case, she will agree there would be no point."

Derrick fumbled in his pocket with his other hand. He didn't have a cell, but he had an MP3 player.

"Why? You can't tell me my sacrifices aren't worthy." Hunter sat back against a tree. "I know the rules. You have to grant me a favor. I brought you two Witchkin."

The woman circled around Derrick and me. Scooting away from her, I nearly fell into a tall fern. The moment she moved from the path, I attempted to lunge back the way we'd come, but two of the birds in the trees dove forward. They shifted and swelled from avian to women before our eyes. If these were fairies, they were bigger and darker than what I'd read about in books. Flickers of memory from the last time I'd been at the fair tugged at my mind. I'd encountered them before. They weren't to be trusted.

The woman stood before Hunter, her back to us. "These two have no traces of magic on them. Therefore, I cannot collect their souls, not now, nor after dark. You, on the other hand, are another matter entirely. The punishment for your crime is to drain you."

Hunter jumped to his feet, staff in hand. "You can't do that to me. I'm a sorcerer. With this staff, I smite thee, evil Fae—"

"Aren't you adorable?" The raven woman laughed, the sound as malicious as the Wicked Witch of the West. "You think a stick is going to save you? The only reason you need a staff is because your skills aren't refined enough to use a wand."

He aimed the staff at her, blue light flashing. Derrick dove in front of me, but the attack wasn't directed at me. Hunter's light shot at the bird woman. She held up her palm, sucking in the light like a black hole.

Hunter cried out in alarm. He shook violently, and his eyes rolled back into his head. The color drained from his face. Light ceased to surge from his staff, and instead, red mist flowed out of it. He fell to his knees. He no longer looked opaque and substantial. I could see through him like a ghost. His scream faded away as the remainder of his form funneled into the staff he held and was sucked up by the raven woman. The staff fell into the moss.

He was gone.

The woman kicked the wood into the stream. "Amateurs."

I clung to Derrick's arm, the hand holding my phone buried in the fabric of his shirt as I stared in horror.

Her smile was coy as she turned back to us. "Let's see what kind of magic you have to defend yourselves with."

"But if we use magic, then you can do the same thing to us," Derrick said.

"I may drain you, yes. Or collect you for our queen so that she may do so." A vicious smile curled to her lips. "But if you *don't* use magic to defend yourselves, I will simply kill you. I offer you a choice."

I held up my phone, using it like a shield. A very small shield. Derrick held out his MP3 player, music coming out of the earbuds. He waved it to the left and right. The bird woman stepped back, her brows drawing together. Feathers ruffled behind us and I turned, keeping my back against Derrick as I held out my phone. I pressed one of the buttons to light up the screen, hoping it made my phone give off more electricity.

"Do you think that will stop us?" The bird woman's tone exuded confidence, but the apprehension in the eyes of the other two women didn't reflect her optimism.

"No, but I will," said a man's British accent from the path. Out of the shadows emerged a man in a tailored tweed suit. His shoulder length hair was styled and elegant. I recognized him.

The school district psychologist lifted his chin, nostrils flaring in anger. "These adolescents have committed no crime. They haven't used magic. Nor would it be legal for you to coerce them into doing so."

He raised his wand. White light fizzed from the tip like a Fourth of July sparkler. It was pretty impressive. I wanted a wand.

I glanced over my shoulder at the bird woman.

She pursed her lips. "Are you saying you don't feel the magic inside them, ready to break free at any moment? It's only a matter of time before they commit a crime. Really, we're doing the Witchkin community a favor."

He stepped closer to me. He waved a hand at my cell phone. "Put that away."

I lowered it to my side, but I didn't put it away. It was my only weapon.

"Are you going to collect them, then?" the woman asked. "Do you intend to bring them both to Womby's School and train them?"

That was the name of the school on the intake form: Womby's School for Wayward Witches.

She raked her talons over the moss-covered ground. "Or shall we make a bargain? You can take the boy to be trained, and we'll hold onto the girl. I know you won't take that one to the school because of the crimes of her mother."

My mother. The school district psychologist had told me she shouldn't have been allowed to raise me. The witch who had kidnapped Missy had said our mom was evil.

"That is none of your concern." The man grabbed me by the arm and Derrick by the other. He dragged us away from the women and back along the path the way he'd come.

Birds leaned closer than I liked, their sharp beaks open as if they intended to peck out an eye. I held up my phone, and they fell back.

The man shoved us along the narrow path, his hand like a vice around my arm. "Do you get it yet? Do you understand why you can't use magic in the Morty Realm?"

"Yes," I said. My voice came out high and tremulous. Now that the immediate danger of the birds was over, I realized how weak and shaky my knees felt.

The path grew brighter, sunlight shining through viridian leaves overhead.

"This is your last warning," the man said. "If the two of you persist in pursuing magic, I will separate you from each other so that you'll be unable to cause any harm to yourselves or others. I'll resort to more drastic measures if I must."

"We weren't using magic," I said. "We were trying to get a professional to use magic for us to prevent someone from dying."

"We thought he was a professional, anyway," Derrick said.

"And see where that got you?" the school district psychologist said.

"You can do magic," I said. "You could help us. There's a prophesy that says I'll kill my sister before her eighteenth birthday. I wanted to find the witch who told her so we can try to prevent it."

"I don't want anything to do with your or your problems. The sooner I'm rid of you, the better."

The distant thunder of cheering and music came from up ahead.

"But why?" I asked. "Why not just take us to your school? What did my mom do that was so bad?"

The man released us and shoved us forward. I stumbled and caught onto a tree before I fell on my face. Derrick tripped into a man dressed as a suitcase and knocked him over. When I turned back, the school district psychologist was gone.

This time, he didn't erase our memories.

We found the rest of the nerd herd at the stage where we'd left them. They watched a man on a bicycle balance five people on his shoulders doing acrobatics. I sat down on the bench next to Jessica. A single raven watched from the perches of a tree next to the small wooden arena. I shivered, thinking about how narrowly we had escaped the Fae.

"We should get going," I said.

"Yeah, there are lots of other stages to go to." Jessica held up a schedule to show me the attractions in different areas.

Mandy turned her gaze from the stage. "What about your mission? Are we done with that?" She poked at her lip ring with her tongue.

"You found that witch you were looking for?" Madison asked. "I knew I should have gone with you!"

"No," I said. "We found some dangerous people. We should leave."

Isaac crossed his arms. "We only got here a few hours ago. I don't want to drive back yet."

"It isn't safe," Derrick said. "We need to go."

Isaac groaned. "No freakin' way."

"Why isn't it safe?" Mandy asked.

Derrick stood, blocking the view of people behind him. "Because Hunter was waiting for us, and he tried to sell our immortal souls to a bunch of badass, shapeshifting fairies who killed him. And they're still here and want to kill us." He gestured to the bird in the tree.

"Oh my God!" Jessica said. "No way!"

"Did you do drugs or something?" Madison asked.

Isaac returned his gaze to the stage. "You are so making that shit up."

"We aren't. We can do this the easy way or the hard way." Derrick sounded like the school district psychologist. He hooked an arm around Isaac's neck in a headlock and dragged him from the bench.

Isaac punched Derrick, though the blows landed on his shoulder. People gave them the stink eye as they blocked people from watching the show.

"Boys! They're so macho." Mandy rolled her eyes. "If you really want Isaac to leave, you should just offer him something better."

Neither were listening. Isaac twisted and shoved Derrick into a man dressed as a yellow ducky standing against one of the wooden fences. The man yelled at them and pushed them toward the exit.

Someone else shouted at them to leave.

"Why are you always listening to Clarissa and taking her side?" Isaac lunged for Derrick.

Derrick dodged away, working us closer to the arena's exit. "I'm not taking anyone's side. I just saw some messed up shit, and *I* want to leave."

The four of us girls scooted toward the exit. People gave our group dirty looks.

Jessica covered her face. "This is so embarrassing."

I didn't want my friends to fight like this. I thought about what Mandy had said a moment ago. I had to offer Isaac something better than cool music and acrobatics. "I'll buy you a marionberry milkshake from Burgerville and a double bacon cheeseburger for dinner if we leave right now."

Isaac turned to me. The anger on his face faded and was replaced by cunning. "Is that all?"

"And onion rings?"

"And. . . ?"

"Whatever you want."

"Cookies. I want you to bake me those chocolate chip cookies your mom made us."

I considered my last cooking fiasco. Fortunately, he didn't know about it.

"Sure," I said.

Isaac dusted himself off. "Let's get this show on the road."

We stopped at Burgerville for an hour in Corvallis and headed back onto I-5 toward Oregon City. We made it to Salem when the car stalled. It slowed as traffic honked their horns at us and passed us by. I thought about the Fae and hoped they weren't behind this.

Isaac pulled over. "I don't know what's wrong with it."

Madison unbuckled her seatbelt. "I can help you check the oil and coolants. Did any lights come on?"

Half of us stayed inside while the rest went outside. I checked my watch. We still had three hours, plenty of time to get home. I could go to Jessica's and ask one of my parents to pick me up from there to make it seem like I had spent the entire day with her. Thirty minutes later, I was sweating buckets after sitting in the back of a car without air conditioning.

"Does anyone have AAA?" Mandy asked.

My parents did. I didn't even have a car, but they made me carry a AAA card around so I wouldn't be stranded somewhere with friends. This seemed like an emergency, but if I used it, I worried they might find out where I'd been.

I looked to Jessica and Derrick. Neither of them had AAA.

"I'm on my parents' plan. I can call," I said.

My cell phone battery was dead, so I used Jessica's. A tow truck arrived forty-five minutes later. The man looked under the hood and decided it was a bad battery and offered to fix it right then and there for a hundred dollars. I was the only one with that much money in my bank account. The car immediately started up.

We were halfway home. The remainder of the trip would take an hour. I still had an hour and a half left before my parents thought the movie would be out.

Then we ran into traffic. The stretch between Salem and Woodburn slowed to fifteen miles per hour. The air conditioner sputtered out, which made the remaining two and a half hours of stop and go traffic hotter than a sauna.

I decided to have Isaac drop me off at home. I was an hour later than I said I would be arriving home.

The moment I walked in the door I could feel the prickly tension in the silence. The television was off.

Mom and Dad sat on the couch, waiting for me. Their expressions were tight and restrained.

"How was the *movie*, honey?" Mom asked.

"Great." I hated lying. My tongue felt swollen and slow in my mouth. I crossed into the kitchen and filled a big glass full of water.

"Lots of fun. Thanks. How was your day?"

"You didn't answer my phone calls or texts." Mom followed me into the kitchen.

I pushed my sweaty hair back from my face. "I'm sorry. I didn't mean to make you worry. My phone battery went dead. I didn't know you called."

Mom's smile was stiff. "I had a call from AAA, regarding some roadside assistance. . . ."

Oh, shit. I was in trouble. "Isaac's car broke down on the way to the movie theater. It was the battery. You gave me a copy of your AAA card in case I was ever in an accident with friends and I thought it was best to . . . um, I'm sorry. Was that bad?" I hid behind the glass as I gulped the water down.

"No, that is exactly what it was for." Mom's eyes narrowed. "To keep you safe. We wouldn't want you to be stranded on I-5 with heavy traffic."

"Okay, great. Thanks." I backed away, trying to leave the room before my mom squeezed any more out of me.

My dad blocked the exit to go upstairs to my room. His arms were crossed, his round cheeks a splotchy pink. He never looked angry like this.

"It made me wonder what you were doing on I-5 since I thought you were shopping with Jessica and Mandy today." Mom spoke casually, waving a hand in the air and laughing, though her movements were stiff and jerky, as though she were trying to hide her anger.

"A little change of plans midway through the day." My words came out in a rush. "We went up to Portland instead."

"Really? Portland? That's funny, because AAA said you were stranded outside of Salem. When you didn't answer your phone, I called Jessica's mom to see if she knew what was going on. She said you girls were with Derrick." She spat out his name like it tasted bad. "And you know where she said you were?"

Please, don't say it, I prayed. Jessica's mom didn't even know where we'd been, I reasoned with myself.

"Jessica has an app on her phone, so her mom knows were her daughter is at all times . . . something we should install on your phone. Mrs. Hazel saw you and your friends were in Eugene today." The words came out of her mouth, stretched like taffy in slow motion. "You were at Oregon Country Fair."

I shook my head, trying to deny it.

"Don't lie to me," she said. "It's bad enough you went there and lied about going. How can I trust you after this?"

I looked to Dad, the more reasonable one out of the two of them. "You don't understand. I was trying to help Missy. I wanted to find the witch who kidnapped her and ask her if what she told Missy was true."

Mom crossed her arms, looking me up and down. "Well?" she asked. "Did you find what you were looking for?"

"No," I said.

Dad turned away, as if he couldn't look at me. "We're very disappointed with you."

I hung my head in shame. This was the last thing I wanted.

"You're grounded for the rest of the summer: no going out with friends, no inviting Derrick over, and extra chores for you," Mom said. "Anytime you aren't in class, you'll either be with me or your dad at work."

Maybe I was descended from an evil witch.

CHAPTER SEVENTEEN
Sucktacular School Days

Never had I been so eager for school to start. Sure, I was busy with the homework from honors classes that gave me college credit, plus an additional online writing class at Clackamas Community College, but at last I got to hang out with Derrick and see him in person rather than a pixelated version of him on Skype.

Derrick was a senior. I was a sophomore. We both took art again, but we had it different periods. Sometimes we ate lunch with the nerd herd, sometimes we sat quietly in the art room, drawing together. Derrick taught me illusions and new juggling tricks, but I didn't press him to show me magic. Every time I was tempted, I reminded myself what had happened to Hunter at the hands of Fae. I thought of Buddy. The day those two teenagers' faces had gotten stuck together remained fresh in my mind. The school district psychologist had warned me of the consequences. I listened.

I didn't want anyone to get hurt.

I kept wondering if that old woman—that witch—at the fair had been right. If I played with magic, I might cause Missy's death. Mom had said magic had a cost. My sister might be the cost. I couldn't allow that. I loved her.

Derrick and I sat together in Mrs. Kelly's room, sketching while we waited for other students to arrive for a literary magazine meeting. Mrs. Kelly had run to the office to make photocopies. I worked on a drawing of an evil raven.

Derrick flipped through his sketchbook until he found a blank page. "Jessica and Isaac, they're going to homecoming together."

"Huh," I said. "As friends?"

"Yeah, I guess." He wiped Cheetos crumbs from his fingers onto his pin-striped pants. The gray and white vertical pattern mismatched the horizontal red and yellow of his sweater and the blue and white plaid button-up shirt underneath, but somehow it all fit together in that funky way of his. He dressed like the wizards in the *Harry Potter* series, trying to fit into a Muggle world.

"Lots of people are going to homecoming," Derrick said. "Why do you act so surprised they're going?"

"It's just weird. I thought Jessica said she'd rather gouge out her eyeballs than go to homecoming. And Isaac said it sounded lame." I thought about it more. Madison had just come out in September and had confessed her love for Mandy, neither detail being any surprise to me. It was obvious she was a lesbian, and it was obvious she had a crush on her best friend. "Are they going because Madison and Mandy are going, to be supportive of their relationship?"

"I bet that's it!" His eagerness fizzled out, and he cleared his throat. He mumbled with the enthusiasm of a hobbit about to jump into a pit of lava, "We could go to homecoming. As friends. You know, to support M and M."

His attitude didn't exactly sell me on the idea. Not to mention the obstacles that lay ahead if I went to homecoming. "I would have to buy a dress." The idea filled me with dread.

Finding a formal dress in my size would be no easy feat. I shopped in the children's section because they didn't make clothes for four-foot-ten-inch teenagers who didn't look like they had hit puberty yet. That growth spurt would be coming any day now, and when it did, it would give me long legs. Breasts would be nice too.

Shopping for homecoming was daunting enough. Then there was my mom to reckon with. A date. Even if it was just with Derrick. I might have considered homecoming if Derrick liked me, if he wanted to go on a real date. The idea of all that work for someone who treated me like a kid sister was too disappointing to bother.

Plus, my mom would never let me go. End of story.

Derrick slouched over his art pad. "Yeah, forget it. Homecoming is lame. I didn't want to go anyway."

I erased the eye on my raven and started over. Derrick fixed his attention on his drawing. I was relieved not to have to think about homecoming anymore.

The silence was quickly broken.

"Wassup?" Josh Hernandez leaned against the doorway. He was a senior, my sister's grade, and a basketball player.

"Mrs. Kelly ran to the office," I said. "She'll be back in a minute."

He flashed a four-thousand-dollar smile. I knew because my dad was his orthodontist. "Lawrence. You. Me. Homecoming. What do you say?"

I crossed my arms. "I've seen *Carrie*. I know how it ends. Thanks, anyway."

"Huh?" He disappeared from the doorframe, whispering something to his friends before sticking his head back inside. "I haven't seen it. Is it any good? We could watch it together before we go on a date. Or after. Whatev. What do you say?"

"I don't want to be the butt of your joke." I turned away. From the way Derrick stared over my shoulder, I knew Josh still stood there.

Derrick lifted his chin. "Get lost, butt munch."

"No one gave you permission to speak, penis breath."

Derrick stood. I tugged on his sleeve. "Sit. He isn't worth the effort."

Josh ducked out of the door again. Derrick sat.

I turned the page in my book and stared at the half-finished elven prince I'd been doodling in my art journal a few months before. His hair was long, and his eyes would be green when I added the colored pencil. I tried to think of something that would make him look less like Legolas and more of an original character of my own creation, but I failed. I glanced over my shoulder. Josh was gone, to my relief.

Derrick continued sketching Cthulhu coming out of a black hole in space and reaching for the planet Earth. "I don't think Josh was playing a prank," he said.

"Yeah, he was. Missy probably put him up to it." Josh was cute and popular and a jock. He hung out with other athletes and popular kids. He could go on a date with any girl he wanted. There was no reason he would pick someone he had spoken to once in creative writing—and that was only to ask to borrow a pencil.

"They aren't even friends." Derrick added stars to the background of his sketch. "It's because you're pretty. He was staring at you in

P.E. today."

"Ugh. Everyone stares at me in P.E. It's because I can't move like my sister." I might have been clumsy, but I wasn't deaf. I heard what people said about how uncoordinated I was. What kind of horrible sadist decided to make physical education mandatory in high school? I looked up. "What were you doing in the gym during first period? You have physics."

He shrugged. "Just passing through on the way to the farthest bathroom from my classroom to kill as much time as possible."

I kicked him under the table. "What is wrong with you? Are you trying to fail your classes so you don't graduate?"

"Pretty much."

"This is about your grandma, isn't it? She's still trying to get you to apply to colleges? It wouldn't hurt you to research scholarships, you know?" This was the kind of behavior that fueled my mom's opinion about Derrick and make her label him as a bad influence. "I know you can be smart when you want to be."

He dumped his Copic Markers on the table and sorted through them, not meeting my eyes. "I don't want to be a physicist. I want to go to art school. Or clown school. I'm already good at juggling. We could go to clown school together. We could work stage magic and illusions into our act."

"Yeah, because my parents will be thrilled when I run away and join the circus."

Derrick glanced at the door where Josh had been a minute ago. "I think he likes you."

"No, he doesn't. No one likes me." I hated it when he teased me like this. I closed my sketchbook so I wouldn't mess up my drawing and smacked him with it.

Couldn't he imagine what it was like to be a geeky girl who'd never had a boyfriend? I was invisible next to my older sister. I wondered what it would be like to be cool and popular, to be asked by a boy to homecoming—not as a friend—but because he liked me. I ached to be liked by someone.

I told myself I didn't need those things. I was happy with my friends and my life. Sometimes I even believed this mantra.

Derrick laughed and ducked away, scattering markers to the floor as I playfully smacked him with my book. "That's not true." He smiled in that puppy-dog sort of way of his and said in a goofy voice.

"I like you." He sounded like Barney the talking dinosaur when he said it like that.

He didn't like me the way I wanted him to. I yearned for a boy—any boy—to fall head over heels in love with me. I dreamed about love at first sight like in the books I read. I wanted a *Jane Eyre* or a *Wuthering Heights* kind of romance that would transcend time and mortality. It hadn't mattered so much in middle school. Boys had been icky then, but I now I was fifteen, and I hadn't kissed a boy. It was so unfair.

"Everyone likes Missy." She had a ton of boyfriends.

He grabbed my sketchbook from me, bonked me on the top of the head with it, and tossed it on the table. "I'm serious. Stop comparing yourself to your sister. Any guy out there would be crazy not to like you." He glanced away, his smile sheepish.

I sat there feeling awkward and unworthy of such praise. He was such a sweet, considerate guy. I didn't know how it was possible he didn't have a girlfriend. His kindness always made up for the black hole of Missy's personality, sucking warmth and joy from the rest of my life.

I threw my arms around his neck. "I'm so lucky to have a best friend like you." He smelled like butterscotch and Cheetos, a pleasant mix.

"Best friend. Heh. Yeah. I'm lucky too." He patted my shoulder.

I released him and stepped back, realizing I probably was acting like a child.

Some kid ran into the classroom with an airhorn, most likely leftover from one of the pep assemblies, and blasted it right next to us before running off. That was high school for you. With all my extra classes, I was going to graduate early from this hell hole. College classes were so much better. People were more mature.

After school, Derrick waited at my locker, his black trench coat unbuttoned to reveal his mismatched stripes. He toed an empty Capri Sun on the floor, looking nervous. Or guilty.

"What did you do this time?" I asked.

"What do you mean?"

I twisted the combination on my locker, eying him suspiciously. When I opened my locker door I jumped back. It wasn't filled with glitter like that one time he'd played a joke on me on April Fools' Day. If he hadn't done anything to my locker, then it had to be something else. Was he nervous about something?

He cleared his throat. "I was thinking, maybe Friday. . . ?"

I shoved my books in my bag, prompting him. "Yes?"

He coughed and mumbled something about math.

"Do you want me to help you with math?" I asked. He didn't usually act embarrassed when I helped him with physics. He said he was happy he had a smart best friend.

He lifted one shoulder and dropped it. "Yeah, sure, that would be great."

We walked home together, Derrick unusually quiet. We traveled along the sidewalk of the parking lot, passing a line of traffic trying to get out of the school. We made better time on foot than the cars did. The lot was full of shouting students and kids revving engines like they thought being loud and obnoxious was cool. I led the way out onto the sidewalk along Beavercreek Road.

"Cat got your tongue?" I shouted over the roar of cars passing us.

"Nope. Just thinking." Red autumn leaves danced around his feet. They spiraled up around him in miniature tornados.

The sidewalk diminished and the shoulder next to Beavercreek Road narrowed. We shifted to single file. Derrick gestured for me to walk ahead like he always did.

I shivered as a gust of wind blustered against us, and I hugged my jacket around me. I turned my head over my shoulder. "Winter is coming," I joked.

Derrick nodded, but didn't respond to my *Song of Ice and Fire* reference as he usually would have. I stepped over a putrid mass of roadkill, something that might have been a raccoon or someone's pet cat. The incidents of finding dead animals were increasing. It was hard not to think of Buddy.

Maybe it had been a mistake not confiding in Mom. It wasn't too late, I told myself. She might be able to help my sister, though it probably would lead to Missy tearing the head off all My Little Ponies this time. It might mean she would be sent away.

A car engine roared behind us. Derrick yelped.

Something wet splattered the side of my face and cold exploded against my coat. I whirled away. A red convertible full of blondes blared a horn as they past us. No doubt it was my sister getting a ride home with her friends.

"Craptacular!" I said. "What was it today?" Something wet soaked my jeans.

Derrick wiped the back of my neck with his sleeve. "Just a milkshake. At least it wasn't tuna fish this time." He glanced at the back of his trench coat. It was amazing how much a chocolate milkshake detracted from his Matrix-like fashion statement.

My Jackson Pollock milkshake splatter probably looked like I had diarrhea all over myself. This was the ultimate walk of shame. We still had half a mile left.

I glared down the road at the car full of demonic cheerleaders. "I hate her. She's my worst enemy." I was pretty sure the feeling was mutual.

"I'm lucky I don't have any sisters." He pulled a napkin out of his pocket and wiped the back of my coat. I could already feel the cold soaking through.

"Pretend I didn't say that—about hating my sister," I said, feeling guilty.

"Already forgotten."

A sporty yellow Audi behind us beeped its horn. I scooted farther off the road into the ditch, afraid some jerk was going to run us over. The car pulled over ahead of us. The window rolled down. Josh Hernandez peered out.

"Did that car just throw something at you? Are you okay?" he asked.

"Yeah, we're fine. Thanks," Derrick said.

"What a bunch of jerks." Josh's gaze flickered from Derrick to me. "Clarissa, you want a ride home? That way you don't have to walk home in wet clothes."

I looked from Josh to Derrick. "Um, well, that's nice of you to offer."

The ice cream had soaked through my jacket, making me sticky and even colder than I already was. It was uncharacteristically humane for a popular jock to notice the existence of an artsy girl like me, much less note I was uncomfortable. Could it be Derrick was right and Josh liked me? He hadn't been trying to play a joke on me earlier?

Derrick smirked in that "I told you so" way of his.

Josh waved a hand down Beavercreek road. "You live down this way? It isn't out of the way for me."

"Okay," I said.

A little thrill went through me at the idea that a cool, cute athlete might like me. I was already imagining I was a character in *Wuthering Heights*.

I should have asked if Derrick could come. That would have been the polite thing to do. But I felt awkward asking if Josh's invitation extended to Derrick.

I opened the door, examining the teal upholstery. "Aren't you afraid I'll get ice cream on the seats?"

"No biggie. It's my mom's car, and she takes it in to be cleaned like every month because of the dogs."

I got in, looking back at Derrick. He waved to me, a strained smile on his face.

"Um. . . ." I gestured toward Derrick, trying to figure out how to ask if he could come with us.

Josh didn't notice my bumbling attempt to communicate like Derrick would have. Why couldn't I have been quick-thinking and less socially awkward?

Josh took off as I fumbled with the seat belt. "So, what kind of food do you like?" he asked.

I was relieved Josh was good at talking because I didn't know what to say. "Italian. Mexican. Thai. Pretty much everything. How about you?"

"Do you like the Olive Garden?"

"Who doesn't?" I pointed to the street coming up on the right. "I live down this road."

He turned, taking the corner sharper than I would have liked. I held onto the door to keep from leaning out of my seat. He didn't use a turn signal. Dad was giving me lessons so I could get my permit. He would have been appalled.

"What do you think about dinner at the Olive Garden on Friday before homecoming?" He kept his eyes on the road as he spoke. "I'll be done with work at Taco Bell at five-thirty, five-forty at the latest. I can change at work and meet you at six. It's just down the street from the Olive Garden. Then we can go to homecoming together."

"Are you for real?" I asked.

He glanced at me. "Totally."

I pointed to the fork in the road coming up next to the identical cookie cutter houses. "Take a right. And you need to slow down to twenty-five. It's residential."

"For sure."

"So, um. . . ." I didn't know the fine art of tact and my words came out in a rush. "Aren't you a little out of my league?"

He winked at me. "Sorry, I don't play baseball."

He couldn't seriously be that stupid. He had to be joking. I smiled, feeling shyer than ever. "I didn't know you even knew I existed."

"How can I not? You're beautiful. The only thing that stopped me from asking you out before was Missy Lawrence. I didn't want to make her mad. You don't know how she can be when she gets angry about something."

"Yes, I do." Every day of my life.

"Hey, you have the same last name, don't you? Are you related? Cousins or something?"

"Sisters." How could he not know?

"Holy shit. She never said."

I could only imagine how Missy might react if she found out he had asked me out. She'd be livid. The idea filled me with guilty pleasure. Making Missy jealous was almost as satisfying as a boy asking me on a date.

"I don't know you very well," I said. "Don't you think it might be, um, weird to go on a date?"

"Look, if you don't want to go out with me, just say so."

"No, I do want to." Only after I said it did I realize how true it was. I wanted a chance to be normal. I wanted someone to like me and not treat me like a pariah. So much the better it was someone in my sister's league of cronies who wanted to accept me into their inner circle.

I couldn't wait to see the expression on Missy's face. Only, I couldn't imagine how I was going to get away with this. Mom had forbidden dating. My chances felt hopeless.

I didn't expect my parents to allow me to go to homecoming. Dad, maybe. Mom, no way.

My mom's car was in the driveway, and Josh came in to meet her. I removed my jacket, turned it inside out, and covered the wet spot on my pants. She hummed to herself, watering her windowsill herb garden as we came into the kitchen.

I felt awkward introducing them. I didn't know where to start.

"Um. . . ." I said. "Mom."

She turned. I gestured from her to him and back again.

"Hi, I'm Josh," he said, extending his hand. "I go to school with Missy and Clarissa."

My mom shook his hand. "Hi, I'm Mrs. Lawrence."

Ugh! Why did she have to be so formal? It was like she had been raised in the eighteenth century or something.

I jerked a thumb at my intended homecoming date, more artless at speech than usual. "Josh drove me home because, um, he's nice." I didn't want her to know about my milkshake humiliation.

So, of course, it was my fate that Josh would blurt, "Some jerk threw a milkshake at Clarissa. I didn't think she should walk home in the cold, soaking wet like that."

My mom's eyes crinkled up with concern. "Sweetie, are you okay?" She hugged me like I was a baby, even though a cute boy was standing there. It should have been obvious she was embarrassing me.

"I'm fine." I extricated myself from her arms. "It isn't a big deal."

"What kind of person would do such a thing?" she asked.

Josh cleared his throat. "It was a red car. A convertible, right? I have a suspicion about who might have—"

I shook my head at him. If he said it was Sarah's car and that Missy was with her, there would be trouble. My mom would confront my sister, they would argue, and Missy would do whatever she wanted in the end anyway. Only, she would be ten times worse to me.

Josh must not have been the dumb jock I'd always thought he was. His brow knitted together as he looked to me. "I mean, I suspect they, um, weren't nice. Right?"

Mom walked around the kitchen island to the cookie jar. "Do you kids want some cookies and milk? Gingersnaps? They're homemade. The ginger is from our garden."

She set out cookies for us at the table. She never offered Derrick cookies when it was just him who came over. My dad was usually the one who showed hospitality to my best friend.

Mom gushed, "That was so nice of you to drive Clarissa home, Josh."

He nodded, his mouth full of cookie.

"Josh asked me to homecoming." My words came out in a rush.

"Can I go? You won't tell me I'm too young, will you, Mom? Please?"

She looked Josh over, studying him like she was trying to figure out if he was a weed or rare flower. "He needs to have you back by eleven. No after parties. And no drinking." She wagged a finger at him sternly.

"No sex, no drugs, but I hope you don't mind some rock and roll," Josh said.

Mom laughed. She didn't give him the stink eye like she did with Derrick. Was it because Josh didn't have blue hair? I was pretty sure Josh's friends smoked pot and got drunk—during the off season when they weren't playing basketball. Not that I cared what he did with his body, but I wasn't into that. It struck me as ironic my mom trusted this preppy kid in his letterman jacket because he looked clean, even if he wasn't, whereas Derrick didn't ever do drugs.

An hour later Missy came through the front door after hanging out with friends. I greeted her in the entryway. "Hi, sis. How was your day? Wow, you look like you're building some muscles in those arms."

She lifted her nose, not even acknowledging my presence.

I leaned against the banister of the stairs, trying to appear casual, despite my excitement. "Guess who invited me on a date to homecoming? Josh Hernandez. Do you know him?"

I knew she did. Everyone knew who he was.

Her face drained of color, and she looked like she was about to cry. "How could you? Why did he ask you, not me?" She stormed off in a rage. "Moooooom! Did you know about Clarissa going on a date?"

I laughed as she tried to tattle on me. She stomped up the stairs a minute later.

I probably shouldn't have eavesdropped on her phone call later, but she made it so easy when she screamed into the phone. I pressed my ear to the wall listening.

"How dare you take her side! She's a lame nerd," she screeched. What she said next made less sense. "No freakin' way! I don't care if Lori broke her ankle and we need another lightweight. Clarissa has zero coordination skills. She has no gymnastic training. She can't even do cartwheels."

It sounded like they were arguing about me being on cheer team, but I had no intention of trying out. I wasn't any good at dance or athletics. She wasn't lying on that point. Then again, I kept hearing stories of how the base girls were always getting hurt catching the girls thrown up in the air during stunts, and several of the cheerleaders thrown had gotten hurt on account of being too heavy to catch.

I was the smallest girl in the school. I had never imagined there was anything that would make my sister jealous. But here it was. I had gotten the date she wanted, and I was about to be accepted into her circle of friends. What would it be like to be popular and asked on dates all the time?

On the other hand, it was hard to imagine Derrick and the nerd herd would ever be interested in joining my rise in the social ranks. I didn't want to leave Derrick behind. Of course, Derrick would be graduating this year, and he would leave me behind. I told myself not to worry. This date with Josh meant I had won a small battle against my sister and the forces of high school evil.

Victory had never tasted so sweet. Only, I wasn't the one who had the last laugh.

I wasn't much for make-up, unless it was for cosplay or Halloween. Mom took me out for a makeover. A couple of days wasn't much time to find a dress in my size, so she hemmed one of Missy's and pinned it into place to take it in. The white fabric glowed against my freckled chest and arms, making me appear dark in comparison. Mom used her makeup to conceal blemishes on my face and even out my skin tone. With her artistry, my eyes became large and sultry, my lips sensually pouty, and my cheekbones defined.

I'd never known I could look this way.

"I used to love playing fairy godmother when Missy first started going to dances," she said.

My sister had gone to her BFF's house to get ready. With Missy at Sarah's, that left me as Mom's dress-up doll. I didn't mind the way Mom fussed and paid special attention to me, but I tried not to act too excited and let it go to her head.

She helped me with my hair in the downstairs bathroom, using the curling iron to give me ringlets that cascaded from a ponytail. I sat on the closed lid of the toilet so Mom could reach. I stared at the pale green paint on the wall and twirled the toilet paper around on the roll as Mom chatted away.

"Are you nervous?" she asked. "I was so nervous for my first ball—I mean—dance."

A ball? Oh God, I was so glad she hadn't said that in front of one of my friends. Sometimes I didn't know what planet she was from.

I shrugged. "I'm more excited than nervous. But I'm afraid I might say something stupid." Like I might mistake oral sex for kissing.

"Josh seems like a nice young man, but I want you to remember, he's a teenage boy. If he tries to pressure you to do something you don't want to do, you need to be firm and say no."

"Mom, I hardly know him. This is our first date. We aren't going to do anything." I hadn't even decided if I liked Josh. All I knew was I liked that he liked me. That wasn't quite the same.

"We should have another birds and the bees talk." Mom pinned a curl into place with a hairpin.

"Not now, please."

"You're right, sweetie. Today is your day to shine like the princess at the ball." She patted my cheek affectionately. "Tomorrow, after homecoming is over we'll talk. Josh isn't going to be the only boy who notices you. Others are going to want to date you." She placed me in front of the mirror and pinned the curls to the underside of my bun.

"Does that mean you're going to let me start dating?"

Dad called from the other room. "Not a chance. No boyfriends until you're thirty."

I rolled my eyes. "Ha ha."

"Or at least sixteen." He stuck his head inside. "You look amazing, sunshine. Make sure we get some photos."

As soon as he left, Mom whispered, "Your father and I will discuss dating. But I don't want you to get any ideas in your head. Especially not about Derrick."

"Derrick and I are just friends. What do you have against him?" I watched her in the bathroom mirror.

Her pink lips pressed into a line. "He isn't good for you. All those magic tricks he teaches you. His witch games. He puts the wrong ideas in your head." She sprayed my curls with glitter hair spray.

I held my breath and covered my face until she was done.

"Derrick is my best friend. He understands me." She never could get what it was like to want to be someone else, somewhere else. I didn't fit in this world. Derrick didn't either. "Plus, we haven't LARPed or played *Dungeon and Dragons* or anything like that in a long time. That was just . . . kid's stuff."

"Stop being so pouty, young lady," Mom said with a wink. She adjusted the straps of the dress and fixed one of the safety pins in the back. "We don't need to discuss this right now. Cinderella gets to have a good time tonight."

I did feel like a storybook character. I looked like a princess by the time she was done with me. Mom made the best fairy godmother.

Mom and Dad dropped me off at ten to six on their way to a movie. I signed up for a table and was told it would be a fifteen-minute wait. I stood inside the front door of the Olive Garden so Josh would see me when he came in. It grew more crowded, and another big wave of diners came in after me, some of them teenagers from our school in formal clothes. I figured I should take the table when the staff offered one to me. It was only a couple minutes after six at that point.

I was almost tall enough to see the front door from my booth over the room of diners and the other tables. Every time the chill of autumn rushed in with a new customer coming through the door, I stood to see if it was Josh. Probably he was running late. Fifteen minutes wasn't enough time to change and drive here if he got off at five forty-five. Then again, he hadn't needed two hours to create an artistic masterpiece of glitter hair.

The waitress came by and asked if I wanted anything to drink. I told her I was waiting for my date. I glanced at my cell. No texts. Did he have my number? I was sure he'd entered it correctly. I texted him and told him I'd gotten us a table. He didn't text back. A sinking sensation weighed heavy in my gut. Twenty minutes after being seated, my worst nightmare showed up.

Missy was on a triple date by the looks of it. Sarah, her friend Amy, and all three of their dates accompanied them. I recognized the boys as soccer players. The three girls wore near identical pink dresses. I was surprised Mom had let her wear something so formfitting, but then, maybe that was why she had gotten ready at a friend's house. I glanced down at the loose dress I wore. It was Missy's from two years ago, but still too big to fit me. Mom had been the one to appropriate it from her closet. My sister had thrown a fit.

Missy left her table and strolled by mine, stopping as if just seeing me. "My, my, what do we have here? Is the littlest dwarf going on a date?" The rhinestones of her pink stilettos winked in the light. The pointed heels looked as lethal as my sister's personality.

I flashed my best imitation of a smile, but it felt tight and uncomfortable on my lips, like the lie it was.

Her mouth curled back in an animal-like sneer. "Where's Prince Charming? Or is this a solo event?"

"He's in the restroom," I said quickly.

"Wow, he must have had to go number two because he's been in there for a while, hasn't he?" She smirked. "Unless . . . you don't have a date." She flipped her blonde hair over her shoulder and sauntered back to her table.

Another five minutes went by and I finally got a text from Josh.

The message said: *Sorry.*

I texted back: *No problem. What time will you get here?*

I can't make it. Sorry.

Why? I texted.

No reply came.

That's when I realized, he'd never intended to take me out. I'd been stood up. Missy smirked at me from across the room.

My stomach roiled. I fled to the bathroom. I barely made it inside before the waterworks exploded out my eyes. She'd set me up? How could she? She was the devil incarnate.

I locked myself in a bathroom stall, hiding in the safety of the metal fortress of toiletdom. I had no date, no way to get home, and I was sure this was the worst day of my life. How could I have been so stupid?

I called my parents first, but their cell phones went straight to voicemail. I sent them texts too. They were the courteous kind of movie patrons who turned off their electronics. I could have called or texted Mandy or Jessica to see if one of them would pick me up. Of course, that would involve admitting I had believed a popular boy would be interested in me. This was humiliating enough as it was. I could have called Derrick on his grandparents' ground line, but talking to him would have been even worse.

The bathroom door creaked open and giggling girls entered the room.

I recognized my sister's voice immediately. "Did you see the look on her face? Priceless! Right?"

I had thought my humiliation couldn't possibly sink to depths any lower than they presently were. I was wrong.

CHAPTER EIGHTEEN
And I'll Get Your Little Dog, Too! Mwah Ha Ha Ha!

For ten minutes, I endured listening to my sister gossip about me. I shrank as far back into my stall as I could, trying to hide. I held my breath so I wouldn't burst into sobs. Probably she had made a beeline for the restroom when she'd seen me flee in one final effort to torture me. This was frosting on the vilest cupcake I could possibly imagine. Poop frosting.

Missy went on and on, taking forever with her friends. I didn't know how much snotty commentary I could listen to. As soon as Missy exited, I needed to leave the Olive Garden. I could slip out unseen and wait behind the building until my parents' movie got out. Of course, that would be a while, and I'd have to hope my dad or my mom actually read their text messages. And I would have to admit what an idiot I was.

I didn't want to talk to them. I wanted my best friend. If Derrick had a cell phone I could have texted him, but he didn't. His grandparents couldn't afford one. I was going to have to endure this torment until the evil cheerleaders left.

"Poor, Josh," Missy said. "Then again, this really is for the best in the long run. That girl's freakishness won't rub off on him that way."

"Yeah, it's too bad about Josh missing homecoming," Sarah said. "Does anyone have any pink lipstick? This shade doesn't match my dress."

Amy, the other girl in their cohort of cruelty, spoke quietly. "Josh won't be able to play basketball this season."

My self-pity turned to alarm. Had something happened to him? He hadn't said why he'd stood me up.

"He'll be fine," Missy said. "I hear smallpox isn't even contagious after the first month."

Smallpox? This had to be a joke. Who got smallpox anymore? Wasn't everyone vaccinated for that?

I didn't understand how it was possible, but I knew Missy was behind this. No one would believe me, of course. My parents didn't believe in magic. People would tell me I was paranoid, and I was just bitter Josh had stood me up.

Missy went on and on about my stupid fashion choices, how my laugh sounded like a hyena on Ritalin—whatever that sounded like— and what emo losers my friends were.

"Yeah, I can't believe I ever thought that girl should have been on cheer," Sarah said.

"I know, right?"

"I hear her parents are hippies or something," Amy said.

Missy laughed, her voice strained. "Whatev."

"That girl needs to grow up. Literally!" Sarah laughed.

"Totally."

That girl. *Her* parents. Didn't they know I was Missy's sister? Hadn't she told them? It was bad enough she made fun of me, but the idea she hadn't told them we were related was a thousand times worse. Was she that embarrassed by me?

I hated her more than I hated anyone else I'd ever met. I wanted to humiliate her as much as she had humiliated me.

Between the cracks in the metal stall I spied the three of them around the mirror, touching up makeup and admiring their reflections as they prattled on. I tried to will magic out of my body and into the air like Derrick did. I imagined Missy's lipstick exploding all over her face or her dress tearing.

Nothing happened.

Not that I had really expected it to. Magic never worked for me. I was calm enough now that I felt more in control of my breathing. I wiped my eyes with a wad of toilet paper and blew my nose.

"Wow. Someone has been on the toilet for a long time," Missy said. Her friends giggled. I knew she knew it was me. She was never like this in front of adults and strangers.

It was easier to stay in the stall rather than face my persecutors. Yet as I waited for them to leave, my humiliation sparked into anger. How dare they treat any human being this way. Fury at the way Missy pretended she wasn't related to me bubbled in my core like molten metal, thick and hot, dangerously close to burning whoever it came in contact with. I would make her pay. I would get back at her the only way I knew how.

Loathing fueled my confidence. I unlocked the door and glared at my wicked sister in the bathroom mirror.

"Oh, goodness!" Missy said in mock surprise. "Were you in here the entire time?"

Amy's eyes went wide. There was genuine embarrassment in her expression. Sarah looked like she couldn't care less. My eye makeup was smeared and my nose red.

I lifted my chin, embracing my inner bitch. "Thanks for letting me borrow the dress, *sissy*."

"I don't know what you're talking about." Missy dug through her purse, feigning interest in the disorganized jumble of makeup. "I don't know you, and I wouldn't give you anything of mine if you paid me for it."

"Mom had to take it in for me, but it worked out great, *sissy*."

"Her name is Missy, not Sissy, you moron," Sarah said.

My lips shaped into a curved half-circle that almost resembled a smile. "Yes, I know my sister's name. Melissa Lydia Lawrence."

Sarah looked me up and down and turned back to Missy. "You've got to be kidding me. You're related to this runt?"

"She's not my sister." Panic flashed in Missy's eyes.

I had exposed her in front of her friends. They all knew she was a liar and the sister of a dork. I hoped they shunned her and made fun of her.

I looked to Sarah, the one she idolized and respected above all the others. Her weakness. "Yeah, it's just a coincidence we have the same last name and same hippie parents."

"I am not related to you! You're adopted," Missy said.

The fear and shame in Missy's eyes was almost enough to satisfy me, but not quite. I twisted the blade.

"Right. That makes a lot of sense considering I'm a natural redhead, like Mom. I look more like her than you do." She didn't look like Dad either.

I strode toward the door.

Missy shoved past Amy, placing herself between me and the exit. "Shut up! They love me, not you. They all love me. Everyone pays more attention to me than you! And they always will, if I have anything to say about it." She said something under her breath, too low to understand. It sounded sharp and guttural as though she were swearing.

"Whoa, this is a major amount of drama I don't need on the night I'm going to be crowned homecoming que—" Sarah started, but her words turned into a cough.

Missy's tantrum wasn't anything new. It was what she had said that gave me pause. Was she really that afraid of not being loved? I didn't know how that was possible with our doting—sometimes overly doting—parents. Could it be that all her cruelty was the result of jealousy, just as Derrick had said? The idea that Mom and Dad loved me more than her was as ridiculous as her accusation that *I* was adopted.

But it all made sense if she had been adopted. I remembered that day she'd made me help her look in Mom's closet.

Maybe it was too generous of me, but I could forgive her in a heartbeat if that was what this was about. "Missy, were you adopted?" I asked. "Don't you see, it doesn't make a difference to me? You're still my sister, and I love you."

I placed a hand on her arm, meaning to console her, to hug her, and try to make things right between us again. Her arm was hot, as though she were feverish. She flicked my hand away. Her eyes flashed red.

Not the response I'd expected. I staggered backward.

"Excuse me—" Amy started.

Missy lifted a hand. Amy silenced. Gurgling came from Amy's throat. She grabbed at her neck. Her face turned red. Chills flashed up my spine.

I tried to dodge around Missy toward the door, but she shoved me back into the wall. She shouted something in another language, the sound harsh and grating. Her words became tangible, bouncing around the bathroom like a rubber ball, hitting the mirror and cracking it, colliding into a bathroom stall and denting the metal, chipping the wood cupboard under the sink. The frenzied anger tore a hole in Amy's dress and cut a gash in Sarah's leg.

Sarah leaned over the sink, coughing and choking, snot running down her face. Her mascara ran. Amy huddled next to her.

I wasn't sure how, but I was impervious to Missy's anger.

Missy's magic.

Missy raised a hand toward me, her fingers slowly closing like she was using a Darth Vader chokehold. Her eyes changed from red to black, the pupils expanding into the iris and beyond into the whites of her eyes.

I was used to finding my sister formidable, but this was beyond the usual evil sister menace. She was the queen of scary town.

Missy snatched up a satchel of herbs from her purse and threw them at me. I pushed forward again, grappling with my sister for the door. She shoved my hands back, her fingers catching on my friendship bracelet. The worn-out threads broke under the talons of her fingers and fell to the floor.

My ears popped. We both staggered away from each other. It felt as if something shattered around me. The warmth and friendship I'd felt every time I gazed at the bracelet faded. All the kind words Missy had once said about protecting me when she'd given the bracelet to me fell away, leaving me vulnerable and exposed.

I later learned that was what it felt like when a spell was broken.

Heat rolled out of my sister's hand. My eyes felt painfully dry, and I blinked to moisten them. I stumbled backward, losing balance in my heels, and collided into a baby changing table. My throat ached the same way it did when I had a bad cold. All moisture wicked away from my mouth. I coughed like I'd swallowed a chunk of stale bread and it had lodged in my throat. I tried to breathe, but couldn't.

Now that the bracelet was gone, I was no longer impervious to harm.

The toilets gurgled in their stalls and splashed onto the floor. Something rattled under the sink. The cupboard doors under the sink basin exploded outward and water gushed onto Sarah, Amy, and Missy. All three of them screamed. The cold geyser hitting them must have broken the spell.

Missy's face looked paler, dark circles under her eyes. She teetered and collapsed into Amy. Amy toppled into Sarah. The three of them fell to the floor like human bowling pins. They kicked and screeched as water sprayed onto them.

I didn't stick around to see how they fared. I fled from the bathroom. Cool air greeted my lungs as I gasped for breath. I dodged into the first place I could find—the men's restroom. My sister wouldn't think to look for me there. And even if she did, I couldn't imagine her following me. In my rush to hide, I walked into a man my father's age coming out.

He smiled politely. "Pardon me, young lady. I think you've mistaken the men's room for the—"

I dove past him and closed the door. Fortunately no one was inside. I hid in the stall.

Now that I was alone, it was easier to think. My sister was a monster. I'd sort of known that before, but this incident had solidified my suspicions. There was only one person who would believe me.

With shaking hands, I dialed Derrick's home number. He answered immediately. I breathed a sigh of relief that came out as a choked whimper.

"Where are you?" he asked. "What's wrong?"

"Promise you won't tell me I'm stupid."

"I won't. What happened? What did he do to you?"

"It wasn't him. It was Missy. She just tried to kill me." I blubbered out my situation. "I'm at the Olive Garden. I waited for twenty minutes for my date, and he didn't show. Then Missy and the cheerleaders from hell walked in. They sat across from me and then followed me into the bathroom when I tried to hide. Missy lost her temper and cast a spell on me. My sister is a literal witch."

"I'm so glad I don't have sisters," he muttered. "Okay, here's what we're going to do. You stay there, but get a seat away from Missy. Don't hide. Stay in public, and remain in a visible place. We both know how your sister is in front of people. She doesn't want to look bad. She's less likely to try something around adults and strangers. I'll borrow the car and come in to get you like I'm your date and take you home. Okay?"

I sniffled. "Thanks. You're the best."

"I know. See you in fifteen."

I hung up. Muffled, high-pitched shrieking came from the women's restroom next door, signaling my sister and her friends were probably still in there. Someone came in to use the men's restroom. I waited until he had finished and exited before I left the stall. I cleaned up my makeup. I had a wet spot down the front of my dress that made it look like I had peed myself. That was the least of my worries.

I peeked out of the restroom. A large puddle extended from the women's restroom. The manager, a woman in her late fifties, carried two rolls of paper towels and a mop toward the bathroom. That wasn't going to be enough to sop up the mess Missy had made.

As soon as the manager strode through the door, I heard Sarah wail. I assumed Missy was still inside too. There was no way she would go out into public looking like a drowned rat. I, on the other hand, couldn't afford to be that vain. I stepped out of my temporary sanctuary, feeling vulnerable in the open as I slunk back to my table.

My table had been given to a family of five. Three high school guys sat at Missy's table, laughing and joking as though they didn't notice the extended absence of their dates. The waitress saw me standing in front of my table looking lost. She apologized profusely for giving away my table.

"Um, I had a stomachache," I lied.

She eyed the wet spot on the front of my dress. A nervous laugh escaped my throat. Looking like a dork in public was the lesser of two evils, I told myself.

"Oh sweetie, is it your first homecoming? I remember how nervous I was my first time." She chatted away, taking my arm and placing me at a table full of dirty dishes. A guy who might have been Missy's date craned his neck to see me around his booth. I ducked lower.

I checked my cell phone three more times. It should have only taken Derrick ten minutes. He'd said he'd be here in fifteen. What if his grandma had told him he couldn't take the car? A hostess cleared the dishes and wiped down my table. Someone brought me water and breadsticks, but I didn't touch them. As soon as Derrick arrived I would be leaving.

I stood up and peeked over the edge of my booth. Missy was still out of sight. Just as I turned back to my table, Derrick slid into the seat across from me. He grinned in his usual happy-go-lucky way.

"Thank goodness," I said. I shoved my cell into the black beaded purse my mom had let me borrow. She said it had belonged to Dad's mom.

"You look pretty," Derrick said. He wore a bow tie that was reminiscent of *Doctor Who*. His blue hair was slicked back, and he wasn't wearing his Matrix coat. The suit jacket he wore looked five sizes too big for him—it was probably his grandfather's.

"You clean up real good yourself." I looked him up and down. "What were you doing when I called?"

"*World of Warcraft.*"

"Ha ha!" I said sarcastically. I waved at his suit. "This isn't your usual gaming attire."

"I threw on some clothes and hurried over."

I started to slide out of the booth, but he grabbed my wrist, stopping me. "What exactly happened?"

I glanced around. Other diners chatted conversationally, paying no attention to us. I lowered my voice. "Josh didn't show up." I launched into the full story. Derrick listened with rapt interest. Not once did he roll his eyes or accuse me of exaggerating like one of our other friends would have. I had just gotten to the part where the pipes had exploded in the bathroom when the waitress set another water at our table. I had to stop talking so she wouldn't overhear the unusual details.

She eyed Derrick with pursed lips. "I hope someone has a good excuse for why he arrived so late."

I sipped at my water, giving him an apologetic smile.

Derrick sighed dramatically, playing along. "This is what I get for trying to please everyone and having two homecoming dates. If only I wasn't so popular."

I snorted water out my nose as I laughed. I wiped my face with a napkin. Multitasking beverage consumption with humorous moments still wasn't my strong suit.

He stretched out his arm and waved a hand in an elaborate gesture that was almost like sign language. The waitress watched his hand. I recognized one of the sleight of hand techniques he'd taught me, but combined with it was something new.

The air grew thick, a warm breeze rushing over us, smelling of curry and cinnamon, like it came from someplace far away. I had the sense subatomic particles were bouncing around, reorganizing themselves for him. Out of thin air he conjured a yellow rose. He smiled shyly.

At the next table over something popped and a glass shattered. I glanced over my shoulder, mostly to make sure it wasn't Missy. It was just a server. He stared at a broken glass at the table he was bussing. His brow furrowed.

Derrick didn't notice. He handed me the rose.

The waitress stared at the flower, a slow smile spreading over her face. She looked to me. "I can see why you keep this wise guy around. Can I get the two of you something to drink?"

"I'll have a root beer," Derrick said.

I kicked him under the table. "We have to get out of here before Missy sees us."

"She isn't going to try anything. Do you want a soda? I'm buying."

I shook my head and waited for the waitress to leave. "Are you crazy?"

"Probably." He scanned the diners. Missy was still out of sight. "Finish telling me what happened. What did she look like by the time she was done casting her spell?"

"Were you listening to anything I just said? My sister tried to kill me *and* ruin my life." It was hard to say what was worse at the moment. Probably the humiliation.

"I was listening. She isn't going to do anything with me here. And you know what? I don't think she can do anything to me. I'm wearing my tin foil underwear." He smiled and winked. "Seriously, she might have powers, but I don't think she's capable of doing anything more. Think about how much energy she must have used. She's going to be weak. Did she look exhausted?"

"I guess. She sort of fell over. Plus, her hair and makeup were messed up." That alone might keep her from venturing out into public. I glanced at the table where Missy and her friends' dates sat. They weren't laughing anymore. The three jocks looked bored, worried. Two of them were texting. Missy, Sarah and Amy still hadn't joined them. Maybe the boys wondered if their dates had ditched them.

I thought about the time Missy's rival cheer team had gotten herpes and how sick she'd been afterward. "How do you think magic works? Where does it come from?"

He swirled the ice around in his water. "Sometimes I think it comes from the air."

"Out of thin air. Right. Har har."

"No, I mean, my breath and the wind and the air. Can't you feel it?" He took in a deep breath and blew it out. Even from across the table it felt as though an arctic wind had been released. Loose hairs from my bun tickled my neck. Goosebumps rose on my arms, and I rubbed them away. Somewhere behind me at another table, papers rustled.

The very atoms in the air felt as though they were rearranging themselves for his bidding. Magic never worked this way for me. I couldn't just exhale magic. It was so unfair. Derrick had magic. Missy had magic.

I had math and art skills.

He pushed his cup of water away. The ice had melted, unlike my cup that still contained large chunks in the water. I didn't understand how his magic worked, but it came from somewhere.

"And if Missy does try anything, I'll huff and I'll puff and I'll blow your sister down." He grinned. "Plus, it would be pretty sweet for her to see you enjoying yourself, despite all her villainous efforts. Am I right?"

His smile was contagious. I always felt so much safer, so much calmer and more sane around Derrick. He made my troubles melt away.

His hand was cool as he set it on mine. "When we see your parents tonight, we need to talk to them about Missy. It's only going to be a matter of time before your sister is refreshed and rejuvenated and ready for revenge. It isn't safe for you to be around each other."

It was difficult to focus on his words with the way his fingers pressed against mine. "They'll never believe me." I wondered if my sister really hated me because she was adopted and felt unloved. Even now, as much as I wanted to hate her, I couldn't help feeling bad for her.

"We'll make them believe us. I'll show them magic." His blue eyes were intense as he stared into mine.

"And then my mom will never let us hang out together."

"We can worry about that later. We need them to see how unsafe it is for you first."

I slid toward the edge of the booth again, but Derrick held onto my hand, keeping me there. The sudden confidence in his eyes faltered. "Let's stay. You're all dressed up. We might as well have a nice evening. You deserve someone to take you out." He swallowed and tried to smile, but his lips quivered. "I should have asked you to homecoming as my date in the first place. Not to go as friends." His hand was clammy on my skin, and I realized he was nervous.

Derrick, the senior, was nervous?

A high-pitched screech from a nearby table made it hard to focus. I knew that grating voice all too well. Don't look, I told myself. I made myself concentrate on what he was saying.

"Um. . . ." I stammered. His words buzzed in my ears. I wasn't sure I had heard him right. "Are you saying, um. . . ?" Derrick was my best friend. I'd always rejected the possibility of him liking me because he was older and cooler than I was. He'd said I was like a kid sister.

"Yes. I like you, Clarissa. You're smart and pretty and a good artist. I can talk to you about things I can't talk to other people about, and you don't laugh at me or think I'm strange. You understand me."

And he understood me.

He sat up taller, as if deciding something. "It is a privilege being your best friend, and I'm fine if that's all you want. But tonight, let's go on a date. And if it doesn't feel right, we can pretend it never happened."

I nodded. My cheeks flushed with heat. I already couldn't pretend this hadn't happened. I had secretly hoped for this, but I'd been too dense to see it could be possible. That day in the literary magazine club he hadn't suggested we go to homecoming because of Mandy and Madison. It was because he liked me.

"I'm sorry. I didn't realize. . . ." I swallowed, feeling more socially inept than ever. "I like you too, I just didn't think you were interested in me like that. If I had known you wanted to go to homecoming with me because you *wanted* to, I would have said yes." Even after hearing him admit his feelings, it was hard to share mine. A small part of me secretly feared he was going to laugh in my face.

But he didn't. His shoulders relaxed.

"Thank you for the flower." I set it on my lap.

He shrugged as if it was nothing. "Breadstick?" He handed me one.

"Thanks."

As I took my first bite, he said, "*En garde!*" He batted the stick out of my hands and onto the table.

I laughed and picked it up, smacking his stick so hard it tore in half. I was glad to see nothing had changed between us. Derrick shoved two breadsticks into his mouth at once and pointed them downward so that he looked like a walrus. That was the moment Missy walked by.

The horrified expression on her face: Priceless.

Also, it didn't hurt that even after what must have been half an hour of effort, her dress was still soaked, her hair looked like a bird's nest, and her makeup was smeared. She leaned heavily against Amy. I didn't know how she had convinced her friends she wasn't an evil witch who had tried to choke them to death. From the terror on Amy's face, it was possible she thought I was the one behind the incident in the restroom. Sarah didn't even look at me.

Dinner was nice. Derrick suggested we share a dish so we didn't have to take any leftovers with us. He knew me well enough to know lasagna was my favorite. We shared a slice of tiramisu for dessert. He held up the first bite to me, a twinkle in his eye. As he leaned forward to feed me the first spoonful, I expected he was going to drop it down my dress or smear the cream on my face or something mischievous, but he didn't. He was nice, sweet. I stared into his eyes, wondering if this is what I'd been missing out on.

I tried to feed him a bite, but I couldn't reach the other side of the table very well. I missed his mouth and got his nose instead. We both laughed.

"I'm sorry! I'm not trying to get food up your nose," I said.

"It's a wonder I let you throw bowling pins at my head when we juggle together." He wiped the cream off his nose and licked his finger. "Mmm, booger flavor, my favorite."

"That is so gross!"

He nudged me with his foot under the table. "So, do you want to go to homecoming or do something else? We could go see a movie."

Ugh. I might run into my parents at the movie theatre. Then I would have to explain why I was with Derrick on a date, the boy they obviously disapproved of, instead of my "nice" date. I would see more of my sister at homecoming.

He spoke fast, nervous. "There's the Anti-Homecoming Party at Atkins' Park tonight. But we'd have to stop at home for warmer jackets because it's freakin' cold tonight. And there might be drinking, which means there might be annoying people. Plus, your parents wouldn't like that. Some punk band is playing, but I know you don't like punk." He ran a hand through his neon blue hair. "I mean, if we wanted to listen to bad music, we could just go to homecoming. It's not like they're going to play anything either of us like. If only I'd followed through with my plan to hack into their system and play waltzes and classical music all night."

I laughed at his rambling. I'd never seen him like this before. I could see what I had been blind to all week. He had wanted to go to homecoming. He wanted to be there with our friends and with me. I couldn't guess how long he'd liked me. I felt too overjoyed for words. He was older and cute and such a good artist and friend. And he was a nice person.

I decided right then he was worth going to homecoming for.

He kept rambling. "I didn't buy tickets, so we'd have to see if they're selling any at the door. Plus, there will be tons of people we hate, and your sister will be—"

I opened my purse and removed the tickets. "No worries. I already have them."

"What? You do?" His eyebrows shot up in surprise. "Why? He was the one who asked you. He should have been the one to buy the tickets."

I sighed in exasperation. It was really something when Derrick of all people chided me on social etiquette. "Don't get all bossy and be in my face. Just be happy I have tickets."

"*MajQa*," he said with a fist pump in the air.

"Was that Klingon?"

"Yes. It means 'well done.'"

We were perfect for each other.

CHAPTER NINETEEN
The Weirdest Day of My Life. The Worst Day of My Life

The decorations in the school gym were made from blue and white streamers and painted cardboard to match the "Under the Sea" theme. Blue spotlights flashed over the horde of dancers in the middle of the dance floor. The music was all pop—not a favorite for either of us—but we weren't there for the music. We were at homecoming to be with friends and have fun.

Derrick and I sat at a table with our friends, shouting to be heard over Mariah Carey and other music I wasn't familiar with. Jessica sat with Isaac. In addition to his Jedi costume showing off the dragon tattoo on his neck, he'd drawn anarchy symbols and pentagrams on his hands with a Sharpie. Mandy held hands with Madison. Both of them wore formal dresses.

I sipped at my punch. It tasted like watered down cherry Kool-Aid. Derrick held my hand under the table. He gave it a squeeze and looked at me as if to ask if that was all right. I blushed and nodded.

It was strange sitting so close and touching like this. Strange and comfortable at the same time. Could it be that we were like two puzzle pieces made for each other, only I'd been too dense to notice?

Jessica locked eyes with me and tilted her head toward Derrick, trying to ask me about us coming together without being obvious. I shrugged. I would tell her about it on Monday at school. It was too loud here.

I pretended I didn't notice Missy with her friends at a table on the other side of the gym, but I snuck glances to be sure she stayed on her side. She looked exhausted. She wasn't even dancing. Derrick followed my gaze.

His eyes narrowed, and he circled an arm protectively around me. "When you get home, we have to talk to your parents. Promise me you aren't going to try to make some excuse for her."

"Why would I make some excuse?"

"Because you're too nice."

I didn't know about that.

As soon as a slow song played, the couples at our table stood and went to the dance floor. Derrick tugged me to my feet. "Dance with me?"

"Sure, but don't get it in your head I'd be okay with any of that gropey stuff." I nodded to a vertical lump on the dance floor that might have been two people, but it was hard to tell with the way they were sucking on each other's faces and entwined in each other arms.

"No way, that's gross." He stood taller and added in a stuffy British accent. "Besides, I don't know if you've noticed, I'm a perfect gentleman."

He was a perfect gentleman. Forget what my mom thought because his hair was blue. He wasn't like other boys my age who made obnoxious jokes about girls' boobs bouncing around in P.E. His idea of partying was staying up all night to read a fantasy novel. He listened when I told him to stop doing something I didn't like, whether it was stealing my tater tots, or to stop telling me how to use watercolor pencils just because I didn't use them the way he used them. For over a year he'd been my best friend.

I felt self-conscious dancing in public. We stood, squished between hordes of sweaty teenagers that smelled like Axe body spray and cheap tropical fruit perfume. I glanced over my shoulder, afraid my sister or someone else would pour punch on my white dress. Or pig's blood. I glanced up. Nothing hung from the ceiling, thank goodness.

The warmth of Derrick's fingers on my waist returned me to the present. He took my hand with his free hand. Our palms were slick with sweat. Every couple of seconds I thought I felt an electric pulse where his fingers met mine, but it might have been my nerves. I stared at his chest the whole time as we swayed back and forth. Neither of us knew how to dance, other than a couple ballroom routines we'd watched on YouTube. None of them seemed appropriate for this venue. Fortunately, everyone else looked about as dorky as I felt, so it probably didn't matter.

The music ended, and we were left standing there, staring at each other. He brushed a stray strand of hair from my face. He slouched lower. He was going to kiss me. Did I want him to kiss me? This was all moving so fast. One minute Derrick was my friend, now we were on a date. Next we would be getting married and having children.

My stomach fluttered and the room shimmered as if someone had just released a glitter bomb. The air changed, something electric buzzing underneath my skin. It smelled like ozone. The blue lights sweeping across the crowd faded. We were left in darkness.

"What's going on?" someone shouted.

"Are we having a power outage?"

"Clarissa?" Derrick asked. "Do you feel it?"

"Magic," I whispered.

My heart pounded against my ribcage. I couldn't tell if this was good magic like his or bad like Missy's. What if we called Fae to us? The spotlights came on again. People looked around, confused. There was still no music.

Something flicked into my ear. I turned around, but no one stood immediately behind me. Something light bumped into my arm, but no one was there. I started at a tap to my shoulder, catching a movement out of the corner of my eye this time. Derrick's brow was furrowed. A piece of folded blue paper dropped onto his head. A bright yellow and red paper fell behind him and a pink flowered one streaked by next. I caught one in my hand. It was an origami paper crane.

I looked up at the ceiling but couldn't figure out where they came from. Students giggled and squealed, catching the cranes or batting them away. Derrick stared up in wonder.

"It's raining origami?" I laughed. "Hanging out with you is always magical."

Derrick's gaze followed the drifting papers. "Weird. I guess some kid's wish in Japan just came true."

"My hair!" someone shrieked. I recognized that high-pitched screech and tried to ignore Missy.

People shifted around us, their feet crunching over the litter of cranes. There had to be a thousand of them, and they kept falling.

Jessica ran up to us and threw a handful of them up into the air. She laughed and scooped up more from the floor. "I can't believe student government made all of these for homecoming. This is the best!"

"It doesn't match our Under the Sea theme," someone complained. "They should have made origami fish."

Folded paper continued to sprinkle down on us like multicolored snow. We seemed to be the only ones to realize this hadn't been planned by the homecoming committee.

Derrick picked a crane out of my hair. "This isn't my usual M.O. I didn't feel . . . well, the air didn't shift. You know?"

If this wasn't Derrick's doing, it might have been mine. There had been a moment when my skin had felt electric. Something inside me had stirred like it wanted to break loose. I didn't want to voice the hope that it had been me, though, afraid he might have a plausible reason it couldn't be.

The speakers exploded into the next song: YMCA. Madison and Mandy made their way toward us. Mandy playfully punched Derrick in the arm. "You better not duck out before this one."

We joined them, singing along and gesturing with our arms. It was so much fun I wished the DJ would play another oldie, but he went back to pop music. Derrick and I were the first to return to our table. I was so hot and thirsty, I gulped both our punches even though Kool-Aid wasn't my fave. It was even worse than I remembered and burned my throat going down. My eyes watered, and I couldn't stop coughing.

Jessica joined us, smacking me on the back. "Easy there, sparky. Try not to inhale the punch."

"No worries. I'll get us some more." Derrick hurried off and presented me with another cup.

The punch tasted different, more like water. I was okay with that.

James and Jessica sat at our table, looking bored. M & M did all the dancing. I waited an eternity for the next slow song. Derrick held my hand in his, stroking my fingers in a way that made my stomach fluttery. The world faded, and it was just him and me. I couldn't tell if that slowing of time and the haziness of the room was magic or chemistry. I didn't even notice the change in the music. He tugged me to my feet, and I sailed into him, wobbling on my high heels.

He wrapped his arms around me and steadied me. It felt nice

hugging him without having to worry about my mom's reaction. Why hadn't I leaned in when he'd looked like he wanted to kiss me? I shouldn't have let the moment pass. Next time I would be ready for it. Unless there wasn't a next time because he thought I didn't want to kiss him now.

I tried to step toward the dance floor, but my knees felt like jelly, and my feet didn't want to cooperate. I waved a hand at the heels. "Sorry, I'm not used to these things. It's my first time." I giggled.

Everyone laughed except Derrick. His brow furrowed as he studied me. He held me under my elbows to keep me from falling over. The heat of the room and the music made me lightheaded.

"Are you okay?" Derrick asked.

Isaac leaned closer. "You're drunk, aren't you?"

"What? No!" I waved him off, my hand floppy.

"Of course, she isn't drunk," Derrick said indignantly. "How would that even be possible? Do you think I would take her to a bar before this?"

Isaac shrugged. "You do have a fake ID."

"No way! You have a fake ID?" I shouted to be heard over the music.

Wouldn't you know it, my voice came out loud over a quiet part in the music. People at nearby tables cast dirty looks in my direction.

"I used it twice when I was sixteen. It was only to buy video games rated 'mature,'" he said. "It's not like I go to clubs or anything."

Isaac smelled my cup and held it out to Derrick to sniff. Isaac went around smelling everyone's Kool-Aid. "Everyone else's is fine. It's just those two cups."

"What about our cups?" My stomach flip-flopped, but it was all good. I was happy, happy, happy.

Derrick slipped his arm around my waist. "We need to get you home."

"Why? I thought you wanted to dance."

"I've changed my mind. It's too loud." He kept a smile on his face, but his eyes weren't smiling. He scanned the crowd, his nostrils flaring when he saw someone across the room. Missy sat at her table with a wicked smile, her eyes dark with her smeared makeup. I was too stupid at that moment to make the connection. Who in that room would want to humiliate me and get me in trouble? Duh.

Derrick looked like a bull about to charge a minotaur in the cartoons. Or was it a matador, I wondered. All the words in my head sloshed together.

I laughed at the image of him charging toward Missy. He was so funny. When had he become so funny?

I hardly remembered walking to the car. I laid my head against the window of the Chevy and closed my eyes. The lull of the engine was like a lullaby, and I fell asleep. I might have remained that way if Derrick hadn't opened the door and unfastened my seat belt. Aside from the porch lights of our neighbors, the street was dark. Derrick had parked one house down, in front of Mrs. Mesker's light up Jack-O-Lantern lawn ornaments, probably so my parents wouldn't see his car in our driveway from the living room.

He helped me stand up.

My stomach churned. "I'm going to be sick."

He kept me from falling flat on my face as I puked in the street. The cherry Kool-Aid didn't taste any better the second time around.

I got bright red barf on the front of my white dress. I would have cried if it had been my dress, but it was Missy's. I snorted out a laugh.

Derrick shook his head. "Your parents are going to blame me."

I wiped my mouth against the back of my hand. "Don't worry about it. They aren't home." The driveway was empty. They were probably at the movies. Or having dinner.

"Keys?" he asked.

I dug through my purse. My fingers felt limp and uncoordinated. I was so tired. Derrick grabbed my keys and held onto my elbow as we walked to the door. He flipped on lights and helped me upstairs to my room. I flopped down on my bed, ready to fall asleep.

"Okay, so here's the plan," Derrick said. "You get changed and go brush your teeth. I'm going to turn the television on and keep an eye out for your parents. If they walk in while you're changing, I'll distract them and act like I just came over to hang out and watch *Star Trek* reruns after you came back from homecoming. I'll take your dress home and wash it, so your parents won't think you were drinking. You can stay up here and then go to bed without them finding out. We'll say you were tired and didn't feel like watching T.V. with me. Got it?"

He was good at making up stories. This was just like when he was running campaigns with his D & D group. I giggled. "You know, that first time you asked me to LARP with you, I thought it was something naughty."

He snapped his fingers in front of me. "Hello? Were you listening?"

"To what? Music?" There wasn't any music here.

He sighed. "I'm going to start phase one of this plan and go downstairs. Can you change out of that dress on your own?"

"Sure." I waved him off.

He closed the door as he exited. I tried to unzip the dress, but I'd forgotten my mom had pinned it together with safety pins to take it in because it was Missy's and three sizes too big. I squirmed, trying to wiggle the back around to the front. It was a lot of work. I sat down on the bed.

Lucifer brushed his tail against my leg. He purred.

The next thing I knew Derrick was shaking me. "Hey, don't go to asleep yet."

"Are my 'rental units home?"

"No, thank God."

He unpinned the safety pins down the front of the dress. I thought my mom had pinned the back of it, but whatev. He stuck his hand down my dress to unpin the hidden safety pins.

"Getting fresh?" I asked.

"Yes, because my idea of a good time is groping the girl I'm in love with when she's covered in puke."

"That's sweet." I smiled. A boy loved me. Derrick loved me. I leaned my head against his shoulder.

"No way, barf breath." He shook my shoulder. "Sit up. I can't do this if you fall asleep."

He unzipped the dress a few inches and unpinned the last two safety pins. I unzipped it the rest of the way and dropped back onto my bed.

He stared, wide-eyed. "Holy craparoni! You aren't wearing a bra."

"Duh. It would show through the fabric."

He wiggled the dress down my hips. "This keeps getting more and more wrong. Any moment your parents are going pull up in the driveway and accuse me of putting ecstasy in your drink." He bunched up the dress and threw it on the floor. "Where are your pajamas?"

I pointed to the armoire. He threw back the doors.

"No, that's where Narnia is. Get my jammies from the drawer."

It was the bottom drawer. He eyed the Strawberry Shortcake set skeptically. "You actually wear these?"

"Yeah. You got a problem with that?"

He shoved the pajama top over my head and helped me into the bottoms. "This is so not how I envisioned our first date. Maybe our fifth date, but not the first." He smiled, and I knew he was making a joke so I laughed, but I was too tired to get it.

He brought me my toothbrush and a cup to spit in. He patted the top of my head as I brushed my teeth. "We're almost in the clear."

A moment later, he tucked me under my blankets and left the room with the cup and toothbrush.

I probably would have fallen asleep except the rumble of a car in the driveway drew my attention. Lights flashed in the window. It was either my parents or sister. I considered sitting up so I could see who it was, but I was too tired.

Derrick walked back into the room.

I waved a hand at the window. "You might want to hide."

Car doors slammed.

He dove onto the bed and scrambled to the window to see better. "Shit!"

He kicked my dress under the bed. Lucifer darted out. Derrick started toward the door and then dashed to the closet. As he pushed the sliding door aside, board games tumbled out. He tripped over to the armoire and tried to squeeze himself inside and failed. I laughed at how comical he looked. I could see why I was the one who would need to be stuffed into a box to get cut in half.

I began. "And for his next magic trick—"

Derrick shushed me.

The front door to the house closed with a thud.

Derrick tiptoed to the door and turned off the light. He was a black silhouette against glow-in-the-dark stars decorating the walls.

"Where can I hide?" Derrick whispered. "Do you have any rope, so I can climb out the window? No, that will take too long."

"Hide under the bed," I said.

"No way. You never vacuum under your bed, and it's disgusting. My allergies will be horrible. I'll sneeze, and they'll find me."

"You can hide in the bed with me." I waggled my eyebrows. Not that he could see me do so in the dark.

Derrick rummaged through something on the other side of the room. He plopped a bunch of dolls onto me and dove under the covers. I could feel him rearranging the dolls over himself.

"Shit! This will never work," he said.

I had to agree. My mother's footsteps padded up the stairs.

"Sweetie? Are you home? You left your keys in the front door," Mom said.

She turned the handle to my door. A ray of light swept over me. I snapped my eyes closed. Derrick froze under his fortress of dolls.

"She's asleep," Mom whispered.

"Come on, Abby," Dad called from the hallway. "We can ask her how it went in the morning."

Mom closed the door, sealing us in darkness. My parents whispered in the hallway. Mom giggled.

"Shh! You're going to wake her!" Dad said.

Finally, their footsteps padded down the hallway.

Derrick let out a long sigh. "Here's the new plan," he whispered. "I'll stay here until your parents go to sleep. Then I'll sneak out."

"Okay," I yawned. I rolled over onto my side and snuggled against him.

"I'm sorry this evening didn't go as planned," he said.

"That's fine. I had a great time. It was the best date I've ever been on." The only date I'd ever been on.

"Really?" he asked.

He stroked my wrist where my friendship bracelet had been, his touch making goosebumps rise on my skin. His arm was warm where it was draped around my waist, safe and familiar. I was so tired I felt like I could fall asleep and never wake up. It was a struggle to fight against that fatigue and stay present in the deliciousness of the moment. I nuzzled my face against his neck. He smelled like Old Spice, which wasn't his usual scent, but he was wearing his grandfather's suit. Derrick squirmed back. I cuddled closer.

"Stop moving," he whispered.

"Why?"

As I flattened myself against him, a bulge in his pants pressed against me. "Is something in your pocket?"

"Um, no."

I burst out, giggling. "Is that your wiener?"

"It's, um, yes." He nudged me away from him. "It's an erection."

184

That made me laugh even harder. I'd read enough in the library to understand how sexual reproduction worked, but it all seemed ridiculous, especially in this moment.

He shushed me. "It isn't funny. I can't help it. I'm in bed with a nearly naked girl, and I can't stop picturing your boobies."

"Boobies!" I laughed. He had such a way with words.

"Shhhhh." He covered my mouth.

The shower started, probably the one in my parents' bathroom. I hoped they weren't going to stay up late.

"So, you like my *boobies*?" I asked. Compared to my sister, I was practically flat chested. I was impressed he'd even noticed I had breasts. Maybe I wasn't as unattractive as I thought.

"Can we talk about this another time?" he asked.

"How long have you liked my boobies?" A giggle escaped my mouth, and I covered it before he could.

"Rephrase that as a question without mentioning your anatomy, and I might answer it." He poked me in the ribs, which only made me laugh harder.

I squirmed away from him.

"Stop making so much noise. And stop moving, will you?" he said in exasperation. "Your parents are going to ground you and never let me come over again if you give me away."

That was a sobering thought that dissolved my case of the giggles. The rush of water in the pipes echoed from farther down in the hallway.

"How long have you liked me?" I asked.

"I thought you were pretty the first moment I saw you in the cafeteria. Once I talked to you I knew I liked you. Then there was a day during art club last year that it was just you and me. You were telling me all the things you would do if you were the principal of your own magical school, and I thought, wow, I'm in love."

I couldn't even remember the day he was talking about. It had to be the most important day of my life, but I didn't even know when this was.

Sleep tugged at my mind, tempting me with sanctuary, but I held on, wanting to savor this moment. It wasn't just that he liked me. He loved me. And I loved him too. He was my best friend. It felt natural we should want to become more than that. I leaned my head against his shoulder.

He rested his hand on mine. "There have been all these moments since then that I kept thinking about it. Like when we went to the movies with Isaac, Jessica and Mandy. I wanted to sit by you so I could hold your hand, but I lost my nerve. I don't even remember what movie we went to see. Waiting for that perfect moment and finding the courage to touch you was all I could think about the entire time. I was worried you might punch me and scream at me if I tried to hold your hand. It would be horrible enough to be rejected, but the humiliation of it happening in front of everyone would be even worse."

I yawned. I couldn't remember which movie it was either, but that was probably because I was so exhausted. "I wouldn't have screamed at you."

"No, you probably wouldn't have. That was my other fear—that you would be so horrified you wouldn't say anything to me at all and start avoiding me. Maybe you think I don't see the way you withdraw when you're embarrassed, when Isaac and Mandy start up with a dirty joke, but I do notice. I've tried not to bring up things that make you uncomfortable. I know you haven't been in health class or taken sex ed yet."

It was getting harder to focus on his words. My body felt as though it were sinking into warm clouds. "You won't tell them I haven't been in sex ed, will you? I don't want anyone to think I'm stupid."

"I don't think you're stupid, just . . . innocent. You're so small and fragile, I kept thinking I would break you if I ever touched you."

I kicked him, but not very hard. My legs were too heavy. "I'm not a porcelain doll, dork brains."

"I know. I'm just saying, that's what I told myself in those moments. And it's okay you're not ready for sex and your mom is overprotective. What parent wouldn't try to shield a kid from the entire world after seeing the way Missy turned to the dark side in every possible way? I like you the way you are. I like *us* the way we are. I didn't want anything to change between us, or for you to feel pressured to do something you'll regret with some guy three years older than you."

"You worry as much as my mom." It took all my energy to lift my head. I wanted to tell him the way I had yearned for him to like me, the reasons I had thought it was impossible, but words didn't feel adequate. Instead, I pressed my lips to his.

He was as rigid as stone, but as I kissed him, his muscles relaxed. He continued to keep his body bent, his midsection pulled away from me, but he wrapped his arms around me and threaded his fingers through my hair. An electric current pulsed inside me. I'd never kissed a boy before. Now that I'd started, I didn't want to stop. My fatigue faded. My skin prickled with energy. It felt like I'd just downed a Red Bull with a side of Monster.

Wind rattled the window. The porchlight outside flickered.

He broke away. He trailed his nose along my cheek, inhaling deeply. "You have no idea how long I've wanted you to kiss me, to want me as much as I want you." He sighed. "But not like this. Tomorrow after you feel better and you're in your right mind, then we can kiss like this." He scooped me up and set me back into the middle of the bed. He remained pressed against the wall, as far from me as possible.

"Are you saying a girl isn't in her right mind if she wants you?"

"Pretty much."

The shower stopped. He rearranged dolls back on top of himself again.

There had been a couple boys I'd had crushes on in middle school. I'd even fantasized about kissing them, but the idea of actual sex sounded disgusting.

Until now. I hadn't been ready for kissing at the dance, but now that we had, I wasn't scared anymore. The idea of him holding me close and kissing me made my belly flutter. I wanted him to love me.

"I'm not tired anymore," I said. "I think I puked out whatever was in my drink."

"I wish."

Something thudded in the other room. At first I thought it was something dropping on the floor in my parents' room. Then the thud came again. And again. I listened, perplexed. It sounded like a drum, only creakier.

Derrick sat up. "I can't believe it!"

"What?" I asked. "It sounds like they're playing a musical instrument."

Derrick fell back laughing. "Your parents are having sex."

"No, they aren't. My parents don't do that." The very idea was absurd. My parents weren't attractive. They were just . . . ick.

Headlights from outside flashed across my room, signaling a car had pulled up in the driveway. That probably was Missy getting dropped off from her date. She was home early.

"This would be a good time for me to leave." He kissed my cheek. "Good night, barf breath. We'll talk tomorrow."

"Do I really smell like barf?"

He sniffed the side of my face. "Not really." He climbed over me, digging his knee into my leg.

"Ow!"

"Sorry." He bumbled around in the dark, accidentally elbowing me as he tried not to knee me. The tent pole in the crotch of his pants poked me again. "Oops. Um, sorry." He scooted off me onto the other side of the bed.

I found his hand and squeezed it. He kissed my fingers. I didn't want Derrick to leave. I also didn't want him to get in trouble for being in my room.

"Kiss me one last time before you go," I said.

"One kiss good night," he said. "And then I have to leave. Hopefully your parents didn't notice my Grandma's car in the street."

Hopefully Missy hadn't either.

He pressed his lips to mine, the kiss chaste at first. I circled my arms around his neck and hugged him closer. Electricity sparked inside me once again. His tongue slid into my mouth. He tasted sweet, like butterscotch candy. Like a cool breeze on a hot day.

Like magic.

I knew I should have come up for air, but I couldn't stop kissing him. I was addicted to his lips. Something deep inside me clenched. A wave of hot and cold prickles washed over me. That lightheaded sensation like when I'd gotten up to slow dance came back. The room didn't feel real. I thought my eyes were closed, but they must not have been because the glowing green stars on the walls looked too bright. Maybe it was my eyes playing tricks on me, but the digital clock on my nightstand flickered. The numbers ran backward. A flutter in my chest seized me, and all the nervous energy building up felt like it would explode. The air smelled of ozone and rain on dry earth.

Derrick pressed closer, his warmth igniting a fire in my core. His erection poked me in the leg. He didn't try to hide it this time, and I wasn't overcome by giggles. I liked the idea he found me attractive.

"I feel magic. . . ." Derrick panted against my face. "I think I understand it now. It happens every time we touch, every time we—"

I kissed him deeply, more passionately. Bright light blinded me. A storm exploded inside me.

Or maybe it exploded outside of me. I couldn't tell.

Suddenly, wind whipped my hair and tore at my blankets. The stuffed animals and dolls on the bed smacked me in my arms and legs, and they tumbled away. I heard yelling above the roar in my ears. Glass shattered and peppered my skin in bursts of pain. I squeezed my eyes closed and tried to turn away from the explosion, but something smacked hard into my other arm. Loud screeches of wrenching metal and screaming wood reverberated all around me. The breath in my lungs was sucked away.

Derrick was torn from my arms. The world around me spun like a dervish. I dug my nails into the mattress, trying to hold on. Thunder rolled, sounding like it came from right above me. Blue light flashed. It was blindingly bright even through closed eyelids.

Just as suddenly as it started, the turbulence stopped. When I blinked open my eyes, I found I was still in my bed, my pajamas in shreds. The blankets had been torn away. Cold night air nipped at my skin. There was no ceiling. There were no walls. I wasn't in my room anymore. It looked like my bed was in the street, but that couldn't be right.

I thought I was dreaming, except that my arms and legs stung from gashes. Shards of glass glittered across the bed. I hurt too much to be asleep.

My ears rang. A car alarm going off in the distance sounded muffled, as though it were under water. The row of houses along our block illuminated the street with their porch lights enough I could see the state of my house.

Or what was left of it.

One wall had fallen in pieces in the front yard. Another wall had somehow been planted in the middle of the street. Our refrigerator was only a few feet away from my bed. A ladle from the kitchen swung from the footboard.

Water gushed out of broken lines where the house had been. My mom ran toward me. Dad stumbled after her.

She hugged, me, sobbing. "You're all right! My baby!" She kissed my face.

I shivered uncontrollably. I felt as though I'd been shocked with electricity.

"A tornado," Dad gasped. "How can we have a tornado? This is Oregon."

My dad was wearing a robe that had been hastily tied. My mom's hair was damp. She wore a Snuggie hanging open in the back with nothing else underneath. Broken bits of glass prickled against my flesh as she embraced me. Only later did I consider this was probably what they'd been wearing in bed when the tornado struck.

I fought to gain control of my voice, to make my mouth work. "W-w-where's. . . ?" I choked on Derrick's name. I glanced at his grandma's car, untouched where he'd parked it one house farther down the street. Our neighbor's light-up balloon pumpkins illuminated the nearest pile of wreckage. At the end of the street stood a figure in a long coat—or perhaps it was a cape. Something about the stance felt male. He stared at the carnage of our house. A chill tingled up my spine. I had the distinct impression the man wasn't looking at the wreckage, but at me. Mom straightened, her eyes fixing on him too.

Lucifer slunk out of the shadows and hissed.

Dad rose from my side and unsteadily made his way to the fallen wall of our house. He dropped to his knees and moaned. My stomach lurched.

Sticking out from underneath a partially intact wall was a set of athletic legs wearing pink heels with rhinestones. The twister had dropped a house on my sister.

CHAPTER TWENTY
Ding Dong, the Witch is Dead

The next few months passed in a blur of sedatives and anti-psychotics.

I couldn't stop thinking about my sister. Or Derrick. I couldn't stop blaming myself for the tornado—or pornado—as I called it in my head. After all, it had happened while I'd been in bed with Derrick, kissing him.

My guilt was the reason my parents forced me to go to therapy at La Vida Loca medical clinic. If I hadn't been pumped so full of drugs, I might have wondered who named a place for mental health and wellness the "crazy life" in Español.

"Dr. Bach will be with you in a moment," the nurse said as she deposited me in the doctor's therapy room.

That was strange. Usually Dr. Bach was already in his room waiting for me.

I walked past the couch and sat down in one of the oversized, fluffy chairs. I clutched the potted plant Mom had grown in her greenhouse and transplanted into a terracotta pot. The orchid was white, with red spots in the center. I didn't know how she knew Dr. Bach liked orchids, but I supposed they talked when I wasn't around.

The room was cheery, with sunlight brightening the room from behind pale, translucent curtains. When the wind blew outside, trees danced, casting flickering shadows against the sheer fabric in front of the windows. A purple orchid stretched toward the window on the bookcase next to the stone Buddha statue. Sunlight spilled onto the pink orchid on the desk behind the chair where he usually sat during our sessions. A philodendron was nestled on a shelf on the wall above the cheery impressionist painting of Vincent van Gogh's *Sunflowers.*

I shifted in the chair, trying to adjust the lumpy pillow. My gaze fell across the file on Dr. Bach's desk. It was probably mine. At one time I might have been inquisitive about what that chart said, but these days, nothing piqued my curiosity.

I felt like a sloth, my every thought thirty seconds behind everyone else's. My movements were slow and lethargic. I didn't care that my ginger roots were showing and I wore jeans with holes in them and sweaters that were too big for me. I passed my online high school classes, did my chores, and stared into space. That was my life.

I tried not to think about what had happened.

Dr. Bach was taking forever. I remembered Derrick's happy-go-lucky smile and exuberance. I reveled in the memory of his arms around me, holding me close. He had gazed into my eyes with such love and tenderness I had known we were meant to be together.

He hadn't believed we were doing anything bad by dabbling in magic. There wasn't a doubt in his mind that I was a good person, whether I was or not. When our lips had touched, something had been drawn out of me, a powerful force I didn't understand.

Something I no longer wanted to name. Magic.

The clock on the wall stopped ticking. The lamps in the corners flickered. The air smelled like freezer burn and ozone. The second hand on the clock lurched backward, thunking irregularly.

Birds fluttered at the window pane, their wings beating at the glass. I prayed they weren't Fae come to snatch me away.

I didn't want to cause another accident. I couldn't allow myself to sink down that dark rabbit hole of evil. I was not going to be a wicked witch. I was not going to be the villain in my own story. Although, at this point, I was pretty sure I already was.

A man stepped into the room, closing the door behind him. He made a gesture with his hand like sign language. The birds flew away, and the room grew as quiet as death.

I didn't know the man. At least, I didn't think I did. It took me a minute to register the shifty look in his eyes. By that point, he'd already slipped behind Dr. Bach's desk. He didn't greet me. He grabbed the file and opened it.

The silence stretched on. I was afraid to break it. He kept reading. I coughed. No response. A bird fluttered in the branches of the tree outside, the silhouette cast onto the sheer curtain.

"Where's Dr. Bach?" I asked.

"Indisposed."

He was tall and lean, dressed in varying shades of indigo. The midnight of his hair flowed over his shoulders, almost seamlessly blending in with his navy-blue suit. The shoulder-length locks had the kind of wave and body teenage girls spent hours trying to replicate. A gray swath of fabric peeked out from under the high collar of his white shirt. There was something strange about the way he was dressed. Old-fashioned.

"Are you a staff member?" I asked.

"Yes." He sat on the desk, reading.

The long line of his nose and frown at the corners of his mouth were familiar. His gray eyes reminded me of the sky just before a thunderstorm. The air around him felt thick and heavy, like rainclouds about to burst. He didn't exactly give off an air of friendliness.

I fidgeted with the hem of my long sweater. "Hi, I'm Clarissa. Nice to meet you." That was what you were supposed to say when you wanted someone to introduce themselves, wasn't it? If only Missy was here. She would have told me. My heart clenched, thinking of her.

The man said nothing.

"Who are you?" I asked.

A smirk curled the edges of his lips upward. "For our purposes today, I am a psychologist." His voice was deep, laced with a British accent.

I could almost place his face, but not quite. "Do I know you?"

He flipped a page in the folder. His voice sounded bored, indifferent. "You may have seen me once or twice, but no. You don't know me."

Maybe I had seen him here at the clinic. No, I was certain I'd seen him at school. The moment I remembered, I smiled, proud of myself. "Wait a minute. I do know you. You work for Oregon City High School. You're the district psychologist." How could I have forgotten that beautiful hair?

"Aren't you clever?" he asked in a dull monotone. "I've read your chart. Hallucinations. Depression and anxiety. Delusions. They have you on several medications. Are they working?"

"Are you my new doctor? Where's Dr. Bach?"

"Have you made anything magical happen of late?"

Was this a trick question? "There's no such thing as magic," I said quickly.

"Right." He tossed the file onto the desk behind him. He circled around and sat on the arm of Dr. Bach's chair across from me.

My dad hated it when I sat on his lounge chair like that at home. He said it would break the armrest. This guy was heavier than I was. I wondered what Dr. Bach would do if the man broke his chair. I could already imagine a *Goldilocks and the Three Bears* scenario. I giggled and then stopped when I realized he was staring at me. These meds made me loopy.

"Are you still under the impression you can cause tornados, pipes to burst, or electrical storms?" he asked.

I hadn't ever claimed to cause electrical storms, had I? My brain was about as sharp as a butter knife. I couldn't remember.

"Um." I tried to focus. "Do you mean, do I still believe I caused the death of my sister and best friend?"

"What I mean is, have your symptoms of magic gone away? Are you still manifesting energies that could harm others?"

No one had ever put it that way before. It didn't sound like something a psychologist would ask.

"I haven't tried to make magic happen since. . . ." Tears filled my eyes.

"No? Well, go ahead. I'd like to see a demonstration of what you can do."

I shook my head. "Mom says magic is bad. It always has a price."

"I thought you didn't believe in magic. If it isn't real, what's the harm in trying?"

I hugged the terracotta pot to my chest. I was probably damaging the orchid, but I didn't care.

"You don't have a plant affinity. That isn't going to work," he said.

"Affinity?" I repeated.

His arms were so long he didn't even need to lean forward to pluck the pot from my arms. He placed it on the seat beside him and dusted his hands off on his navy-blue slacks.

"Now, on to that demonstration. Let's see if the medications are working and if they are enough to prevent you from harming others."

I shook my head. My voice came out a rasp. "I might kill you."

He snorted. "Unlikely. I'm a trained professional."

"Magic isn't real," I whispered. I said it because it was the right thing to say, but even drugs hadn't made me believe this.

With the grace of a stage magician, he used sleight of hand to make a stick appear in his palm. The twisted wood was about a foot long, the ebony matching the dark shade of his clothes. He gestured with his other hand, his fingers dancing like sign language. A shimmer of lights and sparkles wavered around him. I could almost see what he was doing, but my eyes were tired, and my brain felt thick like cotton stuffing. He flourished the stick in the air, and a rainbow poured out of his wand.

"Still don't believe in magic?" he asked.

CHAPTER TWENTY-ONE
Trained Professionals

Holy craparoni! I watched the rainbow spill from his wand like water. It splashed onto me and I laughed. It puddled down the side of the chair and onto the Oriental rug over the wood floor, glowing and brightening the room. I stared in awe. Rainbow dewdrops clung to my skin.

When Derrick had made things happen, the air had moved. Wind blew indoors, bringing with it the scent of faraway places. When Missy had done bad things, water pipes broke, moisture wicked away from my mouth, and my eyes stung like they were dry. The times I thought I'd made magic happen, the air shimmered and waivered. Electric currents prickled under my skin.

This man's magic was more like mine than Missy or Derrick's. The hairs on my arms rose with static. The air felt charged, like before an electrical storm.

Shadows danced over the curtains from outside. Birds swarmed on the other side of the window. I caught a glimpse of one through a gap in the curtains. Black wings. Ravens.

My mom hated ravens. I didn't like them much either after Oregon Country Fair. Although, it was hard to remember what had happened at the fair either time I'd gone. Why were ravens here?

The man waved his wand at me. Rainbows rippled like ribbons over me, cool and refreshing. The sensation reminded me of showering on a hot day, only they didn't soak my clothes.

"How did I do this if magic isn't real?" the man asked.

"Sleight of hand. Stage magic. Illusions." I said the words I knew I was supposed to say. All the while, my heart thundered in my chest. For the first time in months, I felt alive. I felt hope.

I felt magic.

My head was clearer than it had felt in months. The fog in my brain lifted. At least some of it did.

He tapped the wand against his knee, more rainbow beads splattering into the puddle on the floor between us. "Is that what you believe, or what people tell you to believe?"

I wanted to believe magic was real, but if I did, that meant I couldn't deny my part in Missy's and Derrick's deaths. It had been months since I'd thought this much about them. The weight of what I'd done came crashing down on me. The momentary high of magic was gone.

"What did you do to me?" I asked. "With the rainbows, I mean."

"I have cleansed your system of potions and wards. You still have human-crafted medications in your system. I want to see if they're strong enough to keep you from performing magic."

"I don't want to hurt anyone," I whispered.

"That means you aren't completely evil." His words sounded reassuring, but his tone lacked any emotion to indicate he actually cared.

"I'm not evil," I said.

"Yes, yes. That's what they all say." He waved the wand back and forth in the air. The rainbow rippled and flowed in patterns, twisting like a ribbon before it fell to the floor. "Do you know why I can do this?"

"You have some kind of power. You're a witch."

"The correct term is Witchkin, but never mind that. You won't remember it later anyway." He shook the wand, and the rainbow sputtered out. Red and orange droplets speckled the bookcase, clinging to the books. Yellow and green dewdrops fell onto the floor. Blue beads rolled across the leg of his pants and splattered into the rainbow puddle. A single purple bead clung to the white petal of the orchid on the seat. The droplet must have been heavy. It weighed down the head of the orchid, pulling at the white petal.

He went on. "The reason I can do this is I've been trained. I know how to use magic without endangering the lives of others or summoning Fae. You haven't learned how to do that."

I sat forward. "What do I need to do to learn? There's a school? Right?" I tried to remember the name. "Wombat's? Womby's?" Yes, I thought that was the name.

"There are several schools, but it would be best for you not to go there."

"Why? I'm a good student."

"As soon as other Witchkin know about you, it's only a matter of time before someone kills you for who you are. For what you are. You are no ordinary Witchkin." He stared at me so intently it felt as though he could see into me and read my soul.

"What do you mean? What am I?" I whispered. I'd dreamed of this moment my entire life.

"You're descended from the wickedest sorceress in all recorded history." His expression communicated bored indifference. "Nothing you need to concern yourself with if we succeed in hiding your magic."

"My mom isn't evil."

His tone was patronizing. "Of course not."

I vaguely remembered the time my mom had caught Missy and me going through her closet and we'd found Lucifer's adoption paper—only my sister had insisted it hadn't been the cat's paper. Missy had said the old woman at the fair told her I was descended from a wicked witch and she wasn't. At homecoming, she'd said I was adopted. A shiver ran through me.

Before I had enough time for this to sink in, the man went on. "As if your parentage isn't enough to prejudice the Witchkin world against you, your magical mishaps won't do you any favors. Believe it or not, I'm trying to do you a favor by intervening."

"So, you're saying the school wouldn't want me because of the accidents?" I swallowed. "Because I . . . killed Missy and Derrick?"

"Indeed, but rest assured, they won't find out about that. I've made sure of it. If I hadn't, *everyone* would have found out about you by now." He waved me off dismissively. "In any case, you didn't kill that boy. He's still alive somewhere in the Unseen Realm. He'll be found and brought to the school to be trained properly. His magic is perfectly ordinary. Nothing we can't handle."

"Derrick is alive? Really?"

"My life would be so much easier if he wasn't. He'll probably want to tell everyone all about you." He tapped his chin with a long slender finger, staring off into the distance. "I'll have to solve that problem when I come to it."

All I could think of was Derrick now. The man's words were as sweet and tempting as candy. I wanted to believe he was telling the truth—they weren't the hollow, chocolate Easter bunnies that tempted children with false promises. My mom had always warned me not to trust people who said they could perform magic. He might be like the witch who had lured Missy away. That woman had wanted to kidnap my sister. She had told Missy she would take her to another world where she would be safe.

My mom had called that witch a liar, but the old woman had been right about me. Missy could have stayed with her and remained safe. That witch had tried to rescue her.

Guilt churned inside me. All along the witch had been right. Why hadn't I listened and stayed away from magic and kept my distance from my sister? If I had, she would have been alive.

Unless. . . . The man had said Derrick was alive, but he'd made no mention of my sister.

"And Missy?" I prompted. "Is she all right?"

"No. She's quite dead."

My shoulders sagged in defeat. If he was going to try to kidnap me and take me to a magical world, the least he could do was tell me everything I wanted to hear.

"Are you sure she isn't *somewhere* in your magic world?"

"I'm sorry. My mistake. She's somewhere over the rainbow." He raised an eyebrow at me, his tone crabby. "Do you want me to lie to you and pretend she's alive to make you feel better? While I'm at it, why don't I say she's reformed and changed her villainous ways? We lifted the evil curse of teenage hormones, paranoia and a bad attitude, and she'll no longer use magic to try to harm anyone ever again."

Tears filled my eyes. Whatever he was, there was no way he was a psychologist. Besides the fact that he could do magic, he was way too mean.

He cleared his throat. "Try to look on the bright side. You don't need to *completely* blame yourself for the tornado. You can blame Derrick. He was the wind sprite, not you." That actually made sense. "He was as much responsible—or I should say—irresponsible as you."

My hurt sank into the pit of my stomach, compressing and solidifying into anger. It had been months since I'd felt strongly about anything. I was aware of the way my blood pulsed in my veins. Fury grounded me in reality.

"Why are you here?" I asked. "What do you really want from me?"

"Consider this a scientific experiment. Let's see if you can perform magic. If you can't, then I'll permit you to stay in the Morty realm so long as you remain medicated. I'll leave and be out of your life forever."

"What if I can? Will you take me to your school? The magic school?"

"I already told you, no. Don't you listen?" He tsked. "Of course not, you're a teenager."

"What do I get out of it if I can do magic?" I asked.

"You ask too many questions. Let's see if it's even possible first." He waved a hand at me. He stared expectantly.

I suspected I was supposed to do something impressive.

"I don't actually know how to be a witch. It was always by accident before." I wrung the hem of my sweater in my hands. "Sometimes I wasn't even sure I was the one making it happen."

"It happens I know what your affinity is, so I might be able to get you started." He took my hands and placed them palms up on my lap.

"What's an affinity?"

"It's the ingredient that fuels your magic. Thinks of it like petrol for an automobile."

"You mean gasoline? I'm not a machine. How does my magic work? What's my affinity?" This all was too much to take in at once. My brain remained sharper than before his rainbow spell, but the brain fog hadn't completely cleared.

He touched the tip of his wand to my open palm. The twisted wood looked smooth and polished, but it felt rough.

Nothing happened.

"Do you feel anything?" he asked.

"Maybe a splinter?"

"My wand doesn't have splinters." He tapped his chin with a finger. "Insufficient data. You need to try harder. Concentrate on the wand."

Only professional witches had wands. This was like a fantasy novel. "Eleven inches, made of holly, with a phoenix feather core," I said, thinking myself clever and witty. Not everyone could remember such important trivia from the *Harry Potter* series.

His nose wrinkled up. "What are you going on about? How can any stick of wood have a feather in the center? This isn't compressed particle board. This is a *wand*. You have heard of wands before, haven't you? Or has your guardian kept you in complete ignorance?"

I rolled my eyes. Derrick would have understood the reference. The void of depression didn't weigh me down when I thought about him now. I felt hope. I would get to see him again. I just had to show this man I could do simple, ordinary magic like Derrick. Non-dangerous magic. I would convince him to take me to his magical school.

He poked my hand with the wand again. The splinter scraped against my flesh.

"Ow!" I drew my hand away. "This isn't how it works," I said. "I was always touching Derrick when I made magic happen. We didn't use wands."

His scowl deepened. "Of course, you wouldn't. If you had, your magic might not have been as unfocused." The man balanced the wand on his knee. He poked the tip of his finger against my palm. His touch was cold like he'd been outside for a long time.

I still didn't feel anything. He shifted on the arm of the chair, almost bumping the orchid, but his wand remained perfectly balanced on his knee. Reluctantly he placed his hands on mine. My palms tingled.

"Maybe I feel something, but not like I did with Derrick." I thought of the last time we'd been together, when we'd kissed. My cheeks flushed with heat. When we'd been juggling and he'd touched my hands, I'd tingled inside. This man had walked into the room and almost caught us using magic. That one time we'd been drawing together, Derrick had placed his hand on mine and electricity had raced back and forth under my skin. When the origami cranes had rained down on us as we danced at homecoming, I'd smelled ozone like before a lightning storm.

"I never made magic happen when he wasn't around," I said.

"You need that boy to inspire magical feelings in you?" He picked up his wand.

Hope alighted in my heart. "You could bring him here . . . to me. Then I could show you magic."

He waved his wand in the air. Clusters of white light sparkled between us, popping and dying away like miniature starbursts. "You take after your mother. Already you're a manipulative little witch."

I smiled. I didn't even care that he had insulted my mom or me. All I could think about was the possibility of seeing Derrick.

He touched the wand to my temple. "Close your eyes and imagine his face in your mind. Can you see him clearly?"

"This will help you bring him here?" I asked.

He didn't answer. Maybe he was concentrating.

I visualized Derrick's blue eyes, sparkling just as brightly and vividly as his hair. His face was smooth. He smiled with his entire heart, filling a room with sunshine and making his eyes crinkle up. I clasped my hands in front of me, hardly able to contain my excitement as I thought about seeing him again.

"Open your eyes."

I did so. I found myself staring into Derrick's face. He sat perched on the arm of the chair, dressed in a suit that hugged his body as though the fabric had been tailored to fit him. Derrick never wore expensive, fitted clothes, nor would he have settled for such boring colors. He would have been dressed in mismatched stripes and checks like he usually did.

I might have been on three different medications and too drugged for critical thinking skills, but this was a no brainer. This was still the man, only he wore Derrick's face.

I looked him up and down and crossed my arms. "I'm not twelve. You can't fool me."

He muttered something under his breath, waving the wand in a circle around me. The air shimmered as though I was gazing through the rising heat above a radiator on a cold day. My suspicions melted away. He set the wand across his knee again and took my hands in his. I gazed at Derrick as adoringly as I had at the Olive Garden on the night of homecoming. I couldn't stop smiling.

His face was an expressionless calm, not the optimistic smile I was used to. Even as drugged out and enchanted as I was, I knew something wasn't right. I took his lack of smile to be a bad sign.

"You're mad at me?" I asked. "You blame me?"

He didn't answer. He nodded down to my hands in his. I didn't know what he was saying with the gesture. His hands were cool against mine.

I stood up, leaning in closer to examine the vivid azure of his eyes. My shoe slipped in the rainbow puddle, and I skidded forward. He grabbed my arm, his grip firm. He didn't laugh and joke about me being too clumsy to throw bowling pins at his head while juggling like he normally would have. The somberness to his face was unsettling.

I lifted a hand to his cheek and felt the smooth line of his jaw. He frowned. His expression remained cold, nothing of Derrick, and yet, I wanted it to be him so badly it didn't matter. Tears spilled down my cheeks. I threw my arms around his neck and embraced him. The wand rolled off his knee onto the cushions of the seat.

"No hugging." His voice wasn't right. It was the same British accent of the man. The droning monotone jarred with the face I'd come to adore.

It didn't matter. My eyes had seen Derrick's face, and my heart was too overcome with emotion to care. I squeezed him tighter.

"Bloody hell. Let go of me." He tried to push me away. He bumped the plant on the chair, toppling it onto its side and knocking it to the floor. The ceramic pot shattered, shards scattering across the rainbow puddle.

I clutched him more tightly, digging my fingers into the jacket. "I'll never let you go. Please, tell me we can be together. I'll go to clown school with you. Or art school. Or magic school. It doesn't matter." I started to sob, the texture of the jacket rough against my cheeks. I would give anything for this to be real. Part of me knew it wasn't, I just didn't want to listen to that little voice whispering the truth.

He grappled with my hands, trying to pry my fingers off him.

"I'm sorry," I said. "Please forgive me."

He sighed and patted my back, as if in resignation. "Fine. I forgive you. Now stop strangling me."

I loosened my grip from around his neck. I leaned my head against his chest, sniffling. He patted my shoulder. "Do you feel any magic right now? As we, ahem, touch?"

"I don't know."

Someone knocked on the door. He waved a hand and it ceased.

I couldn't tell if I felt magic or not. My stomach cramped, but that might have been anxiety. More than anything, I just felt sad. I stared into his face again. If this was Derrick, my heart shouldn't have felt like it was breaking. I should have been happy, yet worry gnawed at my belly.

Was this Derrick or was it not him? I was so confused. Reality kept shifting around me. I believed he was Derrick, and then I didn't believe he was Derrick.

I leaned in closer. He held me back by the shoulders. "Absolutely not. No kissing. I asked for a small demonstration, not an explosion."

I hadn't been about to kiss him. Well, maybe I had. My gaze rested on his unhappy mouth. I wanted him to smile. My chest burned with yearning. My pulse throbbed hot inside me.

He gently eased me away and sat me in the chair. Sitting this close to him without touching was torment. He brushed potting soil off the seat of the chair and made himself comfortable. He took out a small notebook from his breast pocket, the book expanding to the size of my sketchpad. He made a flourish with his wrist and removed a fluffy ostrich quill from the air and began to write. I watched in fascination.

He muttered to himself. "Theory one: due to scientific advances, the human medications available in this day and age have side effects that counteract magical abilities. Theory two: she has burnt out her magic through trauma. Further research needs to be done to determine the plausibility of either scenario. Theory three. . . ." He fell into silence, but continued to write. Afterward, he closed the book and pushed it back inside his breast pocket. It shrank to fit. His quill disappeared. "There's a chance you might lead a normal life without any kind of magical intervention."

"I don't need normal," I said. "I want to be with you. At the magic school."

I would have everything I'd ever hoped for if I went there with him. I would be with other witches. I could have love and magic. Everything would be all right.

His eyes narrowed, the intensity something I wasn't used to seeing on Derrick's usually cheerful face. He took my hands in his. "I want you to listen, and listen carefully. You aren't going to a magic school. Your presence there would endanger everyone around you. You aren't like the other children. Your powers—your affinity—isn't something Witchkin understand how to control. Do you *want* to hurt people?"

My eyes went wide. I shook my head.

"Do you want to kiss boys and make them die?" His words came out sharp like an accusation.

"No." I couldn't meet his eye. I stared at the rainbow puddle. It was smaller now. The potted orchid lay in the center. It had grown, tendrils of roots stretching into the liquid. They wiggled and writhed. A shoot had coiled up the leg of the chair. Another snaked over Derrick's—no, the man's—feet. I looked up into his face, confused about who I was talking to again.

"Do you want houses to drop onto other girls too?" he asked.

"You said I didn't do that." Had he said that? Or was it the man who had said that? The conversation mushed together in my head. I stared at his hands holding mine.

Something fluttered in my belly. He raised an eyebrow. Could he feel it too? Was that magic?

"Bloody hell. That's your affinity. You still have magic left in you." He looked crabbier than ever.

"Huh?" I said. I still didn't understand what my affinity was.

Another knock rapped on the door. This time it was more insistent. He frowned and waved his hand at the door. The knocking ceased.

"There are two options for you: report you to the Witchkin Council, who will likely bicker amongst themselves about what to do with you until someone leaks to the Fae they have the daughter of the wickedest witch of all time—"

"Stop saying that about my mom!" She wasn't wicked or dangerous. She made me healthy smoothies and bought me a "Spock rules. Kirk drools" sticker for my window. He didn't know what he was talking about.

He went on, ignoring me. "It's only a matter of time before one of the major houses of Fae remove you from the care of the Witchkin. Most likely the Raven Court will claim you as a lost soul."

The Raven Court. I thought back to Oregon Country Fair. I remembered the women with dresses made of feathers. My mom had accused one of stealing Missy. She'd talked about collecting lost souls. More memories solidified in my mind. Hunter had been snatched for using magic.

"If the Raven Queen claims you, they'll make you their slave.

They'll torture you for their amusement. If you go to them willingly and they think you have potential, they may allow you to live so that they can teach you soul sucking spells and succubus magic. That way you can torture people for them. You will become exactly what everyone feared, and all of Witchkin kind will say, 'The bad apple doesn't fall far from the tree,' and they will wish they had killed you instead."

The door rattled as someone tried to open it. Voices murmured on the other side. I thought I heard my mom, but I wasn't sure.

"Listen to me," he said, drawing my attention. "The best-case scenario: before any royal house of Fae discovers you and abducts you, a Witchkin drains you of your powers in the hope you will be able to lead a normal human life without magical complications. You'll live happily ever after. No magic for you. Ever. The end."

The idea of a world without magic sounded horrible. It sank me into the same kind of gloom I had felt when my mom had burned my witch books and toys. The idea of being imprisoned and forced to hurt people didn't sound appealing either.

Yet these two paths were my possible fates. I didn't want him to drain me, but maybe he was right. I had to let a trained professional remove my magic.

I drew in a breath and focused my thoughts. "That's what you're here for. Not to rescue me and bring me to your world. You intend to drain me of my powers."

He leaned back in his chair, releasing my hands. "I'm here to give you a choice, Miss Lawrence. Which will it be: come with me to the Raven Queen and learn black magic, or allow me to ensure you remain mortal and inconsequential to the world of Witchkin and Fae?"

CHAPTER TWENTY-TWO
Son of a Witch

This had to be a test. When it came to math and English, I excelled at tests. But those hadn't been morality tests. The stakes hadn't been torture. The temptation to choose magic was greater than my mom's double fudge brownie bars.

Maybe I had to show him I was a good and moral person. If I did, he would see I wasn't dangerous or wicked like Missy. Would he allow me to see Derrick again if I did?

"I'll make the right decision," I said, rolling my eyes. "I won't use black magic. Remove my powers."

He waved his hand in the air, muttering under his breath. I didn't feel the tingle of magic like when he'd used his wand. "Look into my eyes. This is a face you trust, correct? Someone you'll listen to?"

I tried not to look into Derrick's eyes, but I felt compelled to do so. The door rattled. He held me with his gaze.

"You will never attempt to use magic," he said. He waved a hand in front of me. "Magic isn't real."

I felt myself slipping under his spell. He sandwiched one of my hands between his. I watched him stroke my wrist, dully, as if my body was a thousand miles away. My flesh tingled where his skin met mine. It felt nice, comforting. I smiled dopily.

The spinning bundle of nervous energy in my core flared and slowly ebbed away. I leaned back in the chair, my eyes growing heavy. His hands were hot against mine. Electricity pulsed between his fingers. I waited for him to say I passed the test and he would let me keep my magic.

He didn't.

"You will forget about seeing me. The pain and guilt you've been feeling over Missy and Derrick will melt away."

"Melt away," I repeated.

I was melting like Hunter had when the Fae had drained away his powers and turned him into vapor. The sensation was icky and wrong. I tried to yank my hand away, but my muscles were too tired. I imagined pulling back, the life force flowing from me into him reversing directions. Where his hands met mine, the air wavered. Red pulses of light flickered under my skin and up my arm. I felt stronger.

"Stop fighting me. There is no such thing as magic," he said through clenched teeth. Derrick's face contorted, as if in pain.

My will returned. "Right. These are not the droids you're looking for."

He tilted his head to the side. He was the one who looked addled now. "Pardon me? Droids?"

I took it he'd never seen *Star Wars*. What adult his age hadn't seen *Star Wars*? I was convinced. He had to be evil.

Something snapped inside me. Why did I believe anything he said? Why did I have to take his word that *I* was going to become evil? I hadn't believed him when he told me my mom was evil.

He blinked, looking tired.

The door burst open. There stood my mom, emerald leaves clinging to her red hair. Her skin glowed green. Dust motes sparkled around her. She looked like some kind of fairy sprite.

"Get your filthy hands off my daughter," she said.

CHAPTER TWENTY-THREE
Witchy McWitchface

Mom stood in the doorway, her eyes wild. The receptionist and a nurse stood behind her, their expressions frightened.

"We had no idea there was someone else in there," the nurse began.

"Get away from my daughter," Mom said.

The man with Derrick's face yanked his hand back from mine. "Calm yourself. There's no need to make a fuss and involve the Morties. The last thing I have time to do is erase the memories of an entire medical building."

Mom stepped into the room, the small space filling with the aroma of basil and thyme. The fragrance reminded me of her garden. The door slammed closed behind her, shutting the nurse and receptionist out.

"Clarissa, back away from him," Mom said. "That isn't Derrick."

I tried to scoot back, but my right foot was stuck. A vine had woven through the laces of my shoe. I wiggled my foot out, but another shoot laced around my other ankle. I tore it off. Something clung to my pants.

"I am a trained professional," he said. He stood but swayed and looked as though he might fall over. The shoots from the fallen orchid had coiled up his legs and tangled across his feet. He grimaced and sat down on the arm of the chair.

Mom strode forward, each clomp leaving mud from her gardening boots on the floor. Plants sprouted from each cluster of dirt, snaking over the floor toward him. I stared transfixed. This was my mom? She was *magic*? Some kind of plant witch?

What a hypocrite! She was a witch. And a liar. I knew one thing for certain. She wasn't evil like he'd claimed.

"Clarissa, get back," Mom said. Power radiated from her in waves.

I tried pulling my feet harder. My cotton socks tore. I yanked my feet free of my socks and drew them up to my chest. I scooted onto the back of the chair. Mom raised her hand toward the corner of the room. Behind me a jungle of vines exploded from the philodendron. New leaves sprouted from snaking creepers. It didn't look very inviting to walk across.

"Mrs. Lawrence, we both want what's in the best interest for Clarissa," the man with Derrick's face said.

"No, you don't. You're just like other Witchkin. You want what's best for you."

I pushed away a creeper snaking up the back of the chair.

"I was the one who brought Clarissa to you," he said. "I brought her to you because I knew you would protect her even if you figured out who she was. I'm on your side."

"Don't try to hypnotize me with your mind games. I know who brought her. It was an old woman from the council." Mom stepped forward, but stopped at the edge of plants.

Someone had brought her to me? Did that mean she wasn't my mom?

"Indeed, a toothless old hag," he said. "I disguised myself. It was necessary to be discreet." More vines twisted up his legs, holding him in place. He remained calm, unconcerned. "I have no intention of hurting Clarissa. I'm here to ensure she doesn't harm herself or others. After the incident with Missy, I would think you might understand how dangerous—"

"Incident? Don't talk to me about Missy! It was one of you from the Unseen Realm who tried to steal her away in the first place. One of you who taught her dark magic. I won't let you take Clarissa from me too." Her gaze flickered to the raven fluttering against the window. "I know who you really are. You're one of the Raven Queen's servants."

Raven Queen? Didn't he say she was the one who would force me into slavery and make me do evil magic? He didn't deny the accusation. Now I wondered about his true intentions.

Mom raised her hands. He didn't flinch when the plants in the office burst through the ceramic pots and shot out at him, but I did. I fell onto the seat of the chair, covering my face with my arms.

His expression was more annoyed than afraid. He brushed potting soil off his shoulder. "I have no intention of taking Clarissa from you. The three of us can sit down and talk this out. I'm certain you'll understand my solution is in the best interests of everyone involved." He smiled, a hollow imitation of one of Derrick's earnest smiles. The air shimmered. He was too unconcerned, too confident. Was he working magic on my mom?

"He wants to drain me of magic," I said.

Her eyes widened, and she batted the sparkles in the air away from her face. "Steal your powers is more like it. Suck your soul away and turn you into a vegetable." She gestured for me to move back. "Clarissa, get off that chair and stand behind me."

"How? There are plants everywhere. They'll get me."

"Get over here this instant, young lady." She pointed to the pristine section of floor beside her like she used to when Missy and I were kids and we wandered too far from her in the grocery store.

I scooted onto the back of the chair and eased onto the floor. The path between my chair and the couch would have been the most direct, but too many plants writhed between us. I shuffled around the thickest patch of plants, backtracking. That put me closer to the man. Vines curled around me, and I kicked at them as I walked. I didn't want to walk in front of his chair where he could grab me.

"For the record, I'm not going to turn her into a vegetable." He flicked a speck of dirt off his pants. "Though, with your affinity, I should think you would enjoy having a daughter more closely related to plants if I did."

Mom's brow furrowed. "You would say such a thing. I'm not going to let you hurt my baby."

He went on, airily, sounding bored. "In any case, the council only turns criminals into vegetables. She's just a child, and I'm not on the council." He brushed another speck of dirt off his jacket. "I don't follow their rules. I follow my own."

Mom looked from me kicking away plants to him.

His words reminded me of a stage magician's misdirection. My training with illusions and sleight of hand had taught me to pay attention to details the average person ignored. I knew where to look. Mom watched him smooth dirt off his clothes. It was the other hand reaching behind him that alerted me he was about to do something. He patted the cushions of the chair, trying to find his wand without making it obvious what he was doing.

I'd seen him use magic without his wand, but it had been smaller, less showy. It had been less powerful.

As I scooted around the chair, I spotted it. It had fallen between the cushions.

"Mom, he has a—"

I didn't have time to finish my sentence. His fingers inched toward it. I dove. I bowled him back into the chair in my scramble to snatch it up. The wand fell deeper between the cushions. I shoved my hand down into the crevice. He had me around the waist, pushing me away from the chair, but my fingers closed around it. He shoved me off him.

"Clarissa, get away from him! He's dangerous!" Mom lunged forward again, but she was stopped by the growing carpet of plants.

I tried to wrench away, but the vines held my feet in place. I no longer wore shoes or socks to wiggle out of. The man loomed over me. He pinned my right arm to my side, but my other hand was free. Not that it did me a lot of good. My right hand was the one that held the wand. I could feel it in my palm, but I couldn't see it.

He let go of me in an attempt to grab it. I slipped it down the sleeve of my sweater and continued to move my hand around up high and then down low to distract him. The wand slid down into the waistband of my pants. He snatched up my wrist. Had the circumstances been different, I would have laughed at the bewildered expression on his face when he realized there was nothing there.

My mom kept yelling at me to get away, but I had this down. I had his wand. I was the one with the power.

While he was distracted, I reached into the waistband of my pants and snatched up the one thing that would save me. I held up the stick and jabbed it into his side. He grunted.

He looked down. His eyebrow lifted.

It was a . . . pencil.

"No freakin' way." Where was the wand? I hadn't even stabbed him with the pointy end of the pencil.

He chuckled, the sound low and ominous. He ripped the pencil from my hand and tossed it onto the carpet of greenery. Why hadn't I listened to my mom? I should have run.

He grabbed me by the shoulders, holding me there. I tried to twist away, but the plants didn't give me much room for movement.

Neither did he. Green stems slithered across his chest like snakes. I tore the vines from my arms. More wove around our waists, circling us and binding us together.

Mom held her hands up, coils of plants in her palms. "Release my daughter and agree to leave us alone, and I'll let you go."

A thick stem twisted up my leg. An orchid blossomed next to my thigh. Even if he let me go, the plants wouldn't.

"Fine. I'll let her go," he said. "Call off your garden spell. All will be forgiven."

I didn't trust that shifty look in his eyes. Apparently, my mother didn't either. "Promise me. Bind your intentions to your words with spell craft."

Spell craft? What a great idea! I admired my mom's quick thinking. If only I'd known we had so much in common. She could have taught me so much.

"I don't need to promise anything." The smile he wore on Derrick's face made me shiver. Never had I imagined my best friend could ever look so cold. "Your plant magic is simple. Untrained. Unfocused. You don't even have a wand. The vegetation in this room would just as soon smother Clarissa as me. You need to release us both. At the same time."

From her worried expression, I realized he was right. Mom clenched and unclenched her fists. She paced her little section of floor that wasn't covered in plants.

A leaf tickled across my neck. I tore it away. Derrick's doppelganger remained motionless. He made no attempt to remove the vines circling his throat. He was too confident.

The plants hugged me tighter. They squished me closer to the man. He loomed over me, taller than Derrick, not that I'd ever imagined anyone out there could be taller than he was at six foot one. It was uber awkward pressed this close to a stranger, an adult man wearing my friend's face. Even that night in my room when I'd been alone with Derrick, it hadn't been as intimate as this. Not with the way Derrick kept arching his body away from me, trying to hide his erection. The only moment I'd been close to him, truly close, was when we'd kissed.

My belly gave a little flutter at the memory.

The man's spine went rigid. He leaned away from me. His eyes left my mother and flickered to me. I hadn't noticed before how he'd managed to twist his torso away from mine. My leg touched his leg, and his hands remained on my shoulders, not so much holding me close, but holding me away from him.

Warmth fluttered under my skin, radiating across my arms. My belly kept flip-flopping. The air shimmered. Magic was happening. I didn't know if it was his or mine.

"Mom, please do something," I said. I pushed away tendrils creeping into my hair.

"It's her magic." He shifted a hand, attempting to move it away, but he couldn't. Shoots held him in place. "She's out of control. Having no training, she might kill herself if she explodes again. If you cared for this child at all, you'd call off your plants and allow me to help her."

The place where he touched my shoulders prickled. I was hyperaware of his leg pressed against mine, growing warmer by the second.

Mom bit her lip. "Clarissa, I need you to do something for me. I want you to imagine all the anger and frustration you've been feeling collect in the pit of your stomach. All the grief and joy and everything. Send it there."

Not so difficult. My belly was already churning.

"Don't do it," he said to me. "She's going to make you do something bad." His exterior of calm faded, and for the first time since hearing him speak I heard agitation in his tone. "We don't want anyone to get hurt. I'm trying to help you. You have to believe me."

By draining me.

"Look into my eyes," he said.

The air around his face sparkled. My breath caught in my throat. Something about him felt more like . . . Derrick. I smiled.

"He isn't Derrick," Mom said. "You know that, right?"

I did. Even so, I couldn't stop grinning. I was mesmerized by his blue eyes.

"Would Derrick have ever tried to use you as a human shield?" Mom asked. "Would he put you in harm's way? Keep focusing on the energy inside you."

"Don't listen to her. Does a face like this lie?" He smiled, hopeful, eyebrows raised. It was a poor imitation of Derrick's expression and yet, it was better than no Derrick at all.

I leaned closer to him. He tried to hold me back.

Mom commanded, "Imagine all that energy tumbling around in your belly traveling up your spine and into your arm. Let it collect in your hand."

I didn't know which hand. A knot of energy tingled between my shoulder blades, first swaying to my right shoulder and then the left.

"Push it into him. Take that energy and send it—"

"You're teaching her to harm people with magic." His voice rose. "Once she starts, she won't be able to stop."

I closed my eyes. I couldn't look at Derrick's face.

"Dark magic is forbidden," he said. "I'll report you to the Witchkin Counsel. This is a crime punishable by—"

I punched him in the stomach, sending the energy out my hand. He doubled over and let go of my shoulders. He bonked his nose against my forehead.

I stumbled backward. The plants that had been holding me shrank away.

I was still close enough to kick him. I didn't know much about martial arts, but I'd seen the *Karate Kid* five times. I kicked him as high as I could, which happened to be his crotch. If I was going to be bad, I might as well be very bad.

I must have missed because my foot met air.

"That's enough, young lady. Back away." Mom placed a hand on my shoulder, trying to pull me back.

I punched at his face, or where his face should have been. My fist didn't make contact. His head parted like a cloud of smoke. His body evaporated into swirls of twisting vapor, growing black. I kept punching and kicking at the mist. Fighting gave me energy. It made me feel like I was high. Now I knew what *Buffy the Vampire Slayer* felt like.

"I did magic! On purpose!" I said. "Not accidentally."

"That's right, honey. You did it." Mom looked weary.

"Teamwork!" I held up my hand to high-five my mom.

I jumped, hearing a male voice speak.

"Fine. Have it your way." The reedy voice echoed from somewhere far away. "So long as you continue to use magic, Fae and Witchkin alike will spot you for what you are and hunt you down." He went on in his slow British drawl. "Don't say I didn't try to warn you."

I whirled, but the man wasn't there.

Mom anxiously glanced around. "He'll be back and so will others." She sat me down on Dr. Bach's couch, hugging me to her side.

The plants slowly receded from our feet and back toward the potted plants. The greenery that had spread from the clumps of dirt shriveled up. All that remained were caked clumps of soil.

Tears ran down Mom's cheeks. "He was a bad man. A liar. He tried to trick you into letting him drain you, and he would have succeeded if I hadn't arrived."

"How did you know what he was going to do?" I asked. She had an uncanny ability to stop my magical exploits, whether it was Missy and me in the basement, or Derrick and me at the kitchen table.

She nodded to an orchid on the floor. "Witches have familiars. Most of mine are plants." The flower was brown and withered. Air roots felt along the floor where the rainbow puddle had been. I felt bad for the plant. It looked like it was dying.

"So you're admitting it. You're a witch," I said.

"I'm Witchkin. I'm descended from humans and fairies. I try not to use magic in the Morty Realm. It isn't allowed, so when I do, I have to keep it hidden. If I don't, Fae will find me and collect me. That's why you can't use magic either. They'll collect you as a lost soul. It would be charitable if all they wanted was to drain you to gain your powers. But they won't stop there. They'll steal away your soul and leave you as a vegetable at best. At worst, they'll devour your body as well. That's if they don't decide to make you into one of them."

I tried to swallow the sour taste in my mouth when I thought of Hunter and what the Fae had done to him—what the school district psychologist had almost done to me. I nodded. "That man said I'm different from the other children. I can't go to their special school. My magic is too dangerous."

"That might have been the only true thing he said." She sandwiched my hands in hers. "That's why you can't do magic ever again."

Her words sank into me, heavy and full of doom. "What? No! All my life you told me magic wasn't real, and it was bad, but it isn't. I just saved us with magic. You can't take this away from me."

"Can't you see all the bad things magic has done?" She waved a hand at the window where the birds fluttered against the glass pane.

Black feathered wings blocked out the sun. "Your magic is like a beacon to them. It will be hard enough getting you out of here without drawing attention. They'll come for you again if you use powerful spells."

They would come for me and make me hurt people. "They'll make me like Missy."

She hesitated. "Missy wasn't bad. She was just. . . ." She patted my back. "She wanted to be normal and fit in. She would have been fine living in this world, but she tasted black magic at that fair. She became jealous of your powers. I wish I'd realized that was what had happened sooner. I was trying to protect both of you." She rummaged through her purse and found a tissue. She dabbed at her eyes and blew her nose.

I leaned my head against her shoulder. I loved my sister. Or I loved the person she once had been. If I could have gone back and changed time, I would have never gone to Oregon Country Fair.

"Those are my two choices then?" I asked. "Either become evil and join the bad guys, or become a brain-dead vegetable in order to be a good person?"

Mom's eyes were rimmed with dark circles. "Life is like a forked path through a field. There's the path to the right and the path to the left. People think there are only two paths, but there are always more than two choices. Sometimes we just have to pave our own path through the field. The grass might be high. There might be a bees' nest, a wild dog, or a dip we don't see. The unknown is scary, and we might get hurt. We also might discover butterflies and wildflowers when we take the route no one else has paved for us. You can make another choice."

She rummaged through her purse. "I have another path for you." She removed her planner, wallet, and the nubs of white candles and set them on the couch next to her. Her car keys jingled as she searched the purse. She had enough stuff in there to make Mary Poppins jealous. Finally, she pulled out a glass canning jar filled with some kind of green slush and handed it to me.

"This is a kale and strawberry smoothie. It's made with organic produce from our yard," she said.

"Gee, thanks, Mom." Sustainable living and eating organic were more of her path than mine.

"It's a special smoothie," she said.

"Like Uncle Trevor's special brownies?"

"Yes, except my special food doesn't contain marijuana. It has a potion to help reduce your magical powers. You're old enough to know I've been making this potion for you since you were ten. I only break out the recipe when I feel the magic in you building. If you don't want it, I won't make you drink it, but if you don't, you're going to have to figure out another solution, a different path. You can't play with fire and not expect to get burned."

I took the jar from her. "If I drink this, I won't be able to hurt people?"

"I don't think so. Not with the medications you're on." Her purse rattled as she dug out two bottles. "This potion will cleanse your affinity and help you forget that you used magic today. You'll be able to forget what that man tried to do to you."

I unscrewed the top of the jar. Kale sooo wasn't my favorite. She handed me a pill from each pharmaceutical container, a white one and a pink one. The surrealism of the moment reminded me of *Alice in Wonderland*.

"I already took my pills this morning," I said.

"Do you still feel like you're on prescription medications?"

I thought about it. No, my head was clear. I didn't move like a sloth.

"I think your magic was so powerful it pushed the medications out of your system. Either that or the Witchkin's magic did it."

I needed medications to prevent my magic, but magic could prevent my medication from working. It sounded like a paradox.

I stared at the white pill and the pink one. "I don't like how I feel on medications."

"I don't blame you." She rubbed my shoulder. "We can ween you off the medications slowly, but we need to get your magic under control first."

I wasn't going to be like Missy. I wasn't going to be wicked and hurt people. I took the pills and chugged the smoothie. It was even more vile than her usual healthy shakes.

"Close your eyes, take a deep breath, and repeat after me," Mom said. "There's no such thing as magic."

I grimaced. "That isn't true."

"I know, but we need to undo today. I'm trying to help you."

Everyone was *trying* to help me. But I supposed she was right. If I was to hide in plain sight and blend in like everyone else, I couldn't use magic. I couldn't believe in magic.

I closed my eyes. "There's no such thing as magic."

"Say it again." She took the empty canning car from my hands.

"I don't believe in magic. There's no such thing as witchcraft," I said.

A wave of dizziness passed over me. The air no longer smelled like garden herbs, but artificial air freshener and Dr. Bach's old man cologne. Something about the lighting was different too.

"There is no such thing as Fae or Witchkin," I said.

"What's that?" a man's creaky voice asked.

I opened my eyes. Dr. Bach watched me from his chair in front of his desk. Cheery sunlight spilled in from the window. A new white orchid sat on his desk behind him. It was the one my mom had potted for him. Only, I would have sworn that one had red spots. This one was dotted with yellow.

Dr. Bach said, "Can you repeat that for me?" His thin shoulders hunched forward as he wrote in my folder. His weathered face smiled pleasantly, but a crease divided his forehead in half. "I didn't quite catch that word."

Lightheadedness washed over me. I didn't know where I was or what I was doing. A moment ago I had been doing something. I'd lost my train of thought.

"Did you say Witchkin? What's that?" Dr. Bach asked.

"I didn't say Witchkin. You must have misheard me. Witches. I must have said witches." But there was something about the word *Witchkin* that unsettled me. I had heard it before. Maybe I'd heard Derrick use it. *A Dungeons & Dragons* term?

Usually the thought of Derrick filled me with guilt, but for some reason I felt . . . hopeful. That was odd.

He nodded. "How are the medications? Have you experienced any—"

"Manifestations of magic," I finished for him. I felt like we'd just had this conversation.

He cleared his throat. "I was going to say side effects."

"Oh." I glanced at the window, expecting to see the flickering shadows of bird wings fluttering against the glass, but I didn't. I shifted in the cushioned chair, trying to find a comfortable spot against the lumpy pillows. Something poked my hip.

"I think I'm experiencing déjà vu." Except this was different. Weirder.

"Ah, the sensation you've already experienced this moment. If it disturbs you, we can try a lower dosage."

"No, I'll be all right. I want to see if the medications work." I wanted to be normal, to fit in, and not hurt anyone. Of course, I hadn't hurt anyone. There had been a freak tornado. I couldn't have caused that.

"I'm making progress. I don't believe in magic," I said.

Dr. Bach tapped his pencil against his leg, thinking. "You aren't just saying that because you think it's what people want to hear?"

The wire in the chair, or whatever it was, distracted me and I shifted again in the seat. "No way. It's like this. . . . There's a field with a path, and there are three choices. The first path is to not take my medication and feel depressed. The second path is to take the medication and I'll feel better. I can give up my delusions of magic and stop blaming myself."

"The third path?" he prompted.

There was a third path? I had already forgot where this story was going. These meds made me so spacey. I tried to focus, but all I could think about was the wire in the chair poking me.

I fluffed the lumpy pillow behind my back and scooted away from the side of the chair where something jabbed into my hip. I pulled a stick out from the crack between the cushion and the side of the chair.

"What's that?" Dr. Bach asked, squinting over his glasses.

"A pencil?" I said.

But it wasn't a pencil. It was a stick about a foot long, made of polished black wood. It looked like a magic wand—not that I believed in magic. But it was pretty and the wood was twisted and I liked it. I shoved it into my back pocket and covered it with my sweater.

I was fairly certain I had found the third path. I just didn't know what it meant yet.

THE END

A Sneak Peak of

Hex-Ed

Sequel to
Tardy Bells and Witches' Spells

PROLOGUE
When I Was Five

The other children in my kindergarten class played at stations during free time: the puzzle table, the car corner, the doll house, or the indoor fort. I sat in the book nook alone, reading on one of the beanbag chairs. Wide bookshelves bolted into the floor separated me from the chaos of the classroom, hiding me in the sanctuary of literature.

From between two bookshelves I spied Mrs. Phelps at her desk writing lesson plans. Her assistant, Miss Diane, strolled the perimeter of the room, separating fighting boys and coaxing girls to share with each other. She never had to tell me to stop fighting or to share. I was different from the other children. I knew how to be a good girl.

A tall man in a navy-blue suit stood outside the bookcases, the walls only coming up to his waist. He'd visited my classroom before. On his breast pocket, he wore a badge that read: *school district psychologist*. I could read the words, but I didn't know what they meant.

He removed a small book from his vest pocket and placed it on top of the wall. I returned my attention to my own book on unicorns before glancing up again.

He untucked a twisted stick from his sleeve. When he pulled on it, a feather sprouted out of the wood. He wrote in the book with red ink. The book appeared to be larger than before, not small enough to fit in a pocket.

"You aren't supposed to have pens in the book nook," I said. "Mrs. Phelps doesn't want anyone writing on the books."

"This isn't a pen. It's a self-inking quill." His voice sounded funny, his accent like one of the characters from a television show my parents watched on PBS. "Furthermore, I'm not *in* the book nook. I'm outside of it."

"Oh," I said.

"What book are you looking at?" he asked.

I held it up. "It's about unicorns. There are pretty pictures. I can read the words too. Do you want me to read to you?"

"No." He continued writing.

I read to him anyway. I was a good reader. "Unicorns are pretty. Unicorns are nice. Unicorns dance under rainbows, kiss boo-boos, and make everything better."

He snorted.

"Do you believe in unicorns?" I asked.

"Do you?"

"My mommy says there are no such things as unicorns. My daddy says I can believe in anything I want. I want to see a unicorn."

He crouched down between the shelves, his face level with mine now. His eyes were the color of the stormy sky outside. His shoulder-length hair was wavy and beautiful, like dark water. Everything he wore was dark blues and grays: his long coat, his pants, and the neckerchief tucked under his collar. A little line crinkled between his eyebrows. He didn't look sad, but I could feel it weighing down his frame, tugging at his heart. A black cloud was stitched to his soul. I wondered if he realized it.

"Unicorns don't look like those pictures with rainbow manes and tails." He nodded to the book.

"Yes, they do!"

He went on. "The feral ones are brown and gray, dappled like wild horses, and their horns are sharp."

I balled up my fists at my sides. "You're a liar. Unicorns have rainbow tails. They aren't gray."

He lifted the black hem of his pants and showed me a white line on his ankle. "A unicorn gave me this scar when I was seven because I tried to pet one. Unicorns aren't nice. They like the taste of blood." He said it with certainty.

I looked to the illustration of the sparkly unicorn and shivered. Maybe the unicorn scar was the reason his soul was so dark and sad. I felt bad for the man. I wanted to make him better.

I slid out of the beanbag chair and returned the book to the shelf. I picked out a happier book. "I can read to you about fairies."

"Do you think fairies are any nicer? You should be afraid of Fae. They steal human children and drink the blood of witches. Hasn't your mother properly educated you on this matter?"

I wasn't exactly sure why I thought so, but this adult was more like me than the other children were. He was like my mom, the air around him humming with the scent of herbs and perfumed with notes of music. My senses got all confused when I tried to focus on any one sound or smell.

I hugged my arms around myself. "Do you want to come inside the book nook? It's safe in here."

"No."

"Why not?"

He stood abruptly. "As you said, Mrs. Phelps wouldn't want anyone writing in there."

"I won't tell." I crossed my heart to show him I meant it.

He said nothing.

He was so alone outside the book nook. And I was so alone inside of it. I didn't want him to ache inside. I rushed forward and hugged him around his knees, trying to infuse love and healing inside him. Electricity prickled under my skin.

"No hugging," he said, prying my hands off him. "You need to learn to control yourself. Suppress those feelings inside you."

"Why?"

He pushed me back into the book nook. "You might harm someone."

"Hugging? Does hugging hurt you? It makes me feel better when my mommy hugs me," I said. I could feel a million tiny wounds, raw and painful all over his body. Scars perhaps. I thought back to the unicorns, but this wasn't the same as the scar on his ankle. These were deeper. They sank below his skin.

He went back to writing in his book. I stood on the other side of the bookshelf feeling lost and uncertain.

"Why are you over here instead of playing with other children?" he asked.

I made a face. "They're loud and bossy." That wasn't the only reason, but it was hard to explain the other reasons. "I don't like the things they like. I just don't. . . ." I struggled for words.

"Fit in?" he finished.

Mrs. Phelps' friendly smile was fixed in place as she came up from behind him. "This is your third observation, sir. You've taken such an interest in our little Clarissa."

The man tugged at the bottom of his blue vest, lifting his chin and looking down at her in a superior sort of way. "This one was marked as being a potential concern for autism."

Mrs. Phelps wrinkled eyes narrowed. "She doesn't have autism, and we both know it."

"Indeed. Most of the children I'm sent to observe have been mislabeled. This one should be placed in a Talented and Gifted program." He closed his book and shoved it under his coat. Even though it was far too big to fit, it somehow did. I didn't see his quill anymore, only a stick of twisted black wood he slid into a pocket.

I'd heard the words autism and disabilities, but I didn't understand all of what they were talking about.

He strode toward the door with long confident strides.

"I know who you are," Mrs. Phelps called after him. "Professor Thatch."

His footsteps faltered, but he didn't look back.

She scurried after him. Out in the hallway, I heard her whisper. "I was a student at Womby's School for Wayward Witches forty-two years ago. You taught me wards and self-defense."

I crept out from behind the bookcases, wanting to hear what they were talking about. Miss Diane sat next to a crying boy, trying to wipe his nose. I snuck closer to the door. Mrs. Phelps had to be joking. She had gray hair and wrinkles. She was the teacher. This man couldn't have been her teacher. Even so, she had piqued my curiosity.

"Did you pass my class?" he asked.

I spied on them from the doorway.

Mrs. Phelps' voice was a whisper. "Magic isn't easy."

I wasn't certain I'd heard her correctly.

"Hence the reason you're here living amongst Morties instead of in the Unseen Realm." He looked her up and down. "Who made the wards around this child?" His gaze flickered past her to me. He scowled.

I ducked back inside. The door slammed closed immediately after, separating me from them. I tried the knob, but it was locked.

Good children didn't eavesdrop, but I wanted to know what they were saying. I sat down at my desk and took out the markers. Sometimes unexpected things happened when I used them. I suspected it was because they were called *magic* markers. I drew a picture of the man with a blue pen. I used pink to draw Mrs. Phelps' dress and captured the essence of her hair with gray spirals. Another child wandered by and said something to me, but I ignored him. I concentrated on the ear I drew in the corner. My ear.

My hand slid over the paper, the pen making Mrs. Phelps' mouth move. Her high, sweet voice sounded sharp, confused. "What wards?"

"They're subtle. Expertly made. Obviously not your doing." I could hear the sneer in his voice. "Tell me, did they drain your powers after you left our school?"

"I didn't have much magic to begin with."

"Do you have enough skills left to recognize subtle energies? Have you seen any manifestations of magic in this child? Necromancy? Blood magic? Pain enchantments? Other forbidden arts?" The circle of his mouth opened and closed as the drawing spoke. I couldn't tell if what I was hearing was my imagination or what they were really saying.

"At this age?" Mrs. Phelps asked. "That would be unheard of. Only the child of a great and powerful witch might show that kind of magic this early. Her mother possesses a little bit of garden magic and some kitchen witchery. Her father is a Morty. I'm surprised they could even conceive a child, let alone protect her with wards."

I didn't understand many of the words they were saying. There was only one word I understood and it was enough: magic. He wanted to know if I could do magic. I'd read *Matilda*. Maybe I was like her, only with nicer parents.

The man grunted. "Has she given any indication she knows what she is?"

"Her sister, she knew what she was when I had her. She's the one you should be observing. When she was five, she animated water from the drinking fountain and made it chase after a group of sixth grade girls. I had to hush the whole thing up so the Morties wouldn't suspect her. That girl is an obvious water fury, if I ever saw one. She'd be a candidate for Womby's if only her mother would—"

"I have no interest in the sister."

"What do you mean? Isn't that why you're here? Recruitment for the school?"

"Tell me more about this one."

"Why do you want to know about her? She's far too young to be of interest. She's nothing special."

I clenched my fists at my sides. Mrs. Phelps had told me I was advanced. I could read and do math the other children couldn't do. Didn't that make me special?

"The fewer questions you ask, the better." His footsteps echoed away. "I'll return in a few months for another observation."

"I might have flunked out of your school, but that doesn't make me stupid." Her voice rose. "If you're not here for recruitment, there's only one other reason you could be here. The rumors are true. Loraline had a daughter. This sweet child came from the evilest witch in hist—"

"Don't say that name," he hissed. "Someone might hear."

Loraline. That was a name? When I heard that word I saw long spindly branches and cold winter nights. It gave me the shivers. Loraline wasn't my mom's name. Her name was Abby. Obviously they didn't know what they were talking about.

He whispered, "You don't understand the risk if someone finds out. The Fae would torture you if they thought you knew anything about Loraline having a child."

"Forgive me, professor. I heard how *she*—is it true?" She coughed. "She tortured you? How could the headmaster assign *you* to investigate her daughter? After all that witch did to you."

"I have classes in a half hour. I should be on my way soon. You know how to contact me if there are . . . manifestations."

"The headmaster doesn't know about this girl? Does he?"

"Were you this trying forty years ago as a student? No, don't answer that. I already know the answer."

I could barely follow this conversation with all the strange words. When the man spoke fast I couldn't understand his accent. Sometimes he reminded me of the character from the *Doctor Who* program my dad watched. This man should have worn a cheery bow tie.

"The headmaster doesn't know," she repeated.

"No, and it will stay that way," he said. "It's safer for Witchkin and Morties alike if the Fae think her bloodline has died out. It's safer for you. You will never repeat this conversation. Do you understand?"

"I give you my word," Mrs. Phelps said.

"That isn't good enough. You know what I need to do." The man in my drawing held up his stick.

"Yes, sir."

Pink and yellow magic marker flooded over the drawing, dripping out of the pens and covering the people. The colors grew brighter. The air smelled like burnt hair and autumn leaves. Snowflakes danced before my eyes and then faded. Mrs. Phelps came back into the classroom a moment later.

She looked at me and blinked. I crumpled up my drawing, afraid she would know what I had done. I didn't want to get in trouble for eavesdropping. Mrs. Phelps smiled at me, her eyes dull. "There you are, Clarissa. Aren't you a special girl?"

Part One
Sixteen Years Later

CHAPTER ONE
Yes, We Have No Bananas

I wrote the word "fallopian" on the chalkboard. My face flushed as I spelled the words that would be on the test for the room of high school students.

When the vice principal had burst into the art room where I was student teaching and begged me to fill in for the health teacher who had been in a car an accident at lunch, I'd been grateful to show the administration what a valuable asset I was. Never mind that it technically wasn't legal for an unlicensed student teacher to be unsupervised with students. This was the opportunity I needed to get my foot in the door to teach at Skinnersville High School when the art teacher retired next year.

On the downside, I'd had no idea sex education was part of health class. I could have kicked myself now. I would have been better off telling the students it was a study hall rather than sticking to the heath teacher's lesson plans and fumbling my way through this lesson.

The classroom looked like most of the other rooms in the school: plain, windowless walls covered with motivational quotes and anti-smoking posters, tiny desks with chairs attached, a teacher desk with a stone-age computer that crashed when I tried to take attendance on it, and a class full of sweaty teenagers. The only difference between this classroom and the science room next door was the giant diagram of a male and female reproductive system at the front of the room.

"Clarissa, can you spell clitoris again?" one of the teens with a shaggy mop of blond hair asked.

"It's Miss Lawrence," I corrected. It didn't help that I'd graduated from high school and college early, making me the youngest student teacher in grad school at University of Oregon.

The teens snickered and elbowed each other, not listening to what I'd said. The kid with shaggy hair chuckled. "Can you show us where that is on the diagram? I have a feeling that's an important one."

"Not as important as ejaculation," some other pimpled teen said in the back.

I tried to remember I didn't know this teen's life story; for all I knew his cries for negative attention were because his single mom worked two jobs and was too exhausted to be attentive to his emotional state when she was home.

I turned back to the chalkboard, relieved I didn't have to look at the group of thirty-eight teenagers as I wrote down the word. Nervous energy percolated inside of me. I wished I'd refilled my medication, but it was too expensive. I'd rationalized I hadn't needed it to teach. Art class never made me think about sex to the point of becoming a horndog.

It wasn't like this was the first time I'd taught at Skinnersville High School, but it was the first time I'd been alone in a classroom full of students. I'd never taught this subject and I was hardly an expert on the material. Due to a traumatic experience in high school which resulted in homeschooling and online classes, I'd never taken sex education. I was afraid these kids had more practical applications with the subject matter than I did. The mortified expression on my face probably showed I was a virgin at twenty-one. I bet they could see I was faking my way through this lesson.

Students continued to whisper and joke behind me.

"God, Jon, shut up!" one of the girls said. "Maybe you should learn the word castration."

I stared at the green of the chalkboard. The students teasing each other was starting to get out of control. I was the teacher. I was the one who was supposed to be telling the kids to be mature, but all I wanted to do was run out of the room. Maybe it wasn't too late. I could call the office and say I wasn't well.

But if I did, the vice principal and principal would think less of me. I wanted to show Skinnersville High I could handle any class. I was worthy to take over for Mrs. Johnson next year, and I was ready to fulfil my dream of becoming an art teacher.

I tried to tell myself nothing would go wrong if I stayed. It wasn't like I was actually having sex. Plus, my psychiatrist had insisted I hadn't caused those electrical storms or the tornado by trying to have sex with my former boyfriends. My fear was all in my head.

"When are we going to get to put the condoms on the bananas?" a boy shouted.

The heat in my face crept down my neck. I tried to calm myself with slow yoga breaths, but it didn't work. The chalk in my fingers slipped from my clammy hand. It shattered into twelve trillion pieces at my feet. The air tasted sharp, like ozone. Fluorescent lights above my head flickered. For a second, everything shimmered. I glanced down and did a double take at the chalk. It was still whole. I was certain it had broken.

Magic was not real. There was no room for it in this world of science, technology, and teenage drama.

I smoothed my bleached-blonde hair out of my eyes and pretended nothing was wrong. I was not about to have a psychotic episode. My heart thumped against my ribcage, and I felt lightheaded.

I turned back to the room. One of the students crumpled up a piece of notebook paper and threw it at someone else's head. A boy in the second row made no attempt to disguise the fact he was reading a *Dungeon and Dragons* book. That probably would have been me in high school. Ten students were on their cell phones. A girl in the front was obviously taking a selfie. The duck lips gave it away.

I passed out the worksheets with their crossword puzzles and word searches, navigating through the maze of desks. There was hardly enough room to squeeze by some of the rows. The room obviously wasn't intended to hold this many students. The blouse under my cardigan clung to my back with sweat.

"Miss Lawrence, you don't look so good," Imani Washington whispered to me.

I tried to smile. I knew her from the year before, when I'd done my student teaching at the middle school. That was before the statewide budget cuts had eliminated the art position—and the teacher who had been mentoring me—at the end of the year. Imani was a sweet girl. She sat near two other girls I had taught at the middle school. I wished none of my former students were there to witness my humiliation.

Students moved to other seats and collaborated in groups on their busy work. I helped the students who raised their hands.

Imani waved me over to her table again. "Annie, show Miss Lawrence your book."

The girl next to her showed me her sketches in an art journal. I recognized the blonde girl from the middle school, but I'd never had her in my classes. Most of drawings were anime characters with unnaturally large eyes, but some were pastel drawings.

"This is really good shading," I said, pointing to a charcoal portrait. "I like how you included highlights and midtone values."

Imani nudged her friend. "See, I told you it was good."

For a blissful sixty seconds I forgot about the pack of dire wolves around me as I switched into art teacher mode.

Annie smiled shyly down at her book, turning the pages for me. In addition to characters with unnaturally large eyes, I noticed a pattern.

"All of these people have their hands in their pockets or behind their back. Hmm. What are they hiding?" I teased her.

She shook her head. "I have trouble with hands."

"I used to have a hard time with hands too," I said. "I've got a few *handy* tricks up my sleeves for tackling details like that, if you think you can *handle* them."

"Miss Lawrence is so punny," Imani said.

The girls laughed and rolled their eyes at my lame middle school teacher humor. I liked freshmen. They laughed at my corny jokes.

I gave Annie pointers on drawing hands. She listened with rapt interest. This was why I had wanted to become a teacher. I had thought every moment of teaching would be like this: sharing my passion for art and making connections with the kids. When I experienced little moments of sunshine like this, I told myself it was enough to sustain me through the rest of the year.

You'll get summers off, they said. It will be rewarding and meaningful work, they said. It won't be that hard to find a job as an art teacher, they said. *They* were my college guidance counselors. They had never taught before.

Already I was learning how wrong they were.

I had to cut the art lesson with Annie and Imani to a premature end when the sharp odor of a paint pen caught my attention. Some guy in a studded jacket and a mini Mohawk was drawing penises on his desk. They weren't even anatomically correct. Not that I had a lot of experience with penises, but I did know they weren't shaped like rocket ships.

The heat in my neck crept down my chest. My stomach didn't feel right. I was not aroused by rocket ship penises, I told myself. I liked *Star Trek* and *Star Wars*, but I was more of a Tolkien kind of girl. It wasn't like he'd drawn Legolas naked or anything, right? I could handle this.

I pointed to the paint pen. "Put that away. Get out your classwork."

The student crossed his arms in defiance. "Why? I don't have anything better to do."

I tried to ignore the sensations swelling inside me. Was it my sex-deprived thirst or was it nervousness? I couldn't tell. I waved a hand over the paper at his desk. "You have a crossword."

The teen held it up to show me he had completed both sides. As I glanced around, I realized he wasn't the only one finished.

The activity was supposed to take fifty minutes. Then there would be banana contraception practice for fifteen minutes before their exit activity. As I circulated, I could see the teacher had underestimated the time. Fifteen minutes into the activity, half the students had finished the crossword puzzle.

Oh, God, what would I do with these kids once they were done? I had an hour more of blastocysts, amenorrhea, and menarche.

These ninety-minute block periods were torture.

More than anything I wanted to run out of class, but if I did, how would I get hired as an art teacher at this school if I couldn't demonstrate effective classroom management? I couldn't afford to mess this up when art teacher jobs were so hard to come by.

Forty minutes into class, students were so bored and unruly, I decided it was time to move on to the next activity. Maybe if they were good, I could bribe them with a game like Heads Up, Seven Up. Or Hangman. Then again, maybe not. My stomach felt even queasier at the idea of having to slowly spell out e-r-e-c-t-i-o-n.

The lights flickered again. I tried to clear my mind, to not think of the sexy things that would cause me stress. This wasn't going to be like those other times.

I waved my hand at the class, trying to be heard over the chaos. It was a blessing ten of them were absent. "Everyone, back to your seats for our banana contraception lesson."

"Yes! Finally!" said one girl in the front row.

It was so loud I had to shout two more times before the rest of the class heard me. Students sluggishly trudged back to their seats, glaring at me the entire time, like it was my fault they had to learn. It took a total of four minutes to get them seated again.

I tore the bananas from bunches and passed them out. I felt bad for the students in the back who didn't get the green ones and had to settle for the brown, mushy ones. Navigating the aisles and passing them out took another five minutes. Yes! Only forty minutes of class time left.

I held up a finger in warning. "Now, be careful with these. I only have enough for one per person, and the bananas need to last for the class after this." No sooner had I said that than one of the boys squeezed his banana hard enough in the middle that it squished out from the skin. It was one of the brown, mushy ones.

He howled in amusement. "Can I have another?"

I counted to five before answering. "You can share with one of your neighbors."

He turned to one of his friends. "Bro, that is sick! It's a *ménage à tres*!"

I didn't know if he purposely was mixing Spanish and French, or he thought that was how to say the phrase.

I handed out the packs of condoms. "Wait until I'm done passing these out and give instructions before putting them on the bananas."

"I've got this," one boy said, tearing the pack open with his teeth.

Another student had unpeeled her banana and was licking it suggestively. The students around her cheered her on.

Imani and her friends followed directions at least. I could see where I had gone wrong. I should have given them the demo first, then passed out the supplies. There was always next period to get it right.

One boy with a buzz cut wearing a letterman jacket in the third row unzipped his fly and shoved the banana inside his pants so that it hung out like a penis. His friends laughed and pointed.

At least he'd gotten the condom on without any problem.

"Excuse me," I said. "I need you to put the banana on your desk."

"Whoa, how tall are you?" he asked.

Why had I wanted to become a teacher? This wasn't any different than suffering through the humiliations of high school.

He slapped his desk. "I mean, you can't even be five foot. Am I right?"

"Remove the banana from your pants," I said through clenched teeth.

He pretended to tug on it. "Sorry, dude, it's stuck."

I couldn't imagine my day getting any worse than this.

The little creep winked at me. "Hey, maybe later, you'll tutor me a little more on this subject."

The teen next to him, who had written his vocab words in Sharpie across his arms, grabbed the banana and tried to yank it out of his friend's pants. "What the fuck—"

"Watch your language," I said.

Mr. Buzzcut punched Sharpie-arm in the shoulder. "Knock it off. That hurts."

They both let go of the banana. It remained sticking out of his pants.

The condom rolled itself up and flew off the banana without anyone touching it. The latex shot itself at a girl with a nose ring and hit her in the back of the head.

She turned around. "Fuck you."

"Excuse me," I said, about to correct her potty language.

My attention was drawn back to the boy with the banana. Mr. Buzzcut held up his hands, but the banana hanging out of his pants flopped around of its own volition. My jaw dropped. The group of teenagers all stared in wide-eyed confusion.

One of the students started, "How did you do—"

"Dude, I didn't—"

Before my very eyes, the banana unpeeled itself, and there inside the husk was a pale white banana in the shape of a penis. That wasn't the weirdest part, though.

A little mouth opened in the side of the banana penis and sang in a tiny, shrill voice. "Yes, we have no penises. We have no penises today. We have vaginas and ovaries and testicles, gonads and cervixes and—"

I stared in open-mouthed horror. Students screamed. This couldn't be real. Surely, the doctors would tell me this was all in my head, like they had before. The fluorescent lights buzzed and flashed on and off above me, the flickers following me like a magnet as I backed away from the students. I should have refilled my pills, but I thought I would only need them if I was going to have sex.

One of the students had actually managed to get a condom on one of the penis-shaped bananas. He high-fived a friend. "This is awesome!" he said. "This is way better than when Mrs. Richardson teaches class."

He was the only student in class who appeared to think this was a fun prank.

Students jumped away from me. Some ran out the door. I thought it was because of the singing banana. Nope. It was because *all* the bananas were dancing. As I made my way across the room, more bananas came to life. Some unpeeled themselves to reveal penis-shaped fruit within. A young woman held one of the brown mushy bananas away from herself, flopping it around like a flaccid penis. Or maybe it was flopping itself around.

"Oh my God! Oh my God!" She panted. "How is this happening?"

"It's witchcraft!" a kid in a jersey said, pointing to a Goth girl.

"It isn't me." Her eyes swept over the chaos, me being at its epicenter. "It's the sub! Look!"

Horror-stricken faces turned to me.

The bananas bounced on the desks around me in a dance, following me like the pied piper of penises. More bananas sang along to the song, some of them more muffled than others with the bright blue or neon green condoms covering them. I had to stop this, but I didn't know how. The rising screams and shouts of students drowned out the song.

On the plus side, students were all too freaked out to take dick pics of their bananas. They pushed and scrambled for the door. One of them slipped on a banana peel. Two jocks tripped over the fallen student. Someone collided with a garbage can, toppling its contents all over the floor.

Not real. Not real, I told myself. Magic only existed in those fantasy novels I liked to immerse myself in to escape from the mundane world.

I would have liked a little more mundane at the moment.

Imani and her friends scooted to the other side of the room. Her wide eyes said it all. She was seeing this too. Everyone was seeing this. Unless I was hallucinating that too.

That was the moment the principal marched in with Skinnersville Public School District's psychologist. The principal's jaw dropped as he stared at the chaos. I couldn't tell if they'd seen what I'd seen. The bananas had stopped singing. Smashed bananas and used condoms littered the floor. The overpowering perfume of fruit and latex lingered in the air. A cluster of girls wept against the back wall. The classroom was eerily quiet now that most of the students had vacated.

The psychologist crossed his arms and frowned at me.

I'd bumped into the school psychologist on multiple occasions while student teaching. He was tall and lanky, his black hair the long, disheveled hipster style so many others had in Eugene and Skinnersville. At first I'd found him handsome, with his long, aquiline nose, chiseled jaw and deep-set eyes. The snotty sneer that crossed his face when I tried to talk to him changed my mind pretty quickly.

One of his dark eyebrows arched as his gaze fell on me. The room was eerily silent.

The student with the banana sticking out of his pants sobbed. He pointed to me. "She did this to us! It isn't like this when Mrs. Richardson teaches the sex-ed unit."

The school psychologist spoke in a dry British monotone. "Don't be ridiculous." He strode forward and pointed to the student. "Remove that banana from your pants and zip up your fly."

The student did so with far more compliance than he'd done anything else thus far. On the plus side, it appeared his anatomy was back to normal. I suspected he'd be in therapy for years, though. The two adults in the room rounded on me.

The principal found his voice. "What the hell happened here?"

This had to be the weirdest day of my life. Well, now that I thought about it, probably the second weirdest day of my life.

To read more, go to Sarina Dorie's website to learn about
Hex-Ed, including where it is available:
https://sarinadorie.com/writing/novels

If you enjoyed this Cozy Witch Mystery *in the Womby's School for Wayward Witches Series* please leave a review on the online retailer where you purchased this collection. You might also enjoy free short stories published by the author on her website: http://sarinadorie.com/writing/short-stories.

Readers can hear updates about current writing projects and news about upcoming novels and free short stories as they become available by signing up for Sarina Dorie's newsletter at:

http://eepurl.com/4IUhP

Other novels written by the author can be found at:

http://sarinadorie.com/writing/novels

You can find Sarina Dorie on Facebook at:
https://www.facebook.com/sarina.dorie1/

You can find Sarina Dorie on Twitter at:
@Sarina Dorie

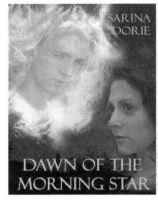  

Seventeen-year-old Sarah's life changes forever when a man falls from the sky—and she falls in love. As if teenage romance isn't hard enough in the times of the Puritans, imagine falling in love with an alien!

Magic. Jehovah's witchnesses. Karmic collisions. . . .Two unlikely friends—a witch and a Jehovah's Witness—discover the magic of friendship, as well as real magic.

Gothic Romance. Mystery. Ghosts. Imagine a whimsical fairytale world with the feel of Jane Eyre . . . only working in a house of were-wolves.

For more fantasy, science fiction and romance, go to: www.sarinadorie.com

ABOUT THE AUTHOR

Sarina Dorie has sold over 150 short stories to markets like Analog, Daily Science Fiction, Magazine of Fantasy and Science Fiction, Orson Scott Card's IGMS, Cosmos, and Abyss and Apex. Her stories and published novels have won humor and Romance Writer of America awards. She has sold three novels to publishers. Her steampunk romance series, *The Memory Thief* and her collections, *Fairies, Robots and Unicorns—Oh My!* and *Ghosts, Werewolves and Zombies—Oh My!* are available on Amazon, along with a dozen other novels she has written.

A few of her favorite things include: gluten-free brownies (not necessarily glutton-free), Star Trek, steampunk aesthetics, fairies, Severus Snape, Captain Jack Sparrow and Mr. Darcy.

By day, Sarina is a public school art teacher, artist, belly dance performer and instructor, copy editor, fashion designer, event organizer and probably a few other things. By night, she writes. As you might imagine, this leaves little time for sleep.

35067629R00135

Made in the USA
Columbia, SC
19 November 2018